At the
Far End
of
Nowhere

At the Far End of Nowhere

A NOVEL

CHRISTINE DAVIS MERRIMAN

GREEN WRITERS PRESS | *Brattleboro, Vermont*

Printed in the United States

10 9 8 7 6 5 4 3 2 1

At the Far End of Nowhere is a work of fiction. Apart from the actual historic figures, events, and locales that provide background for the narrative, all names, characters, places, and incidents are products of the author's imagination or are used fictitiously.

Green Writers Press is a Vermont-based publisher whose mission is to spread a message of hope and renewal through the words and images we publish. Throughout we will adhere to our commitment to preserving and protecting the natural resources of the earth. To that end, a percentage of our proceeds will be donated to environmental activist groups and The Southern Poverty Law Foundation. Green Writers Press gratefully acknowledges support from individual donors, friends, and readers to help support the environment and our publishing initiative. Green Place Books curates books that tell literary and compelling stories with a focus on writing about place—these books are more personal stories, memoir, and biographies.

GREEN PLACE BOOKS   GREEN WRITERS press

Giving Voice to Writers & Artists Who Will Make the World a Better Place
Green Writers Press | Brattleboro, Vermont
www.greenwriterspress.com

ISBN: 978-0-9987012-8-8

COVER DESIGN: Asha Hossain
BOOK DESIGN: Hannah Wood

PRINTED ON PAPER WITH PULP THAT COMES FROM FSC-CERTIFIED FORESTS, MANAGED FORESTS THAT GUARANTEE RESPONSIBLE ENVIRONMENTAL, SOCIAL, AND ECONOMIC PRACTICES BY PRINTOPIA.

FOR MY PARENTS AND MY BROTHER

CONTENTS

ACKNOWLEDGMENTS

I would like to thank:

The late Dan Jones, for validating and nurturing me as one of his creative writing students at Towson State University.

The late George Cuomo, for guiding me through my MFA thesis at the University of Massachusetts Amherst so many years ago.

Steve Eisner, for relating so warmly to my characters and encouraging me to carry their story forward.

Peggy Moran, John Tiholiz, Cathryn Lykes, and Emma Irving who applied elegant and sensitive editing to my manuscript.

Jay Neugeboren, my former MFA professor, and David Milofsky, my former MFA classmate, for remembering me after all these years, and for so kindly reviewing and finding value in my debut novel.

Dede Cummings, my publisher at Green Writers Press, for her amazing energy and unbridled enthusiasm for all things positive.

Alex, my son, my muse—in some ways a reincarnation of his grandfather.

My husband, Jack, for his unfailing love and support.

At the
Far End
of
Nowhere

CHAPTER ONE

TURNED ON MY DADDY'S LATHE

WEST BALTIMORE, 2015—Flashing blue-light police cameras mounted on lamp posts. Suddenly flaming cars, shattered glass, an unhappy community in the streets, protesting the untimely death of one of their own. Then lines of riot police, curfews, closed schools. For days, these images are projected by all the major news channels on TV screens across the nation, threatening to seal Charm City's transmogrification from "the city that reads" to "the city that bleeds," hometown of NBC's *Homicide* and HBO's *The Wire*.

Amid the sorrow and the anger and the smoke, the specter of an older neighborhood rises; and on a deserted street, the wounded face of a row house emerges—broken windows, a boarded-up front door, its number, 629, no longer visible beneath the plywood.

The violent burst of light and sound and color on the TV screen carry me back in time to that same place, when things were so very different—but oddly, in some ways, so very much the same. The present repeats something of the past, urging me to pull out childish belongings—packed-away dreams and photos, yellowed letters bound with crumbling pink ribbon, a discarded card game, a young woman's diary, an old man's words—and turn them over in my mind until characters begin to reveal themselves in imagined conversation like

3

the scrabble of birdsong released after the rain. Now, it is time to examine memories more closely, establish a frame of reference, and move forward to a new point of departure, a broader truth.

West Baltimore, 1955—Televisions have just begun to flicker their black-and-white images in the front rooms of some of the houses across the street, but radios still dominate the airwaves with music, news, and popular drama and comedy shows. Here, at 629 Franklintown Road, an old man in a blue overcoat waits on the white marble front steps of a brick row house, smoking a cigar, watching anxiously for his daughter's safe return from kindergarten.

I am that little girl—Little Red Riding Hood wearing a red coat, hat, and mittens that my daddy has picked out for me. Red is our favorite color. When I am wearing them, my daddy can see me from afar.

My big brother, Spence, has run on ahead, but I am skipping down the block from the bus stop, counting the cracks in the side-walk, careful not to step on them. Now past Harlem Avenue, twelve more cracks, then home safe to my daddy.

Our house is near the end of the block, right next door to a small grocery shop where you can get bread, milk, donuts, candy, popsicles, and those strawberry and vanilla ice cream torpedoes on a stick.

Miss Beulah, an old-maid lady across the back alley, tends her roses and hates cats. Two doors down, the red-haired lady is drunk again, screaming at her husband. Above the corner bar, Natty Boh's one eye blinks on, watching, watching.

The world is not always safe—except when my daddy takes me back with him to *once upon a time*, where everything is magical and you can make true whatever you want it to be. He takes me with him to the far end of nowhere, where everything begins.

When I am born, my mother, Jimmie, gives me to my daddy. He names me Lissa, after his grandmother. My daddy is very old. Jimmie says he is seventy-two when I am born. She says that some people don't understand why she is married to a man so much older. She says it is a different kind of love they have.

Other kids think my daddy is my grandfather. When I tell them he's my father, they tell me that cannot be.

My mother calls my daddy Stouten. He calls her Jimmie. I call her Jimmie, too, because that's what Daddy calls her. I have a brother, Spence, who is two years older than me. He calls Jimmie Mommy. Spence belongs to Mommy.

Jimmie says I belong to my daddy, and I am always to respect him and never hurt his feelings. "Your daddy is a genius. He knows everything there is."

I like to sit on my daddy's lap and listen to radio shows with him: *Amos 'n' Andy, Gunsmoke.*

My daddy likes to listen to the news on the radio. Gabriel Heatter is his favorite. Daddy says, "he tells us the good news, and we need to hear more of that."

I hear another man's voice speaking. "Do you know who that is, Lissa? That's President Truman. He was our president when you were born."

For a living, my daddy fixes watches and clocks. He can make any part of a watch. Sometimes he shows me the parts inside a watch and tells me their names—mainspring, barrel, hairspring, balance wheel…. He likes everything to be precise—to within one thousandth of an inch.

One day, my daddy takes me downtown to see the big clock on the Bromo-Seltzer Tower. He lifts me up and puts me on his shoulders so I can see above all the grownups.

"Lissa, hold on tight, so you won't fall." He holds my legs steady, and I grab onto his ears. He wears his gray hat. He always wears a dressy hat when he goes downtown. In the summer, he wears a straw hat.

He points at the top of the tower. "I fixed that clock many years ago, and she's been running ever since. After I die, I reckon all the clocks are going to stop running."

My daddy likes to ask me this riddle: "What's rounder than a riddle, brisker than a bee, the prettiest little thing you ever did see?" The answer, he tells me, is a watch.

My daddy works in the big front room of our house. That's where he keeps his magical machines. He touches each one and tells me its name. The little whirring one: "This is my watchmaker's lathe." The one that's as big as a horsie and takes up one whole side of the room: "This is my woodworking lathe." And the funny-looking one that has buttons Daddy can push, handles he can turn, and arms he can slide: "This, Lissa, is my special creation for making cams."

"What's a cam, Daddy?"

"A cam, Lissa, is a tiny sliver of magic. I make all the cams for the gas and electric company. These little mechanical miracles go inside the boxes on people's houses, and measure how much electricity folks are using. Cams are like the stars that God places in the universe to make music among the heavenly spheres. I put just the right number of points on each one to make the meters hum." My daddy also has black monster machines that live in the basement because they are too heavy to stay upstairs. He uses them to cut and shape and shave pieces of metal. I pretend they are not monsters at all, but friendly hippopotamuses. I am not allowed to pet these hippos—or any of Daddy's machines—because they might nip me and hurt me, or the sweat on my hands might make them get rusty, which would ruin them, Daddy says.

My daddy invents things. In a special drawer in his workbench, he keeps some of his favorite inventions—the world's smallest steam engine, and one even smaller than that. Both of them can fit side by side on a dime. And they really work when you blow into them. "That," says my daddy, "is one of the most difficult feats in mechanics."

"Feets? Like ogres' feets? Their feets are hairy."

My daddy laughs. "These kinds of feats are things that are hard to do—unless you put your mind to it. You know, Lissa, when I first came to Baltimore, the streetlights didn't go on by themselves. I invented the mechanism that made them go on when it got dark. I also figured out a more efficient way to temper steel."

"Temper steel? Does that make the steel mad?"

My daddy laughs again. "This kind of temper makes it strong."

"I don't want you to be like all those other children," my daddy tells me. "You must always be perfect like all my other inventions—perfect within one thousandth of an inch."

My daddy tells me I am beautiful because I look just like him in the face, and my hair is red-brown like his—except now his hair is mostly gray and white, with little patches of red in it that shine like copper. My daddy wants me to grow my hair longer and longer—so long that I can sit on it. He won't let Jimmie cut it—*ever*. I also have my daddy's stick-out Celtic ears.

My daddy likes to span my little wrists and my little ankles with just his thumb and his first finger and say, "I turned you on my lathe, and you are perfect just the way you are." He can span my waist easily with his two hands. "You have my mother Lovenia's wasp waist," he tells me.

One day he gives me his mother's gold watch. "Now you always take good care of this watch, Lissa, and it will always take care of you. It's a fine wristwatch—14-karat gold." I think fourteen would be a lot of carrots to put inside a watch. He makes the bracelet part of the watch the smallest it can be, to fit on my wrist. It's still a little loose. "You'll grow into it someday," he says. And he laughs when I call it a "witch-watch."

I kiss my daddy all over his face to thank him for the watch. Jimmie says I shouldn't be kissing him on the lips, so I don't do that anymore.

Every week, my daddy takes the streetcar downtown to Regal Jewelers to do business. Sometimes he takes me with him, to visit some of his watchmaker and jeweler friends. I like to ride the streetcar. It's nice and smooth, but I don't like buses because they sometimes jolt you, and the fumes make me sick in my stomach.

Regal's has glass cases filled with jewelry—diamonds and emeralds and rubies—oh, my! My daddy's friend, Mr. Weinstein, owns Regal. He always comes out of his office to shake my daddy's hand. One day, my daddy tells Mr. Weinstein it's my birthday, and he gives me a gold ring with my birthstone, a real topaz.

We always go to the back of the store, to a tall counter, where all the watchmakers sit. We say hello to Mr. Wagenheimer, my daddy's best man at his wedding. Daddy drops off some fixed watches and picks up some broken ones. He zips them up in a little brown leather case.

Mr. Wagenheimer wears very thick black glasses, plus a funny little thing that looks sort of like the spool of thread Jimmie puts on top of her sewing machine. But this has a thick piece of glass at the end to make the watch parts look bigger. My daddy calls it a watchmaker's loupe. Daddy wears one just like it at home when he is working on a watch. Mr. Wagenheimer also wears a green shade over his eyes that my daddy calls a visor. Mr. Wagenheimer's watchmaker's loupe is attached to a band around his head, and he can flip up the loupe when he doesn't need it to look at a watch. He flips it up and smiles at me. "You know, we always give your daddy the watches nobody else can fix."

Sometimes, we have our lunch at Mr. Chen's Chinese restaurant. My daddy orders chicken chow mein, and for me, chicken noodle soup.

Mr. Chen asks, "Where's you little brother?" He means Spence, who is really my big brother.

My daddy says, "He didn't feel like coming today." Then we buy almond cookies for dessert and take some home for Spence.

But we usually have our lunch at the Oriole cafeteria. Here, they put me in a lift-up seat and give me an orange balloon. The balloon has a picture of the oriole bird on it; he's wearing his baseball cap.

Then we go to the five-and-ten-cent store, where my daddy buys me candy. The candy lady scoops out whatever kind I ask for and weighs it on a scale.

Then Daddy takes me to a movie on Howard Street. There's a picture of a big penguin on the glass door that says *Come in, it's COOL inside.*

I ask my daddy, "Is that Chilly Willy?" He's my daddy's favorite cartoon character.

"He's the air-conditioning penguin."

We see the movie *A Man Called Peter.* During movies, my daddy likes to chew a whole box of Chiclets, or even a jumbo pack of Juicy Fruit gum. He says he likes "a big chaw." One time, a lady in the row in front of us shushes my daddy and says, "Do you have to chew that gum so loud? I can't hear the movie." I don't like it when anybody shushes my daddy. But my daddy is hard of hearing. So maybe he doesn't hear her.

After the movie, we walk to the Kettle Korn. It's all syrupy sweet and warm inside, and there's a big kettle brewing caramel for the popcorn. The popcorn lady's face is pink from stirring the hot caramel. She's short and round, and has the softest fur on her face. She reminds me of the mama bunny in *Peter Rabbit.* My daddy tips his hat to her, and she smiles. They are old friends. She puts the sticky golden popcorn in a white paper box and ties it shut with string. My daddy lets me carry it home to Jimmie.

I try to skip all the way home, but I get a pain in my side and have to stop. My daddy calls it a "growing pain."

I go to kindergarten at School 65. Every morning, before I go there, my daddy breathes out his "consciousnesses" into his hand and gives them to me to swallow, to protect me through the day. Consciousnesses, my daddy says, are a person's soul, a person's spirit, and they ride on the breath. One by one, I take my daddy's consciousnesses into my hand, and *gulp, gulp, gulp,* I swallow three of them—sometimes more if I'm really scared. "Now you are inside me, Daddy, protecting me all day. And nothing bad can happen."

My daddy and me are just alike—two peas in a pod. We can read each other's mind. Daddy says he is clairvoyant. That means he can see things that are happening in another time or place. I can do this, too, but only with some things that Daddy is doing, or when he tells me stories from the past. Today, when I am taking my nap at kindergarten, I can see him sipping a double malted milkshake at the drugstore lunch counter.

After kindergarten, my daddy is, of course, there waiting for me on the marble steps. He is sitting on the top step in his long blue overcoat, smoking a cigar. His consciousnesses are just about used up by now, so I am glad I'm back home with him.

"Lissa, can you guess what I had for lunch today? I went to the drugstore lunch counter."

"You had a double malted milkshake, I bet."

He nods and grins—he still has all his teeth—except the two bottom ones in the middle, where food sometimes spills out on his chin and down his shirt when he's eating. His teeth are all worn down and brown-yellow—it's from the tobacco, he tells me.

I scrunch up next to him on the step. Daddy slides the pretty paper ring off his cigar, which he calls a panatela, and puts the ring on my first finger—the only finger, not counting my thumb, which isn't really a finger, that's big enough for the ring.

"Make smoke rings, Daddy." My daddy puffs out gray and purple rings, and I try to put my finger through them before they come apart and float away. The wind is starting to get blowy now. It brings us the smell of fresh bread coming from Hauswald's Bakery down the block. My daddy puts his arm around me and snuggles me warm.

"Daddy, why do you say you're clairvoyant? I can read your mind sometimes. I want to learn to be clairvoyant, too."

The night shadows are starting to come down on us. I close my eyes, and in my head, try to see two blocks over to where Mr. Ludwig is closing up his drugstore. Next door to him, the shoemaker, Mr.

Gambini, calls to me, "Good night, Lissima, *bellisima*," and shuts down the mechanical man who works all day in his shop window. Over and over, the little shoemaker is taking a nail from between his pinched lips, jerking his head to one side, hammering the nail, and fastening a Cat's Paw heel onto the bottom of a tiny shoe held upside down on what my daddy calls a shoemaker's last. "Goodnight, little shoemaker," I whisper. Natty Boh's one eye blinks on above the bar down at the corner. In the mornings, me and my brother treasure-hunt there for coins dropped in the dirt outside the door. The streetcar barn is three blocks away, but I think I can hear the pigeons there rustling in the rafters, settling in for the night.

My daddy takes me inside, and I sit on his lap in his big gray chair. He only shaves once a week, and I like to scratch his whiskers when they start to grow out. They tickle under my fingernails and make me laugh.

My daddy looks me very deep in the eyes for a while. Finally, he says, "So you want to be clairvoyant, do you?" I nod and tickle his whiskers.

"Well, my little Lissa, you need to be careful what you wish for. I found out I was clairvoyant when I was just a little tacker, not much older than you.

"My mother was Roman Catholic, very devout, and she wanted me to become a priest. To please her, I started out as an altar boy. I was such a serious boy—high-strung, and maybe wound a little too tight.

"One Sunday during Mass at St. Ignatius, after genuflecting and approaching the altar, and after taking Father Martin's *biretta* from him and putting it aside, I felt the sanctuary suddenly grow very warm, then cold, then warm again. But I kept up with the Order of Mass. I knelt beside Father Martin and made the sign of the cross, just the way the priest did. I bowed with Father Martin when he said the Three Persons of the Blessed Trinity. I bowed toward him and recited the *Misereatur tui omnipotens Deus....* I bowed down and recited the Confiteor. I struck my breast three times and recited *mea culpa, mea culpa, mea maxima culpa*—and then I passed out.

"When I came to, some of the ladies at St. Ignatius were fanning me. One church lady said it was the scent of the hyacinths on the windowsills that had made me faint.

"Later, when I walked home from church, a gust of strong, hot wind swirled around me; a dust devil circled around my feet. It was carrying a ring of dirt and loose brush, and it whirled like some kind of entranced dervish. It rose, fierce as a demon, to engulf my whole person. It stung my eyes, twisted my hair, and made my head spin.

"Then the most curious vibration rose up my spine and exploded out the top of my head. It was then I heard a woman's voice calling, 'Urchie's dead.' Then, as quickly as it had risen, the wind subsided and left me in a space of profound stillness.

"I walked the rest of the way home, and it was like walking in a dream. When I got to the house, I found my mother weeping in the kitchen, wiping her eyes with the corner of her apron. She had just gotten news that her sister's youngest and only remaining son, Urchie—he lived over the ridge, about eight miles to the south—had succumbed to swamp fever that very morning.

"When my mother said, 'Your cousin Urchie's dead,' it was like an echo of what I already knew. I had tapped into another realm, and I could see clearly. That's what it means to be clairvoyant."

"I want to be clairvoyant, Daddy, just like you."

CHAPTER TWO

COLORING LEFT-HANDED, MOUSE AND CANNON, COMPLETELY BLUE KITE

ONE day I am sitting on the floor, coloring in my coloring book. My daddy takes the crayon out of my hand and puts it in my other hand.

"Lissa, use your *right* hand."

I try to color with this other hand, but it makes me want to rub my teeth together. It makes me nervous, like when a little boy I know at school scratches his fingers across the blackboard. My right hand doesn't work right. The lines won't go where I want them to go. Every time I start coloring, my left hand wants to pick up the crayon.

"Lissa, just try using your right hand. It will take just a little practice."

Daddy pulls me away from my coloring, holds me on his lap, and tells me, "We live in a right-handed world, Lissa. Machines and tools are made for right-handed people. Using your left hand will make you clumsy. And when you get older, when you try to write with a fountain pen, you will smear the ink across the pages and make a mess. No one will be able to read what you write. In this part of the world, we read from left to right. We write from left to right. You got your left-handedness from your mother. As she can tell you, when she was a young girl in school, her teacher made her use her right hand. And she's the better for it. So now you, too, must learn to write with your right hand. If you learn to write with your right hand, Lissa, I'll buy you an ice cream cone."

I want to make my daddy happy. And I do like ice cream. "Okay, I will try." Over and over, I try to print LISSA with my right hand. But it just doesn't want to do it. The letters are all crooked, and my teeth want to scrape at each other.

One day, my left hand takes over, and I print the words of a story on the lines of my kindergarten notebook. I call it "The Mouse and the Cannon."

A little gray mouse lives under the stairs. He has a very big cannon in the basement. He pushes the cannon all the way to the top of the stairs. BOOM. He shoots off the cannon at his worst enemy, a big man at the top of the stairs who sets mousetraps. The End.

My kindergarten teacher, Miss Wareheimer, reads us a story today about a magical blue kite. Now we are drawing a picture of that kite. I sit at a round table with three other children. Each of us has a big piece of brown drawing paper and a fat blue crayon. The girl across from me is making many tiny blue kites. The boy next to me is using a ruler to draw the outside lines of his kite; he fills it in with a few zig-zag lines. I draw a big kite that takes up most of my paper, and then I try to make it completely blue. I try and try to cover all the brown patches of paper with the blue from my crayon, but I can't get all the brown not to show. I try and try.

All the other children at my table are finished, but I keep trying to make my kite completely blue. The teacher comes to me and says, "It's nap time. Time to stop coloring."

All the other children in the class are unrolling their mats on the floor. But I keep coloring. I want to get my kite completely, perfectly blue—or something bad will happen.

Finally, my teacher takes my crayon away from my left hand, and I try to take a nap. I try not to let anybody hear me crying.

That night, I can't eat my supper. My mother feels my head and takes my temperature. She says my temperature is normal. I tell her I don't want to go to school tomorrow. She says, "But honey, you've always *loved* school."

I tell my daddy I don't want to go to school tomorrow. He tells me I don't have to if I don't want to. He tucks me in and tells me a story.

"You know, Lissa, when I was your age, most all the children in our neck of the woods went to a single-story, board and batten, one-room schoolhouse presided over by Schoolmaster Olan Langsford. At that time, children of all ages shared the same classroom. We learned by rote—as best we could, and at our own pace—how to read and write and count and do arithmetic.

"One unseasonably hot May afternoon, Master Langsford, parched from lecturing to us children, went over to get a drink from the oak water bucket he kept in a corner near his desk. He took the tin dipper down off its peg on the wall and wielded it like God Almighty parting the Red Sea. But the dipper scraped bottom and emerged with barely a swallow's worth of water.

"'Stouten!' he intoned, pointing at me—that would be the little freckle-faced, redheaded boy sitting in the front row. 'Go down to the spring and fetch me a fresh bucket of water.'

"I leaped up from my desk, grabbed the empty bucket from the for-midable schoolmaster, and ran—swift-footed as a young Achilles—down the hill to the spring.

"The sun's light flashed like a dagger on the cool, fresh water. Just as I was about to dip the oaken bucket, a movement in the grass on the opposite side of the spring caught my eye. A frog! Green and shiny, it hopped along the bank. As I watched, an urge came over me, an urge I couldn't resist.

"Compelled, I chased after that little green fellow, trying to pocket myself a pet frog. But the frog was too quick for me, and hopped into the spring. Pursuing my little-boy instincts, I got down on my belly, dipped my hand into the water, and tried to grasp that elusive amphibian. Try as I might—swirling and splashing spring water in all directions—I could not catch that nimble little critter.

"All of a sudden, I remembered my teacher's command!

"I abandoned my quest for the frog, dipped the wooden bucket in the spring, and raced back to the schoolhouse.

"Solemnly, and with as much dignity as a small boy could muster, I carried the filled bucket up the middle aisle—past all the rows of desks, and all the other pupils' staring eyes—as Master Langsford watched my approach. He sat with unquestionable authority behind a massive desk on an elevated platform at the front of the classroom. I placed the bucket full of water before him, like an offering to the Lord, and high-tailed it back to my seat. Master Langsford descended from his throne, filled the dipper, raised it to his parched lips, and took a full draught of water.... He stopped mid-swallow, his face registering the look of someone performing a difficult cipher in his head.

"The class sat, mesmerized, silently watching a most unusual performance by their venerable schoolmaster. Master Langsford emitted a series of coughing, sputtering, and gagging noises. As a grand finale, he emitted a tremendous groan, paused as if for a drumroll, then spat out the water all over the front row of pupils, including me.

"I could feel my jaw drop like a lead weight. Some of the bolder pupils tittered.

"'Stouten! I can't drink this water. It's full of mud!'

"I hung my head in shame. I could feel the blood creep up my neck and all over my face. I was terrified that Master would take off his belt and flog me.

"When the teacher's ruler came down with a hearty crack on my fingertips, I was actually relieved. Master Langsford often quoted Samuel Butler's line, 'spare the rod and spoil the child,' seeming to take those words to heart and at face value. And so did I, at the time. Much later, come to find out, most probably that line of verse was written to poke fun and not to be taken so seriously."

I hug my daddy. "I'm sorry he hurt you, Daddy."

"Well, you know, Lissa, school wasn't all bad. Sometimes, good things happened at that schoolhouse.

"I remember one day in early spring; the sun was very clear and bright, and the last of the snow was melting. A man from the county seat—it was still over at Port Tobacco at the time—came by and administered what he called intelligence testing. He got all the boys and girls to answer a series of questions and do some ciphering. He claimed our scores on these tests would tell him how smart we were.

"Well, at the end of that day's testing, the man pulled me aside and told me I was the most intelligent boy he had ever tested. Imagine that, Lissa!"

"Do you think I'm smart, Daddy?"

"Yes, Lissa. Sharp as a briar. Just like your daddy."

My daddy tucks me in. I kiss him on the cheek and say, "Goodnight."

I do go to school the next day. I know it's what I'm supposed to do.

Today, we go to Gwynn Oak Park. It's one of my favorite places. I wear a minty-green puckery dress with white stripes. Jimmie calls it my seersucker dress. Spence wears matching shorts. Jimmie makes most of our play clothes, and she likes us to match, so we pretend, sometimes, that we are twins.

Gwynn Oak is full of rides and noises and people and smells—merry-go-round music, the big wooden roller coaster going clackety-clack, kids screaming, a fat lady laughing at the funhouse, and pretty pink cotton candy getting spun on cardboard sticks.

First, Jimmie takes me on the caterpillar ride. It's scary when the cover goes over us. Then my daddy takes Spence and me over to the goat cart rides. Spence goes first, then me. The goats are supposed to run around a track that has a fence around it. Spence's goat stops at the first turn in the track to nibble at the grass. Spence uses his reins, but his goat won't budge. Then it's my turn, and the man lets my goat go. My goat goes fast-fast and runs right past Spence's cart. I get to the finish line, and then watch with my daddy while Spence keeps trying to get his goat to move. Finally, the man goes and swats Spence's goat to get it going.

After that, I watch with my daddy while Spence rides the sail plane. It goes up and flies in a circle with the other planes. Spence can steer his plane and make it dip left or right.

I say, "I'm going to get bigger and bigger for that." And my daddy laughs and holds me up so I can see better over the fence.

"Don't get too big," Daddy says. "You won't be able to sit on my lap anymore."

Next, Jimmie takes Spence on the roller coaster. I'm afraid of the roller coaster, but Jimmie and Spence are not afraid to go on any of the rides. Jimmie gets sick to her stomach, and we have to leave early.

The park is crowded now and we have a long walk back to the Oldsmobile. It's getting dark by the time we get to the car. The rides are lighting up like it's Christmas all over the park.

My daddy can't see very well at night, so Jimmie has to drive us home—even though she's sick.

When it's very hot, me and Spence beg my daddy to take us to Pasadena Beach on a Sunday afternoon. Jimmie packs a picnic hamper and a thermos bottle and a cold watermelon. My daddy blows up our inner tubes. Mine is a red-and-white ring with blue clowns on it; Spence has a big yellow duck with a head that quacks when you squeeze it.

Me and Spence put on our bathing suits in the back seat of the car. We have lunch at a green picnic table, and then we have to wait an hour before we are allowed to go in the water so we won't get cramps and drown. Spence and me crawl on top of an overturned rowboat, and Jimmie snaps our picture with a camera that folds out in front like a tiny accordion.

My daddy holds my hand while I wade out into the water. Spence goes splashing on ahead of us. Later, we take turns going down a big sliding board into the water. I would be scared, except my daddy is waiting at the bottom, holding up my inner tube so I can slide right into it—safe—at the bottom of the slide.

Sometimes we go to another park on the other side of the water. We take the streetcar downtown and wait on a wooden platform—my daddy calls it a pier—for a steamboat named *Bay Belle* to come and take us across the water. My daddy says we are crossing the Chesapeake Bay. The air is wet and cold, and wind hits us in the face and blows our hair around. The seagulls screech at us. I hold my daddy's hand. We are on an adventure together.

Then we are at a magical place called Tolchester that has gondola swings and pony rides and a child-sized steam train and little boats you can ride on. I fall asleep on the way home. Then I wake up just enough to feel my daddy carrying me up to bed and tucking me in.

One day, my daddy comes back from downtown with presents—a pair of matching kids' fishing rods—one for me, one for Spence. The next afternoon, he packs up our rods, along with his own fishing pole. My daddy tells us he had it specially made for himself from a very fine wood, which I think he calls *my hog's knee*. He keeps his pole in a fancy case, in the big trunk in the back of the Oldsmobile. We ride over to a little river near Gwynns Falls. Daddy shows us how to put worms on our hooks, and we stand on the bank and fish all afternoon until it starts to get dark. I catch two fish. Spence doesn't catch any.

As we walk back to the car, Daddy brags, "Look at what a good fisher your little sister is, Spence!"

Spence hangs his head and kicks a big stone at the car's tire.

There is a playground just a few blocks from our house with see-saws, baby swings, big-kid swings. Jimmie walks there with me and Spence on sunny afternoons while my daddy stays at home working on watches.

One day, a little boy with chocolate skin knocks me over—on accident—when I am standing too close behind the big-kid swings. I start to cry, and his daddy runs over and apologizes to Jimmie. Then the daddy takes off his belt and whips his little boy hard, and the boy screams and screams. Jimmie says he doesn't need to do that, but he does it anyway. The daddy looks scared of us and really angry at his little boy. He keeps apologizing to Jimmie and beating on his son. I wish he wouldn't do that.

Me and Spence are not baptized. My daddy thinks we should decide for ourselves what church to join when we are older. For now, Jimmie takes us to Sunday school at Emmanuel Lutheran Church, just a few blocks past the playground. In the summer, we go to Bible school there.

Jimmie takes me up to meet my Sunday school teacher. I hide behind Jimmie's skirt when the teacher tries to hug me and make a fuss over me.

She says, "I'm a real mother hen." She is short and puffy, but she's not like the little small red hen in my storybook.

"What's the matter, Lissa? Cat got your tongue?" she asks me, and tries to smooth my hair.

"She's fine," Jimmie says. "She'll talk a blue streak soon as she gets home."

My daddy teaches me to say my prayers every day. At home, before every meal, I sit on my daddy's lap or stand up next to his chair at the head of the table and say grace: "Bless us, O Lord, and these Thy gifts, which we are about to receive, from Thy bounty, through Christ, our Lord. Amen."

Every night, before I go to sleep, I kneel beside my bed and pray: "Now I lay me down to sleep, I pray the Lord my soul to keep. If I should die before I wake, I pray the Lord my soul to take. Amen." Then I say a list of God blesses that gets longer and longer: "God bless Daddy. God bless Jimmie. God bless Spence. God bless...."

I don't like the taste of milk. So, Jimmie gives me coffee-milk. It starts out as warm milk with a little bit of coffee added for flavor. As I get older, I ask for more and more coffee in the milk.

My daddy makes me a little rocking chair—just my size—and paints it pink for me. After supper, I like to rock in it, sip from my mug of coffee-milk, and read out loud from a big storybook called *A Patchwork Quilt of Favorite Tales.* The book is full of pictures of all the storybook animals and people. I like to feel the words as I shape them with my lips and send them out to float across the room. I pronounce all the words just so, and put all the ending letters on them. I make the animals and the people in the stories talk in different voices.

If I mess up a sentence, I get upset with myself and read the sentence again and again before I can go on.

"If you keep going," Jimmie says, "you can figure it out." She gets impatient with me sometimes and calls me a fussbudget, or "Miss Priss."

My daddy calls me "an old soul."

If I don't know a word, I show it to my daddy and he pronounces it for me. My daddy likes to look up words in the dictionary, and he knows all kinds of magical-sounding words—like asafetida and excelsior and psithurism.

Ours is the last house on the block, next to a store. The other houses have backyards shaped like rectangles, but the store cuts off part of our backyard into the shape of a triangle. I have an imaginary jump rope. I turn my arms around and around and pretend to jump it. I can count to one hundred and not miss. I like to watch Miss Beulah across the alley in her yard. She wears a sunbonnet when she comes out to water her roses.

Miss Beulah calls over. "What are you doing, child?"

"I'm jump-roping."

"Your mother ought to go get you a real jump rope," she says and goes back inside, toting her watering can.

Sometimes, I pretend I'm the little small red hen from my storybook. I dress just like the little hen. I wear a little apron, a shawl, a sunbonnet, and Buster Brown lace-up shoes just like hers that my daddy bought me from Mr. Gambini. I carry a little pair of scissors in my apron pocket just the way the little small red hen does in the story.

While I am outside, walking "picketty-pecketty" and pretending to gather sticks, I leave my door unlocked. The cunning fox sneaks in, hides behind the door. He jumps out at me and I fly up to the rafters—this is when I flap my pretend wings and run up to the top of the back-porch steps. The fox runs around and around below me until I get dizzy and fall off my perch. That's when the fox catches me, stuffs me in a sack, swings the sack over his shoulder, and carries me back toward his den. But the fox gets very tired in the hot sun. He is lazy, and stops to have "forty winks."

So then, while the fox is napping—just like the little hen—I use my scissors to cut my way out. I play a trick on the fox by pushing a big stone into the sack. Then I run back home.

The fox wakes up, carries the sack back home, and dumps the big stone in the pot of water Mother Fox has "on the boil." So, just like the little red hen, I outsmart the wicked old fox. Instead of boiling me for supper, he and his wife get terribly scalded and die.

I am safe at home, living a quiet life, and sweeping the hearth in front of my pretend fireplace. The End.

Jimmie goes to the Food Fair once a week, and usually I go with her. She tells me to hold onto the back of her skirt so I won't get separated from her and get lost. It's just a few blocks down the street, so we walk there. We roll the grocery bags back in the big baby carriage I used to ride in as a baby.

One day, I let go of Jimmie's skirt in the store and wander down a long candy aisle. I see a big bag of M&Ms; it's open, and pretty candies are spilling out. My sweet tooth gets the best of me, and I go over and start eating the spilled candies. When Jimmie comes back to find me, she gets very upset.

"Stop that, Lissa. That's stealing!"

I don't know I am stealing, but I feel very guilty. I will never do that again.

Another day, when we take our groceries up to pay for them at the cash register, the checkout lady tells Jimmie the store is having a coloring contest. They will be giving prizes to the winners. Jimmie takes one of the Campbell's Kids coloring books home for me to color. I know that Daddy still wants me to color right-handed, but I want to do a good job and win the contest, so I color the pages when Daddy's not around. But I keep falling asleep when I'm coloring, and all the pages have to be colored by the end of the week. Spence finishes coloring them for me.

Weeks later, I am the winner for my age group. My prize is a pair of ball bearing roller skates, but they're way too big and fast for me. Because Spence helped me with the coloring, Jimmie gives him the ball bearing skates. She buys much smaller skates for me—without the ball bearings.

Spence likes to go fast, and he doesn't mind falling down. My daddy says he is reckless. Spence, Daddy tells me, tumbled down the stairs all the time as a baby, and once, when he was just four years old (which I can't remember), Spence fell off the edge of the front steps, hard, right onto the pavement. Jimmie is always scolding Spence for running around barefoot and coming home with big gashes in his feet from stepping on broken glass. Jimmie patches him up, and then out he goes again!

Spence learns to roller skate in a just couple of days. I can hear his skate wheels whizzing on the cement as he zooms down the pavement, all the way down to Edmondson Avenue.

My daddy always tells me to be careful, and I am afraid of hurting myself. The first time I put on my little skates, they roll out from under me, and I fall smack on my butt. I stand up and try to hold onto the brick wall of the grocery shop next door, but my feet keep wanting to roll out from under me.

"You gotta let go of the wall, Liss," Spence tells me.

"I don't want to."

Spence grabs me around my waist and tries to pull me away from the wall.

"Just hold onto me," he tells me. But I'm too scared to budge.

Finally, Spence helps me sit down on the sidewalk.

"Here, let me take off one of those skates, Liss. Then you can practice on just one skate."

Spence shows me how to wear my skate on my right foot and use my left foot to push myself along. With just one skate, I can go all the way up to the end of the block. Not as fast as Spence, but pretty fast. Fast enough for me.

I turn the corner at Harlem Avenue. A girl is standing on her front steps, bouncing a little red ball against a wooden paddle. The ball is on an elastic string that looks like a long rubber band. This girl can keep the ball going, almost forever, without missing. "What happened to your other skate?" the girl asks me. "You can't skate with just one skate."

"Yes, I can," I say, and keep on scuffing along down Harlem Avenue.

With my Bazooka bubble gum, I can blow a bigger bubble than she can. One time, Spence has me compete with her. He grabs me by the arm and tugs me along to her front steps. The paddleball girl is standing with her big sister on the top step. Spence and me stand on the pavement at the bottom of those steps.

"Here's my sister, Lissa," Spence says to the big sister. Her name is Ella. "I bet my sister can blow a bigger bubble than your sister."

"How much you want to bet?" says Ella.

"Yeah," says the paddleball girl. Her name is Juanita.

"How about a nickel?" says Spence. "You can use it to buy more bubble gum."

"Okay," says Ella. "It's a bet!"

"Yeah," says Juanita. "It's a bet!"

Me and Juanita stuff as much bubble gum in our mouths as we can. We chew and chew to get the gum all soft and wet.

"Ready, set, blow!" says Spence.

I blow and blow. I see Juanita's bubble getting bigger and bigger. It gets about as big as her face, but then she stops blowing. I keep blowing until my bubble gets even bigger than my face.

"The winner!" Spence says and pulls up my right arm as far as it will go.

I forget to stop blowing. Then the bubble pops and sticks all over my face.

Spence gets the nickel from Ella and takes me home to Jimmie.

Jimmie scolds me for making such a mess of myself. She has to scrub for a long time with a washcloth and use witch hazel to get the gum off.

Then Spence takes me around the neighborhood and brags about me. He tells me to blow another bubble to prove how big I can blow it. This time, the bubble gum gets stuck in my hair, and my daddy has to get it out with benzene he keeps under his watchmaker's bench to clean watch parts. After that, I just blow normal-size bubbles.

CHAPTER THREE

MAYBE, MAYBE NOT

SOMETIMES on weekends, Jimmie drives us way, way out into the country to visit her mommy and daddy on their farm. She drives our big black Oldsmobile. Me and Spence sit in the back seat. It's as big as the davenport in our living room. Daddy stays at home. He doesn't like to go out to the farm.

"I prefer city life," he says when he kisses me goodbye.

We drive out from the city where all the houses and stores are close together and there are lots of big buildings and cars and pavements. The farther we go, the farther apart the houses and stores are. Then the roads start to go up and down more and get skinnier and there are steep hills and curves, and for a long time there are hardly any other cars. We go past long fields with wheat and tall green cornstalks so thick you can't see through them. Then there are cows and horsies and barns. I know we are almost there when we get to a little town Jimmie calls Grangerville. It has four gas stations and a drugstore and a hardware store and a Twin Kiss soft ice cream place and four stop signs where two roads come together that Jimmie calls the Crossroads. Then we turn left at Sweeney's grocery store and go a little farther past what Jimmie calls the Nike Missile Base. It's behind a tall chain fence, and a soldier in a little house guards the big double gate. Jimmie says they keep missiles there to protect us from the Russians who are our enemies.

We turn right and go what Jimmie says is seven-tenths of a mile, and then we are at Granddaddy Friedrich's and Grandma Magda's chicken farm. We drive up the bumpy driveway. The old house has a big front porch that pokes out under two big trees. Jimmie says they are Norway maples that Granddaddy planted there for shade. The windows at the side of the house seem to watch us as we drive around to the back and go in through the back porch to the kitchen. The kitchen is where the grownups sit around a big round table, eating or talking. The dining room is next to the kitchen, but it's kept closed up most of the time, except in the evenings when Granddaddy goes in there to watch the television.

One day, Grandma and Jimmie send me into the dining room to take a nap on the sofa in there. Grandma closes the door so she and Jimmie can talk about grownup things they don't want me to hear. When I wake up, I play by myself for a while under Grandma's big dining room table. I pretend to be a kitten, and pounce at the light as it dances through the lace tablecloth. After a while, I crawl out from under the table, across the scratchy rug to the door, and call out, "Meow?" Where is everybody?

Spence must be outside somewhere with Granddaddy. I can hear Jimmie out in the kitchen, helping Grandma Magda fix supper. I am tired, and I don't feel so good. I want something to eat. I go out to the kitchen and tug at Jimmie's skirt.

"I'm hungry," I say.

Jimmie is talking to Grandma Magda. They don't seem to hear me. So, I tug harder at Jimmie's skirt and shout as loud as I can, "I'm hungry!"

"Jimmie, make that child stop whining," Grandma says.

I am very angry now. Why are these big people ignoring me?

Grandma Magda is very large and very fat. I heard Daddy say once to Jimmie, "I feel sorry for your father, Jimmie. He's henpecked. It's your mother who rules the roost."

So now I pretend Grandma Magda is a big, fat hen perched on a big roost above the kitchen table. The roost is drooping and swaying under her fatness.

"You need to discipline your daughter now before it's too late," Grandma says.

"I think maybe she just needs a little something to eat to tide her over till supper's ready," Jimmie says.

"Mark my words, Jimmie. You're going to spoil that child if you don't punish her."

I don't like the sound of that word—punish. It makes my heart hurt. I'm so hungry I'm getting dizzy and my head aches. I pull at Jimmie's skirt harder. Jimmie pushes me away. I let go and let myself drop to the floor. I scream and cry and start to roll around on the floor. Grandma Magda is bending over me now. She slaps my face. I scream and kick and hit back at the big, fat hen who is hurting me.

In my head, I hear words I've heard somewhere. Some of them are repeating, repeating, repeating inside my head:

One, two, buckle my shoe
Three, four, open the door
Five, six, pick up sticks
Seven, eight, lay them straight
Nine, ten, a big, fat hen...
A BIG, FAT HEN
A BIG, FAT HEN
A BIG, FAT HEN!

"She's throwing a tantrum," Grandma Magda says. "Put her out in the car until she calms down."

"No! No! Don't! Please, Jimmie! Don't!" I cry and scream as Jimmie carries me out to the Oldsmobile. It's parked in the driveway under one of the big Norway maples. Jimmie locks the car door on me. I scream and scream and watch her walk away, up the front-porch steps, back into the farmhouse.

I scream until my throat hurts and my sides hurt. I am panting hard. I'm trying to get the air to come back inside me. My skin is sucking in against my ribs. I can't breathe! I think I may *snuffocate* to death.

I press my face to the car window. I watch and wait for the white door on the front porch to open, for Jimmie to appear. It seems like forever. I'm still waiting. I am too tired to cry anymore. I just wait and wait. Something inside me seems to break. My heart wants to split open and stop ticking.

Finally, the white door opens and Jimmie comes out to the car.

"Are you ready to behave?" I hear Jimmie's voice through the glass on the car window that separates us.

I just nod. I am too tired to say anything. I am like a broken watch. I stop ticking. Jimmie leads me back inside. I will try not to cry so much anymore. I will be-have, be-have, be-have.

Later that year, when my Grandma Magda dies, I don't cry at all. Now I am *being have*.

I am a very good reader. I love to read. My mother, Jimmie, lets me read out loud to her when she is combing my hair. I read to her from *The Bobbsey Twins* and *Old Man Rabbit's Dinner Party* and lots of those Little Golden Books, stories about Snow White and Cinderella, and Mother Goose rhymes. I like the one that goes:

> *There was a crooked man, and he walked a crooked mile.*
> *He found a crooked sixpence upon a crooked stile.*
> *He bought a crooked cat, which caught a crooked mouse,*
> *And they all lived together in a little crooked house.*

But, for some reason, it does bother me that everything is crooked and not perfect.

Jimmie calls the people who live in the house right next to us colored people. Daddy sometimes calls them a name that starts with an n, but Jimmie says I mustn't repeat that word because it isn't nice.

"Why are they called colored people, Jimmie?"

"Because they aren't white like us. Their skin is a different color, it's dark, and they have different ways."

Sometimes, when Daddy is smoking his cigar out on the front steps, he sees a very dark colored man named Curtis washing and polishing a big shiny black car at the curb. Curtis wears a rolled-up lady's stocking over his hair. He waves at Daddy and calls out, "How you doin', Mr. Power?" He has a big white smile and seems very friendly.

Daddy is not very friendly back. He just nods and halfway tips his straw hat and mutters something about Curtis always showing off his Cadillac with the whitewall tires.

One day I leave my *Lady and the Tramp* coloring book and my new box of giant crayons on the floor in the little room right behind the front door that Daddy calls the vestibule. When I come back, my crayons are gone. I see a little colored boy running away with them down the block. I tell Jimmie and Daddy, but the little boy is gone, and I never get my crayons back.

Another time, I leave my red tricycle out front on the pavement while I walk with Spence up to the grocery shop. Next thing I know, a little colored boy comes running past us, gets on my tricycle, and rides away as fast as he can pedal down the block. Spence runs in and tells Daddy a little colored boy just took my tricycle, but Daddy is working on a watch and gets mad and starts cursing and using the n-word I'm not supposed to say. So Spence tells Jimmie, and she walks with me and Spence around the whole neighborhood to look for my tricycle. We go up and down alleyways, and finally I see my red tricycle in a backyard. Jimmie talks to a colored woman who is pinning up wet clothes on a line. Jimmie tells her what happened and shows her the special number my daddy carved on the handlebars to show that it belongs to me. The woman looks tired and sad. She just waves her hand at my tricycle and says, "Go on, take it." One of the back tires has a slash in it, but Daddy fixes it for me.

Daddy says our house is called a row house because it stands up like a brave soldier in a row of other houses with no spaces between them. That is why, one day, our house almost catches on fire. Jimmie smells grease burning in the kitchen in the house right next to us, where Curtis lives with his sister Mabel and her children. There is just a wall between us and that house, and the wall starts to get hot, and Jimmie smells smoke. I watch while she runs over to the yard next door and raps on the back door. Nobody answers. Jimmie calls the firemen, and they come in a big red firetruck and break down our neighbors' door and spray water all over the place.

Later, I hear Jimmie and Daddy talking about it. Daddy uses the n-word and says, "All this push for desegregation while it's *those* people who are ruining the neighborhood." I'm not sure what desegregation is, but I can tell Daddy doesn't like it.

At School 65, in first grade, they give all the children tests to see how smart they are. They put me up with the second graders. My new teacher, Miss Eriksen, puts me in a special reading group with two other kids who are extra good readers. She makes us read out loud, faster and faster.

At home, my daddy lets me read the newspaper with him in his armchair. I sit on his lap, and we read the funnies together. He lets me help him with a newspaper puzzle he does every day. You have to unscramble some words, and some of the letters have circles around them. You put those letters together, and unscramble them again to find out the surprise answer to a cartoon riddle. I am learning to do it, very fast, all in my head.

One morning, I come downstairs for breakfast and I find Jimmie, sitting on the davenport, talking on the phone. Usually, by this time of day, she is wearing a housedress and has her hair pinned up in a bun. But this morning, she is still wearing her pretty nightgown—it's smooth and glossy and the color of black cherries—and her hair winds long, black, and wavy down her back.

Jimmie hangs up the phone. She is crying. I hate to see Jimmie cry.

"Why are you crying, Jimmie? Did your daddy die?"

Jimmie looks up at me and stares. "Yes. Just last night. He had a stroke."

"Don't cry, Jimmie." I stroke her hair. "I hate to see you cry."

"But how did you know Granddaddy died?"

"Because I know how much you love your daddy. I think he was missing Grandma."

I ask to go to Granddaddy's funeral. Jimmie thinks I'm maybe too young to go, but my daddy lets me. He stays home with Spence. Jimmie goes to the Methodist church early to help with arrangements. I ride with my Uncle Frantz past miles and miles of farms. He drives very fast around the curves, and slams on the brake at the very last minute. I reach out both hands to keep myself from falling into the dashboard.

Uncle Frantz grins. "Did I scare you?"

The church is very small and plain compared to Emmanuel Lutheran. All of Jimmie's brothers and her sister are here, along with a bunch of other country people. Uncle Frantz takes me to sit next to Jimmie on a hard wooden pew. Jimmie is crying into a handkerchief. Her nose looks red and swollen.

"Do you want to say goodbye to Granddaddy?" Jimmie asks.

She takes me up the aisle to where Granddaddy is asleep. He is tucked into shiny white sheets in a narrow bed surrounded by baskets of soft white lilies. Granddaddy is a farmer, and he usually wears over-alls and an old felt hat. But today, he is all dressed up in a black suit.

"Why is Granddaddy wearing lipstick?"

"The undertaker fixed him up to look nice," says Jimmie.

I sit back down with Jimmie. Now everyone seems to be crying. The organ plays, and we sing sad hymns. The preacher talks about a house with many mansions where we will all go some day. I keep my eyes on Granddaddy. I know, for sure, he will wake up at any minute, sit up straight, and surprise us all. And everyone will laugh and hug, and we'll all be happy. And maybe even Grandma Magda will come bustling through the back door behind the altar. She always loves big family reunions.

When school closes for the summer, Daddy sells our house in the city because Jimmie inherited her parents' property, and we move out to Grandma and Granddaddy's spooky old farmhouse in the country. It has a big front yard, and all kinds of trees and bushes and flowers, and gardens all around it, and you can sit on the big front porch in the summertime. The house has pointy parts on its roof that my daddy calls gables.

We have an incubator in the cellar where we keep baby chicks, and we have three chicken houses: a little house for the pullets, a bigger one for the broilers or fryers, and the biggest one for the layers. We also have a rooster and a couple of broody hens.

Spence and me have to do regular chores now. Jimmie teaches us how to feed the chickens every morning and evening, and how to get the eggs every day.

My daddy pays Jimmie's brothers to change Granddaddy's old garage into a woodworking shop, and turn part of the barn into a garage for our big black Oldsmobile. Daddy even has a phone put up on a post out in the woodshop.

When school starts up again, I have to go to a brand-new school in the county—an Annex school for just first and second graders, away from the bigger part of the school where my brother goes for fourth grade. The Annex is a little brick school with only four classrooms— lower and upper first grade and lower and upper second grade. They put me in second grade here even though I was in second grade last year in the city. They go by different rules here in the county.

First, they put me in the lower second grade, but soon they move me to the upper second grade across the hall. But then they keep me stuck in the middle reading group. I can hear the kids in the top reading group, and I hear them stumble over words I know how to read, but I think I am invisible to Mrs. Breton, my new second grade teacher.

In front of the Annex school there is a playground with swings, a jungle gym, and a big circle with a white line drawn around it. The circle is for playing games. At recess time, when the circle is empty, I sometimes skip around and around it, following the white line—all by myself. When the other children are playing in the circle, I like to just stand and watch them. If it's windy, I get cold just standing there, but I don't really know how to play with the other children. I miss being at home with my daddy.

I am the new kid at the Annex. All the other kids went to first grade together. I am very shy, and don't know how to make friends here. I find friends in the storybooks I read, or I make up imaginary friends in my head. I have a gold plastic Snow White ring that I got in a cereal box. I wear that ring to school every day. I talk to Snow White sometimes when I'm by myself on the playground.

After school every day, as soon as we get home, Jimmie and Daddy make us change into our work clothes, so our school clothes don't get messed up when we get the eggs and feed the chickens.

I hate it when the teacher makes us play Quizmo. It's like a bingo game, but you have to do arithmetic to get the answer. I don't like adding and subtracting all those numbers. I don't understand number games, and I think I may be afraid of some of the numbers.

In class, I am afraid to raise my hand to tell the teacher when I have to go to the bathroom. One day, I wet myself at my desk. The back of my dress is soaked, and there's a big puddle around my feet. When it's time for recess, I go to the girls' bathroom. My shoes got wet and they make a little track, which I hope no one will notice. I squeeze out the back of my skirt into the toilet, the way Jimmie uses the washing machine wringer to get the extra water out of our wet clothes when she does the laundry.

All during recess, I stand up against a wall to hide the back of my dress. I hope it will dry out before we have to go back inside.

But then recess is over, and we have to go back into class and sit at our desks for Quizmo. An old man, the janitor, comes into our class and shouts out to Mrs. Breton, loud enough for everyone to hear, "Where's the little girl who wet herself?" Mrs. Breton points me out, and the janitor comes over with a bucket and a string mop and wipes up all around me.

The only good thing is that Mrs. Breton doesn't call on me for Quizmo.

At home, my daddy sometimes lets me read for him what's in the big black letters—the newspaper HEADLINES. There is something called a Sputnik that just sent a dog up into outer space. There are people called Communist dictators in a place called the Soviet Union. My daddy blames the bad headlines on the Soviet Union and its crooked politicians. He hates crooked politicians. He says they are bad because they tell lies.

He says, "President Roosevelt trusted his 'Uncle Joe' Stalin, and Uncle Joe lied and walked all over us. Now we have that rascal Khrushchev to deal with."

My daddy tells me, "Lissa, you must never tell a lie. You must be straight as an arrow."

Whatever my daddy says to me is very important; it goes around and around in my head, and it won't go away. I scrape my mind trying to figure out how I can ever be really sure I am not lying. How can I ever be sure about what is really true? To stay safe and never tell a lie, I always say, "Maybe, maybe not." I answer every yes/no question that way. Other questions, I say, "I don't know."

If my teacher asks me a question, like do I like the story she is reading to us, I say, "Maybe I do, and maybe I don't." If my mother asks me if my alphabet soup is hot enough, I say, "Maybe it is, and maybe it isn't." How can I ever know for sure what is hot enough or not hot enough?

At night, a mean witch visits me. She balloons up and out from under my bed, clutching something that is very important to me. She runs away with it, cackling like the wicked witch in *The Wizard of Oz*. I wake up screaming and Jimmie asks me, "What's the matter? Are you okay, honey?"

I tell the truth the best I can. I say, "Maybe I am, and maybe I'm not." That way, I don't tell a lie, and I am safe for now. If my daddy asks me if I am finished with my homework, I say, "Maybe I am, and maybe I'm not."

This goes on and on. My big brother, Spence, says I'm acting goofy. My teacher sends a note to my parents that says I am having some kind of problem.

In February, all the kids put Valentine cards for their friends in a big cardboard box. I still don't have any friends here. Jimmie gives me a card for the teacher, and I put that in the box.

On Valentine's Day, Mrs. Breton's favorite student—a boy with a big forehead who is not shy at all—is the postman. He delivers all the cards to our desks. I only get two cards—one from the teacher and one from a little girl whose mother makes her give cards to everyone in the class.

Finally, in spring, my daddy takes me out to sit with him in the red porch swing he built for Spence and me. He painted it red—me and my daddy's favorite color. It's evening, and the wind is tickling the leaves on the maple trees the way I tickle my daddy's whiskers. In the swing, we look out over what used to be my Grandma Magda's tulip garden.

Daddy asks me, "Lissa, why don't you ever give us a straight answer anymore?"

"Because I'm afraid I may tell a lie, and you say I should never tell a lie, Daddy. So all I can say is maybe, or I may be telling a lie, and then you will be mad at me."

"Well, you know, my little tadpole, just do the best you can, and I won't be mad at you. Sometimes, the truth is kind of hard to get at—like trying to figure out what color a tulip really is, or whatever really happened to old Fringe-a-Frock."

"Fringe-a-Frock? Did it happen in *once upon a time*?"

"Yes, Lissa, once upon a time, way back when I was a little boy. So, come back with me to the far end of nowhere…where everything begins. There, you can decide for yourself what happened, and the truth is whatever you make it out to be."

I let out a big breath, and with it, all the maybes and maybe-nots, and snuggle up closer to my daddy.

"Lissa, you see the tulips here? Some petals are a pure velvet red, but others are a mix of colors—like those over there—red, stippled with gold, and maybe even a little purple if you look very close.

"The tulips are in full bloom today, just as they were at this time of year on Tulip Hill in Southern Maryland when Fringe-a-Frock decided to force a log through the saw at his lumber mill. Now, Fringe-a-Frock was not a tailor, as his name might suggest; he ran a sawmill down near Criderstown, off a tributary of the Loco Moco River. He was sawing lumber to build a house for his new bride, and he wanted it done quickly.

"When a stubborn log bogged the saw, he yelled at his steam engine, 'More steam! Give me more steam!' as he stoked the fire. The log began to move again; the saw began to chew, then bogged again. 'More steam! Give me more steam.' He increased the pressure on the boiler. The saw groaned a mighty groan, then bogged again.

"Again, Fringe-a-Frock increased the pressure. Then with a final, terrible groan from the saw, the boiler blew, sending the steam engine and Fringe-a-Frock flying every which way. The only visible remains of Fringe-a-Frock were some fragments of his shredded clothing hanging from a nearby tree, which, some say, was a tulip tree."

"I bet it was a tulip tree," I say.

My daddy nods, and says, "And I bet you are right, Lissa."

Afterward, Jimmie makes me raw fried potatoes for supper, and I go to bed. The witch doesn't come to visit tonight. And in the morning, the maybes and maybe-nots are gone away—for now, anyway.

One day, we have an air-raid drill at the Annex. The air-raid siren goes off real loud—BREEEET, BREEEET, BREEEET, and the teacher tells us to get our coats from the cloak room and crawl under our desks with our coats overtop of us. If someone is really dropping a bomb on us, our coats will protect us from the flying glass.

"Walk quickly, class, don't run," Mrs. Breton tells us. "No pushing or shoving."

I get jostled and pushed by some of the bigger kids in the cloak room. We have to stay under our desks until we hear the all-clear sound.

Sometimes, I dream at night that a big bomb in the sky is falling on me. It's very scary. Soon after this, the counting begins.

CHAPTER FOUR

THE COUNTING BEGINS

A T the farmhouse, we inherit my granddaddy's television set. Gray shadows are blinking on the TV screen. That's when the counting begins. If I count to twenty-four, I am safe. I like the number four. Numbers that have four in them are safe.

On Saturday nights, after supper, we all watch TV in the darkened dining/living room. Every Saturday night is the same. I am on my daddy's lap in his armchair. Jimmie is in her chair, and my big brother, Spence, is on his mother's lap.

First, we watch *The Lawrence Welk Show*. Jimmie loves the man who plays bouncy accordion music. Daddy gets a chuckle out of the way the band leader talks and how he counts out the beat when he conducts, "Ah, one, and ah, two, and ah, three!" I like it at the end of the show when the "Champagne Lady" goes out into the audience with Laurence Welk, and they dance in the ballroom with all the bubbles coming up around them.

Then we watch *Gunsmoke*. Matt Dillon is always in a shootout, and he always wins. Sometimes, bad guys come to Dodge City and make trouble for Miss Kitty at the Long Branch Saloon. Now I am counting to be safe—one, two, three, four…. All this counting is inside my head. Counting is my secret. No one—not even my daddy—knows about it. Counting to just the right number—but not going past it—keeps me safe. If I pass the top number I set, I have to start all over again. So sometimes I count to this special number over and over again. If I don't do it, something bad will happen.

Sometimes, I have to go to the bathroom while the others are watching TV. The bathroom is at the top of the stairs. To get there, I have to walk by myself through the dark hallway, past the closed downstairs bedroom where Jimmie's mother and then her father died. I think that the ghosts of my grandparents, and maybe other dead relatives, maybe even some of my daddy's relatives, too—his mother, Lovenia, and his oldest brother, John, who slit his wrists long before I was born—are in that downstairs bedroom.

At night those bedroom walls melt away and the room turns into a big meadow with hills and flowers and shady trees and a shiny stream where all my dead relatives meet to have a picnic together. All my pets are there, too—my turtle who got squished under the cellar door, and my parakeet who flew away and never came back, and one of my cats who got run over. That bedroom becomes a special place in heaven where my dead relatives all meet and are glad to see each other again.

I tiptoe past that bedroom door, careful-careful not to disturb them. I cannot open the door and peek in, or they would all have to disappear. There is a wolf that hides in the shadows, near the bottom step. I turn on the light switch at the bottom of the stairs, run quick-quick up the fourteen steps to the bathroom, and turn on the bathroom light.

But then I have to go back down the stairs to get back safely to my family. If I don't make it back down the stairs and back into the dining/living room before the toilet finishes flushing, the wolf will eat me. I flush, wash hands, and run down the stairs and through the hall as fast as I can—1, 2, 3, 4, 5, 6, 7, 8, 9, 10, 11, 12, 13, 14—through the hall, 15, 16, 17, 18, 19, 20, 21, 22, 23, 24—STOP counting to be safe. Now I'm back safe in the dining/living room.

Besides repairing clocks and watches, my daddy makes wooden inlaid lamps, plates, and jewelry boxes. He made me a jewelry box of rosewood with a pink rose inlay on the top and a gold key shaped like an "L" for Lissa.

My daddy is such a perfectionist that if he discovers the littlest flaw in a piece of cherry or walnut or mahogany, he starts to swearing and plucking the hairs out of his head. After a while he tosses that piece out, no matter how far done he is, and starts over. He keeps telling me, over and over, "Lissa, you are my best and most perfect creation. I turned you on the lathe myself." He tells me I must be ladylike at all times—I must be quiet, obedient, and perfect in every way that he thinks is perfect.

I am skinny. "You eat like a bird," Jimmie tells me. And my ears poke out. Jimmie makes me wear a scarf tight over my ears at night to try to make them grow flat against my head. My hair is getting very long now. Jimmie pulls it back tight and puts it into two long braids so it won't get so tangled. My daddy thinks I am the prettiest girl in the world.

My daddy never makes a fuss over Spence the way he makes a fuss over me. He expects Spence to follow in his footsteps and become a craftsman. Daddy is disappointed; Spence would rather stare for hours into his microscope, or tinker with his chemistry set, than work in the woodshop with my daddy. My daddy yells at Spence whenever he does something wrong.

Sometimes, I make Spence so mad he punches me. Then I cry and run to my daddy, and Daddy always takes up for me. He scolds Spence and tells him he must always take care of his little sister.

"She's just a little girl," he tells Spence.

Daddy tells me not to cry. "Your face gets ugly when you cry. If you cry too much, it will grow that way." So I try harder than ever not to cry. I don't want to be ugly.

And me and my brother have both learned *never* to slam a door—not when my daddy is working on a watch.

Some days, when my daddy's clock repair business is good, the old farmhouse echoes with musical chiming, and bonging, and ticking, and whirring—on the hour or half hour or even sometimes on the quarter hour. Daddy keeps the fixed clocks on a long, flat table in what used to be Grandma Magda's sun parlor. He likes to keep the clocks running for at least a week before his customers come to pick them up. That way, he can be sure they are working well and keeping time.

A French mantel clock may swing its golden sun-shaped pendulum; an anniversary clock may twirl four shiny chrome balls, clockwise and counterclockwise, showing off its polished workings underneath a glass cover. A carved wooden bird may pop out of the oval-topped door of its carved Black Forest house, flutter its painted wings, and let out a rowdy "cuc-koo, cuc-koo, cuc-koo" to tell you the number of the hour. A spice clock may keep up a quick steady tick, tick—as comforting as a baby's heartbeat. A mahogany mantel clock with a heavy brass pendulum may make a loud gong, gong, gong that you can hear all over the house.

The clocks my daddy fixes come in all different shapes—banjo clocks, chariot clocks, clocks with columns and pedestals, a clock that looks like Felix the Cat and rolls its eyes and swings its tail.

Sometimes, other, larger clocks come to stay for a while at our house. A tall Regulator wall clock with a long pendulum has a tick that's so loud it breaks into the silence at night. A sweet cherrywood grandmother clock rotates bright phases of the moon through a hole in her face—as the weeks go by, you can see the moon's faces, changing ever so slowly.

Grandfather clocks. Well, they are so big, my daddy usually goes to the owners' houses to fix them. Sometimes, one of the finials—those things that stick out the top of the grandfather clock's head, like two curvy horns—is broken off or missing. Then Daddy turns a brand-new finial on the lathe in his workshop. He makes the new one so carefully, carefully; it must match its twin, in size and shape and color and grain, exactly. Then he goes back to visit the clock at its home, and gently, gently, he attaches the new finial, just so.

"Clocks need to be tended to, Lissa. Cleaned, oiled, and adjusted. You should keep them wound, but not too tight. Some clocks you need to wind every day. Some will run for eight days without stopping, but you should wind them before they run all the way down.

"Now, an anniversary clock can run for an entire year without winding, but it won't keep the most accurate time."

One rainy Saturday, Spence shows me how fun it is to jump up and down on his bed. We can almost hit the ceiling when we jump. We jump higher and higher. Spence can touch the wallpaper above the bed and make squiggles on it. Jump, jump, jump....

"What the hell's going on up there?" It's Daddy's voice! We both freeze, standing on Spence's patchwork quilt. We hear Daddy's heavy steps creaking on the stairs.

He throws open the door and shouts at us. "Goddammit! You children nearly made me ruin this watch." He's holding up a gold pocket watch. Its uncoiled mainspring dangles from its barrel in Daddy's trembling hand. "And I could have put my eye out with this mainspring."

We had forgotten—or maybe we didn't even realize—that Spence's bedroom is right above the room where Daddy keeps his watchmaker's bench and works on watches. That room is lit by one of our grandma's old Victorian chandeliers. The chandelier hangs from that room's ceiling, right below Spence's bed.

"The ceiling was shaking. The chandelier was swinging. It could all have come crashing down on my head!"

"I'm sorry, Daddy!" I say, but he isn't listening. He turns away and makes his way back down the stairs to finish fixing the watch.

"Boy, is Daddy mad," I say to Spence. But Spence has moved on to something else.

"You know how you say you have claustrophobia, Liss?"

"I know I do. I don't like being stuck in little tiny places where I can't escape. It makes me feel like I can't breathe. It's like when Daddy tells me I mustn't cover up my head at night, or I might asphyxiate myself. He says that means I won't be able to get enough air to breathe while I'm sleeping."

"Well, claustrophobia is just a kind of fear you need to get over. And I know a way to cure claustrophobia," Spence says. He points to an old trunk at the foot of his bed where Jimmie stores winter woolens and extra blankets. He pulls everything out of the trunk and dumps it on the floor. Moth balls roll out from the woolen folds.

Spence takes out an old wristwatch from his desk drawer. Daddy gave it to him. It has a second hand for timing things.

"Get in the trunk, Liss. If you can stay in there for a whole minute, you'll be cured of claustrophobia."

"I'm scared to, Spence!"

"You'll be fine for just a minute. Underwater swimmers can go a lot longer than that without air. Come on, get in."

He holds open the curved lid of the trunk, and I get in. He closes the lid. All is can smell is mothballs. And I'm all scrunched up inside. I hate it! I can hardly move! I try to push up on the lid, but Spence is sitting on it. I start beating on the lid.

"Let me out! Let me out!"

Finally, after what seems like a long time, Spence gets off the lid and I push it open and get out. "I couldn't breathe in there! Why'd you sit on the lid?"

"Jeez, Liss." Spence looks at his watch. "You were in there for less than fifteen seconds!"

"I hated it!"

"Jeezy peezy, Leezy. Take it easy! You're never going to get rid of your claustrophobia that way. I was just trying to help you."

***

Usually, I run to tell Daddy whenever Spence does something I think is mean. But I don't tell him about Spence trapping me in the trunk; Daddy is already mad at both of us for disturbing his work. That night, when my daddy comes to tuck me in I ask him, "Are you still mad at me and Spence?"

"No. I can't stay mad at you children. Sometimes I lose my temper."

Then Daddy tells me a bedtime story from long ago.

"On windy days, some folks claimed they could hear ghosts whispering and moaning over in Fallen Angel Swamp. And so, it happened that one fall afternoon, after working late in the fields, I started the long walk home through Piney Woods due north of Fringe-a-Frock's old sawmill. I was hungry for a good hot supper. In the distance, I could see the sun sinking behind Tulip Hill at the far western edge of my Pappy's tobacco farm.

"My ears perked up. The wind was rising. I turned up my collar against the cool evening air and descended a long slope down, down into the marshy wetlands to escape the turbulence. Halfway down, I lost the sunlight. At the bottom of the slope, I began to feel a powerful tugging at my boots. I heard a gulping noise—like a scaly underwater creature transforming itself into a fierce amphibian, breathing heavily, gasping for air, emerging after centuries of struggle from the murky waters, trying to suck off my boots, gobble them up, and swallow me.

"Just then, on the verge of crossing Crider's Creek, I halted midstep at the sound of a deep, eerie voice, crying out 'Knee deep, knee deep!' Was this an omen warning me of the water's depth? Or was it the hideous swamp demon many folks believed had dwelled for generations in the depths of Fallen Angel Swamp?

"Well, just as a precaution, I stepped back onto the safety of the creek's mossy bank, and found me a sturdy ash branch. With my pocket knife, I sharpened one end of that branch to a point and whittled a barb into it, sort of like a harpoon. Then I rolled up my britches to above the knee, grabbed my spear, and began once again to ford the creek, ready to do battle with that ferocious swamp monster.

"Again, mid-step, I heard a voice, a different voice this time, one that warbled with the crippled twang of a very old man. 'You'll drown, you'll drown!' creaked the voice. Surely this was the voice of a wise woodland spirit or guardian angel or holy saint, warning me not to cross these cursed waters, this River Styx!

"So rather than venture across those dark waters, I pulled myself up the soggy creek bank and spent the night sleeping on higher ground.

"As the sun rose next morning, I could plainly see that the water was indeed shallow, no deeper than my ankles, and that those otherworldly voices had been nothing more than the false warnings of a couple of croaking bullfrogs!

"I crossed Crider's Creek in safety, and got home in time for breakfast. 'Course, my Mammy was right anxious about my welfare, and she scolded me something fierce, even while she served me up a helping of cornbread and clabber. I reckon she had a bad temper, too. Runs in the family, it seems."

At the end of Daddy's story, he gives me a big hug. The croaking frogs make me laugh. Daddy's tall tale and his hug take the fear out of bad tempers, and make me feel safe again.

CHAPTER FIVE

MOON ROCKET

Our first year living on the farm, Spence gets a compass for his birthday, and Daddy teaches him how to read it. Spence goes on long hikes around the neighborhood and uses the compass to draw up a map on a big sheet of Daddy's mechanical drawing paper. When he's done, Spence shows me his map.

"Look, Liss, if you don't want to get lost out here, you need to learn the lay of the land. See? I wrote the four directions along the edges of this map—north (left), south (right), east (top), and west (bottom). You need to know the four directions so you can read a compass. I put different size rectangles with labels to show where buildings are.

"This is us," he says, "Our property." Spence and me are sitting cross-legged next to each other on the front-porch floor, and he has the map spread out in front of us. He points to our twelve acres. Our place is nested right in the middle of the map—farmhouse, grape arbor, Daddy's woodshop, three vegetable gardens, barn and corn crib, three chicken houses, and two big fields that run all the way over to the east and south woods at the top and right edges of the map. At the top-right corner of the map, an arrow pointing beyond the east and south woods says *To Grangerville Crossroads*.

"Out past Grangerville is the Long Green Valley. But I ran out of room, and couldn't fit that on the map," Spence explains. "Mommy says that's where some of her Amish Mennonite relatives live on big farms."

Another arrow labeled *Horse Country* points north. "That's what Mommy calls My Lady's Manor," Spence tells me. "That's where, a long time ago, the King of England gave a big parcel of land to the first Lord Baltimore, and later on, another Lord Baltimore gave this manor part of it to his wife, who was a lady."

"Daddy says I must always be a lady, and not use bad words and be quiet and obedient."

"Well, Liss, this is a different kind of lady, with a capital L, who is married to a lord. Lords and ladies are all rich. Mommy says the ones who came here were from important English families who were friends with the king. They came over here and set up big horse farms, and went to the Episcopal church that's still here. And at Thanksgiving, they still wear their fancy red or black riding coats and riding hats or top hats and shiny boots, and bless their hounds and mount their horses and go hunting for foxes."

"I feel sorry for the foxes, Spence, even though, in my storybook, sometimes foxes are bad and trick little small red hens."

"Well, I think foxes are pretty smart. Maybe they have fun playing tricks on the horses and hounds."

"Maybe. But I don't guess they like to be chewed to death by the dogs."

Spence shrugs, "Who knows?" I can tell he's ready to move on to the next thing. Daddy has told me Spence doesn't like to go too deep into his feelings. "He's like his mother that way." I'm not so sure about that. I like to think maybe Spence and Jimmie are just trying to be practical, or even brave.

But now, Spence *has* moved on. He's pointing out Aunt's Essie's place, next to ours, on the map. "See Liss, that's just north of us, and there, even farther north and over toward the east, is Mr. Clay's dairy farm." Mr. Clay has been farming our fields since Granddaddy got sick and died.

Spence has drawn a pair of curvy lines to show the road at the bottom of our front yard. Across the road is Brenner's place—a house and barn with fields all around. There are woods behind it that run up a hilltop all the way to the west edge (bottom) of the map. In the evenings, we can see the sun going down behind Brenner's woods from our front porch. The Methodist church (a box with a triangle drawn on top) is at the bottom-left corner of the map. We can see its steeple from the upstairs windows on that side of our house. In good weather, Spence and I walk there for Sunday school.

As the year goes by, Spence takes me along with him to explore our twelve acres. Out in the east woods, we discover a hillside where rusted old cars are half-buried under dirt and dried brown leaves. We call it the Car Graveyard. Down a pathway between the east and south fields, we find a beautiful tree with big greenish-yellow blossoms shaped like tulips growing all over it. Some of the flowers have dropped to the ground, and we bring them home for Jimmie. "I see you've found the tulip tree," she says, and smiles as she puts the flowers in a big glass Mason jar on the kitchen table.

One day, we find glittery rocks in the east field, and tote two of them into the kitchen.

"Look what we found, Mommy!" Spence tells Jimmie. "Look at all the sparkly speckles buried in these rocks! We found gold!" Jimmie is washing dishes. She dries her hands on her apron and examines the small flat rocks.

"Sorry to disappoint you, Spence. But that's just fool's gold. It's not really valuable. You'll find it all over the property, especially in the woods and in the fields."

"Liss!" Spence shouts, all excited. "Let's excavate the rest of these ancient ruins. We'll do what archeologists call a *dig*!"

Spence finds an old coal shovel in the cellar. We use it to dig around the foundation of Daddy's woodshop. We find pearly white shells with glossy rainbow colors inside, poking up through the mud, and run to show them to Jimmie.

"Look what we found behind Daddy's shop!" Spence says, lifting up a shovelful.

"Oh," Jimmie says. "Those are oyster shells. Your Grandma Magda loved oysters. She used to toss the shells out there when she was done eating the oysters."

Daddy has built a bookcase for us in the hallway. We clean up the oyster shells and polish them. I color pictures on some of them with crayons. Then we use the shells to decorate empty spaces between the books on the shelves.

With Spence, the adventures and ideas just keep on coming. Behind the barn, we find all kinds of neat stuff, piled in an old rubbish heap nearly a story high—broken concrete, chipped cinder blocks, scraps of rusted metal farm tools, a cast-iron and white enamel bathtub, rotting planks, a thrown-away icebox, rolls of chicken wire, old tires, and thrown-away car license plates.

"We can use pieces of this old junk to build a rocket ship," Spence says. "I can be the pilot, and blast off to the moon. We'll use some kerosene from the tank for rocket fuel.

"Liss, next Saturday, let's get up real early. You can help me build a spaceship behind the littlest chicken house. By nighttime, we'll have it ready, and I can blast off to the moon."

After supper and homework, I sit in my bedroom at the oak desk my daddy built for me and begin to write a story, printed in pencil in a composition notebook, about our moon rocket project. There are four main characters—Spence, me, Perry (Spence's best friend at school), and Perry's little sister, Jeannine, who's a year younger than me. Spence asks me to call him Captain Rewop (power spelled backward).

By Friday evening, I am up to Chapter Three of my story. I am not good at drawing, but I sketch some pictures in crayon to illustrate my story, including one with me, Perry, and Jeannine on the ground waving goodbye to Spence, who peers out the round window of a pointy-tipped spaceship as it blasts off into space on a trail of flame and smoke.

Before going to bed, Spence and me set our alarm clocks for four A.M.

Saturday morning is rainy and foggy. We sleep through our alarms. I get up before Spence, as usual, when Jimmie calls me to help make breakfast. I always make my daddy's breakfast—coffee and oatmeal. In the pantry, I stand on a two-step stool my daddy built for me. As I do each step, I recite it inside my head:

1. Fill the saucepan with water up to the place on the inside where the handle is attached.

2. Scratch a wooden matchstick on its box—it's easier and safer for me, my daddy says, than using a little cardboard match.

3. Light the gas stove and be careful not to burn myself.

4. Bring the water to a boil in the saucepan.

5. Dig the oats out of the cardboard box with the Quaker Oats man's picture on it, one fistful, another fistful, then one-half of a fistful—Jimmie only fills her fist once, but her hands are much bigger—and drop the oats in the boiling water.

6. Turn down the flame.

7. Stir the oats around with a big spoon.

8. Let the oatmeal simmer while I make coffee in the blue and white speckled enamel pot.

When I'm done fixing Daddy's breakfast, I get Spence up to feed the chickens. Daddy takes his place at the head of the kitchen table, beneath the Regulator clock. I sit on his lap and say grace.

After breakfast, I watch TV with Spence—*The Lone Ranger* and cartoons, and we snack on cereal right out of the box. Finally, Daddy comes in and chases us outside.

"Too much television will rot you children's brains," Daddy says. "There's a cathode ray tube inside the television making those pictures you see on the screen. Who knows how much radiation is coming at you through that TV screen."

Jimmie gives us a basket and tells us to go get the eggs and give the chickens some more feed.

In the big henhouse, the gray speckled hen is nesting on her eggs. I hand the basket over to Spence. "I'm scared of that hen. She always tries to peck me when I try to get the eggs out from under her. If you get the eggs, I'll scoop the chicken feed out of the bin."

"Oh, all right," says Spence. "You're such a sissy, Lissy." Spence plunges his hand under the gray hen. She makes a fuss and pecks at Spence, but he retrieves her eggs and moves on to the other nests.

The feed bin is built into the wall of the henhouse. The bin's almost as tall as I am, and when I open the lid, I can see that the feed is low and the scoop is way down inside there with the grain. I hoist myself up against the front of the bin. I hold onto the top of the bin with both hands, balance myself just below my waist, and flip the whole top of my body forward and down into the bin. That's the only way I can reach the bottom. It's getting dark outside, and I have to feel around for the hard metal of the scoop, but what my fingertips touch is something cold and scaly. And it moves!

"Spence! There's a snake in the bin!" I yank my hand away and swing back up and down onto the henhouse floor.

Spence comes running over and takes a look down into the bin. "Yep. It's a snake, all right. A big black snake coiled up down there. Looks kind of like an old rubber boot."

We head back to the house with the basket of eggs and report the snake to Daddy and Jimmie. Jimmie goes back to the chicken house with a sharpened hoe. Spence goes along with her. I follow along, but keep my distance while Jimmie chops up the snake, tosses it out in the field, and comes back to feed the chickens. Me and Spence forget all about our moon launch. And before we know it, the day is gone.

On Sunday, I walk to Sunday school with Spence. Spence and me wear our perfect attendance pins fastened to our Sunday best clothes. Sometimes we stay for the church service, sit together on a hard pew, and secretly time the minister's sermon with Lovenia's gold watch.

My daddy and Jimmie always stay home on Sunday mornings. After church, we have a big Sunday dinner with fried chicken, all kinds of vegetables, and Jimmie's special lemon meringue pie for dessert.

On Sunday afternoons, I like to read, or watch old Shirley Temple movies on TV. If it's windy, I like to go out in the field and let the wind blow me around. One Sunday, I find a flattened patch of wheat in our south field, hollowed out by the wind. I bring a library book with me, but I don't read it. It is late in the afternoon, and the sun, like the wheat, is golden. I lay me down to sleep, and hear the wind singing my name.

When I wake up, it's getting dark, and the wind is blowing stronger. I stand up in the field, spread my arms, and dance with the wind. Daddy says the soul rides on the breath. I think the wind must be the earth's soul. It's so powerful! It holds me up when I lean against it, and I think I can feel God's soul riding on it.

I hear the wind whisper, "Soon, Lissa. Soon." But then it's just Jimmie, calling from the back porch, "Supper. Supper's ready!" From here, she and the house look small and far away.

Then it's Monday—Blue Monday, my daddy calls it—and there's school and school and more school. And before I know it, we're helping Jimmie plant the vegetable gardens and rake the straw off the early spring strawberries.

My daddy all-of-a-sudden decides to help Jimmie with the tilling. He hooks up the disc harrow and cranks up Granddaddy's old tractor. He needs somebody to sit on back of the harrow to weigh it down, so the discs can dig into the soil and slice up the plowed earth. Spence is off somewhere else.

I volunteer to sit on the board at the back of the harrow, but my daddy makes too sharp a turn with the tractor. The harrow careens up at a steep angle off the ground, and I'm too light to hold it down. I just sit there—still as still—until Daddy backs up a little, and the tiller goes back down flat and even on the dirt.

"You saved my life," my daddy tells me. "If you had gotten scared and jumped off, that tractor would have flipped over on me. You are a brave little girl." Even Jimmie says, "Yes, that was brave of you. You are a brave little soldier." I don't usually feel very brave, but what my daddy and Jimmie say makes me feel good about myself.

In June, the yellow school bus drops Spence and me off from school one last time. We run up the driveway, change into our summer shorts, toss our loose-leaf notebooks on the trash heap out by the grape arbor. Spence lights a match to all our school papers. We dance around the fire, slap our palms to our mouths, and let out Indian war whoops, "Whoooo! Whoooo! Whoooo!" We are released from school—me from second grade, Spence from fourth grade—for the summer!

In the summer, Spence and me help Jimmie sell vegetables from her gardens. We hang up a little blackboard sign by the road at the bottom of our front lawn. *Fresh Vegetables. Picked While U Wait. Sugar Corn 60 Cents a Dozen.* When a car comes rolling up our driveway, Jimmie finds out what the customer wants, and then we run out and help Jimmie pick it fresh. Jimmie always prices the corn ten cents more than what the local store is selling it for.

"Customers are willing to pay a little more to get their vegetables fresh," Jimmie tells us. "And we always give them a baker's dozen, thirteen ears, in case there's a bad one."

We put the money from the customers in a big piggy bank that we keep on a shelf in the pantry. By the end of the summer, the piggy is stuffed with coins and one-dollar bills. Jimmie lets us use the money to buy our school supplies in September.

Jimmie has taken over her dad's chicken-and-egg route. On Friday nights, she and her sister, Aunt Essie, kill chickens out back, then pluck them and clean them in a big washtub beside the back-porch steps.

My daddy doesn't take part in any of this. He doesn't like to kill things or see them killed.

"You can tell a lot about a person," Daddy says, "from the look on his face when he kills a helpless animal. Some folks will frown or will look perturbed, or intent or resolved—or even pained—when they lay a chicken's neck on the chopping block and drive the hatchet down. But others...yes, I've seen some others who seem to take pleasure from killing.

"I saw one man down in Charles County, a grizzly-looking farm-hand, smile as he wielded the hatchet. I saw his face split into a wide, triumphant grin as the blade found its mark and blood erupted from that chicken's severed neck.

"And there's some men that take sport in watching beheaded chickens squawking and running in circles—run, flop, run, flop—until they collapse into a trembling feathery heap. Some actually make bets as to which chicken will run the longest before it drops."

So that's why, on Friday nights while Jimmie and Essie are out back killing chickens, Daddy holes himself up in the dining/living room, shuts all the windows and doors tight, and tries to block out unwanted sounds coming from the chicken massacre that's going on outside. He reads article after article from his watchmaker's journal or from *Popular Mechanics*. I've even seen him read the same page over and over again, the same way I sometimes count certain numbers over and over to ward off evil thoughts and keep myself safe.

Jimmie is the one who catches the chickens and chops off their heads. I watch her, and she doesn't smile when she does it. She just looks determined to get the job done in time for Saturday's delivery. Essie helps with the plucking and cleaning, plopping the naked white chickens into a big metal washtub to soak. Sometimes, Essie and Jimmie sing old Methodist hymns while they work. It's usually past my bedtime before they're finished.

On some Saturday mornings, after I fix Daddy's breakfast and say grace on his lap, I walk over a little footbridge to Aunt Essie's next door for breakfast. Jimmie stays behind to load up the trunk of the Oldsmobile with chickens, and, in the summer, fresh vegetables.

I carry a tin of chewable milk of magnesia tablets in my dress pocket. At Aunt Essie's, I have squash pancakes covered with super-thick syrup that sometimes makes me get carsick. One time, I had to throw up out the car window right after our first stop. That's why, now, on chicken route days, Daddy always makes me take a tin of milk of magnesia tablets with me, in case I start to feel sick in the car.

I sit up front next to Jimmie as she drives along the route. Our first stop is at what Jimmie calls a "mansion." We drive up a long curving driveway, past tennis courts and a swimming pool, to a big beautiful stone house.

Jimmie raps on the screen door at the back and calls out, "Hello, anybody home?"

A lady in a white uniform—Jimmie tells me she is the cook—comes to the door and holds it open for us.

I am carrying paper bags of peas and string beans I helped Jimmie pick early this morning, when everything was soaking wet with dew.

"You can put those bags over there," the cook tells me, and points to a big round wooden table.

Enormous copper pots and pans, polished shiny bright, hang from a thick wooden beam above the table. The kitchen has a gigantic stove and an oven big enough to cook Hansel and Gretel at the same time.

Jimmie carries in chickens, boxes of eggs, and bushel baskets of fresh corn and tomatoes.

After that, we drive across a bridge over a big lake that Jimmie calls The Reservoir.

"Jimmie, what's a reservoir?"

"It's a big pool where people get their drinking water. This one is man-made."

"Can you go swimming in there?"

"It's not for swimming. But some people go fishing there."

"Oh, yeah. I see some rowboats out there."

After The Reservoir, we are in the suburbs. We stop at a few homes where customers live in new ranch houses and split-levels. Then we drive downtown to an old neighborhood with big shade trees and wide sidewalks.

Mrs. Tyson, one of our regular customers, lives on Mount Royal Avenue in what Jimmie calls "a brownstone apartment building" that has wide front steps, a balcony with a fancy black railing, flowers in window boxes, and a turret like a castle. Mrs. Tyson is an old lady who does sewing.

"Hello there, Lissa," she says. "Would you like to see what I'm working on now?"

I nod, and she pulls out a miniature trunk and opens the lid for me.

"Look, see what I've got tucked in here." One by one, she pulls out a whole collection of doll clothes—an apricot-colored silk slip and matching panties, a crocheted traveling outfit, an embroidered satin coat, and a fur muff.

"Do you know what this is?"

I just shake my head and say, "It's beautiful!"

"This is what you call a bridal trousseau. It's all the outfits the bride doll takes with her to wear on her honeymoon.

"And this," she points to a tiny pink satin heart at the bottom of the trunk, "is a lily of the valley sachet. It makes everything smell nice. Would you like to meet the bride?"

"Oh, yes!" I clap my hands.

Mrs. Tyson opens a small cabinet and pulls out a bride doll dressed in a white wedding dress with a lacy white petticoat and a full-length veil.

"Can I touch her, Mrs. Tyson?"

"Certainly, Lissa," she says, and holds the doll out to me.

"Lissa, let's make sure your hands are clean," Jimmie says. She inspects my hands. "Okay, go ahead. But be very gentle with her."

I cradle the doll in my arms.

"I'm raffling her off for my women's society. The proceeds will go toward a fund for homeless girls. It's five dollars a ticket, and if you win, you get the bride doll and her trousseau. I've sewn everything by hand."

"Oh, Jimmie, please, please. Can we get a ticket for her? She's so beautiful."

"Well, honey, five dollars is kind of steep for us right now. I don't know."

I can tell that Jimmie would like to get the doll for me, but she doesn't like to spend a lot of money.

"Tell you what," Mrs. Tyson says. "How about you throw in an extra tomato or two—you know how I love your tomatoes—and I'll let you have a ticket half price, two dollars and fifty cents."

"Well, I do like to support a good cause," Jimmie says. "It's a deal!"

I'm so excited. Maybe I will win, and maybe I won't. But even if I don't win, I'm happy, happy, happy. Jimmie did this for *me*.

Tonight is one of those hot, sticky summer nights. After supper, I sit on the front porch, across from Spence, in the red swing. My daddy made it with all the edges rounded, so it wouldn't hurt us.

Spence's and my feet are pumping the swing. We are wearing shorts, and sometimes our bare knees just touch. We are pretending we are traveling to the Land of Oz.

I can hear the creak-creak of Aunt Essie's rocker on the floorboards. Jimmie sits next to her in a green metal porch chair. Jimmie's skin is tanned as dark as Tonto's on *The Lone Ranger*; her fingers move over peas or limas or mending—it's too dark to for me to see what.

The lighted front porch is safe, like a fortress with a concrete railing that protects our family from the spooky night shadows, the whispering leaves, and the lonely road. From time to time, a car whooshes past, and I can see the tire swing Daddy roped up for me and Spence on one of the front-yard maples.

Like most nights, Aunt Essie comes over from next door after supper to visit with Jimmie. Aunt Essie is a widow, and she doesn't have any children. She's wearing an apron, and she has an almanac spread open on her lap. She licks the first finger on one of her plump hands, turns the pages, and reads out loud. She works her way through the weather forecasts, and then all the ads—salve for boils, and praying hands for your dashboard, and where you can send away to get your horoscope charted.

My daddy doesn't care for Aunt Essie's company, so he excuses himself and goes inside to smoke a cigar and read the evening paper in his armchair.

In my head, I can see exactly what he's doing inside. He's doing his rituals. First, he's screwing his watchmaker's loupe into his left eye socket, clamping down on the loupe to keep it in place. Now he's folding the newspaper precisely—my daddy insists that things should be precise. He uses the nails on his thumb and forefinger to make sharp creases in the folds and to get the paper folded into exact quarters so it is an efficient size for reading. Most every night is the same.

Tonight's an especially hot night, and the air is thick with lightning bugs. I overhear my aunt saying there will be a new moon. I lean forward in the swing and whisper to Spence, "I'm going to look out for that new moon. I've never seen one."

Spence shakes his head and gives me a big brother I-know-better-than-you laugh. "You're a real dummy, Liss. You will never see a new moon. It's invisible from the planet Earth."

Spence reads all kinds of science books, and he fills his notebooks with pencil sketches of planets and solar systems and rocket ships. Even though we didn't get Spence's spaceship built last fall, Spence stills says he is going to be the first man on the moon when he grows up. I figure he ought to know what he is talking about, and I give up on the idea of ever seeing a new moon.

Just as Spence and me are pumping faster and faster to travel as fast as the speed of light over the deadly poppy fields, I hear leaves shivering and branches snapping in the treetops. Then I hear a rebel yell so loud it almost explodes my ears. Our dog, Jupiter—we call him Jupy, and Spence says he's a mutt, a mixed breed, part greyhound—is lying on the porch steps. Jupy throws his head back and howls. I am so scared I draw back into myself, kind of like a turtle, away from Spence and everybody.

Jimmie calls out, "Who's there?"

"Oh, that's just Lonny, jumping around in the trees," Aunt Essie says. "That boy loves to climb trees. He can jump from one tree to the other."

Jimmie says Lonny is the neighborhood orphan. His mother died when he was born, and his daddy used to beat on him. Then, when he was a teenager, his daddy got killed from driving drunk and crashing into a cement culvert on this very same road. Aunt Essie takes pity on Lonny. In return for helping her out with chores, Aunt Essie gives him an allowance, and lets him live in an old beat-up aluminum trailer that sits on cinder blocks out behind her apple orchard.

Now, I see—in a flash of heat lightning—the white parts of Jupy racing back and forth between the tree trunks, circling the trunk on the right, leaping up on it. His body is long, and he stretches it up the tree trunk. His front legs are slim like my wrists, and they climb way up the trunk. The nails of his front paws scratch at the bark. He is yapping up at Lonny.

Jimmie calls up to Lonny, "You ought to be careful up there, or you're liable to break your fool neck." Her voice is strong and sure—just the opposite of mine. She's not afraid of Lonny the way I am.

But he's so tall—already a six-footer. He's too young for a driver's license, but he has a shiny black souped-up Ford that he works on in Aunt Essie's driveway; he put a Hollywood muffler on it. Whenever the fire department siren goes off, Lonny revs up his car and roars off to chase the fire engine.

Lonny's voice is low and deep, and he has a sullen way of walking—not straight and proud, but hunched over and scowling. Sometimes, he's nice to me and gives me rides on his bicycle handlebars. At the Sunday school picnic, he tries, I think, to protect me. He tells Jimmie she ought to get me out of Dempsey's pool because I am turning blue. I don't know how to swim, so I just stand in the shallow part and shiver.

I am glad Jimmie knows how to put Lonny in his place. She can also drive a tractor as well as any man, and she wears her hair tied back in a knot and doesn't worry about how she looks all the time or frizz her hair or rinse the gray hairs blue the way Aunt Essie does.

My daddy tells me Jimmie's people don't trust him. They are not Catholics; he calls *them* holy rollers. They think he is too old to marry Jimmie; she is much younger. And my daddy doesn't like Jimmie's people, either. He calls Aunt Essie sanctimonious. He says her hired hand, Lonny, is a juvenile delinquent who ought to be put in a reform school. One time, Lonny shot holes in Daddy's shop windows with a BB gun.

I hear my daddy say to Jimmie, "If I say a single word against that boy, Essie just clucks her tongue like an old hen and tells me, 'Who are you to judge? Only God can judge.'"

"Well," Jimmie says, "she *is* my only sister."

CHAPTER SIX

CIRCUS

ABOUT one hundred feet behind our farmhouse, a lopsided red wooden barn leans away from the wind. One part is fixed up as a garage for our Oldsmobile. The other part has old stables in it, with splintery wood walls and three empty stalls. The feeding troughs have moldy hay in them. The floors are made of dirt and you have to walk across bird droppings and rat droppings to get across. One of the stalls has a rusty cow stanchion that's hanging like an empty noose over a skinny trench that somebody must have dug a long time ago to catch cow pee and poop.

Another part of the barn is where we keep my granddaddy's tractor and some rusty farm tools that Jimmie knows how to attach to the back of the tractor. There's a plow to turn over the dirt in the fields, a disc harrow to break up the big clods of earth after you plow, and a drill for dropping seeds. There's also a corn crib about two-thirds filled with field corn. Above the stalls, loose planks make a floor for the hayloft.

Every Tuesday, while school is out, the county library's bookmobile parks in the drugstore parking lot about a mile from our house. After I finish second grade at the Annex, Jimmie starts taking me and Spence there to borrow books. I like to carry my books up to my secret place in a corner of the barn loft. Here, I can read and take naps and dream up my own stories.

During the summer months, Essie's hired hand, Lonny, works the fields for our neighbor, Mr. Clay. In the middle of summer, Lonny invents a game he calls circus.

Lonny's circus begins one drizzly afternoon when the fields are mired with rainwater and fog is filling up the ground hollows. Right after our noon meal, I climb up the wall ladder to the loft, toting my latest Nancy Drew mystery book. I'm hooked on Nancy Drew! She's a girl detective who can do all kinds of things—ride a horse, drive a blue roadster, swim, everything! Nancy and her friends get into all kinds of scrapes and adventures, and she always solves the hardest crime cases. She's very brave. Kind of like Jimmie.

Just as I get to the next-to-top rung, who do I see propped up against a hay bale, puffing away at a cigarette? Lonny!

"What the hell are you doing up here?" Lonny hurries to snuff out his cigarette on his pants leg. I want to escape back down the ladder, but Lonny's voice is so deep and gruff now, it paralyzes me.

"Get on up here, girl," Lonny's voice booms. I am too scared to budge, so I just stare at Lonny's thick black eyebrows and slanty green eyes.

"You're not gonna tattle on me, are you?" Lonny comes over to the edge of the loft and sticks his head down at me. I look at the splinters in the ladder rung where my hands are holding on. I start to shake all over.

"Don't you cry, girl." I screw up my face and try not to. "You don't cry, I'll give you a stick of peppermint gum. Here."

I climb the rest of the way up the ladder and into the loft, take the gum from Lonny's hand, and stick it in the back pocket of my pedal pushers. They are my favorite new outfit—yellow with red-and-white striped piping. Lonny moves away and sits back down, cross-legged. My eyes sting from the pressure of holding back tears. I'm not brave like Nancy Drew or Jimmie.

"You're getting to be a big girl now, aren't you? You probably don't remember, but I used to play with you when you was just a baby. But you're a real big girl now. How old you getting to be?"

"Seven," I say, and bend to trace a seven in the straw dust on the loft floor.

Lonny leans back against a hay bale and lights another cigarette. "You're not going to tattle now, are you?" I shake my head and draw a line through the seven in the dust.

Lonny blows out a stream of smoke and peers up at the rafters where a rusting pulley system is mounted on a metal track that runs the length of the barn roof. A corroded hook, fastened to the pulley mechanism, dangles from a thick braided rope.

"You know what that rope's for?" I crane my neck and shake my head.

"Your granddaddy used to use it for lifting bales off the hay wagon up into the loft. See that hook on the bottom end of the rope?"

I nod.

"Well, it's rusted away now. Can't use it no more. But that used to hook into the hay bales."

Lonny half-closes his eyes and studies the rope. "I got me an idea how we can use that old rope and have us some fun." He pulls an empty dirt dauber's nest off the wall and crumbles it in his fist. "Go get your brother. Tell him I want to see him."

I climb back down the ladder, carrying my Nancy Drew book under one arm, knowing that my secret reading place is spoiled forever. I tell Spence, "Lonny wants you to come to the loft."

Spence climbs the ladder to the loft. I follow along after him. Lonny tells us, "I got me a brand-new game that'll be lots of fun. It's called circus."

Me and Spence watch Lonny use his pearl-handled penknife to cut off the rusty old hook from the lower end of the rope. The rope is a dirty brown-yellow color.

"This will be our trapeze," Lonny tells us, and he ties a big triple overhand knot at the rope's bottom end, stands on the knot, and jounces it.

"It'll hold."

He gets Spence to help him pile hay bales in the loft's back corner. "This'll be our takeoff and land platform."

Lonny grabs the rope knot and flings it out to test the rope's swing. It swings like the pendulum of a huge clock. The rope swoops down over the plank floor, then out over an open space, above my daddy's new garage. The rope knot crosses over the concrete floor; then up to less than a foot away from the far wall; then it comes back across to the hay bale platform.

Lonny stands on the rope and pushes off. He shrieks a rebel yell as he swings out. He wears his hair combed back into a ducktail. When he flies through the air, two strands of his hair flap over his ears like greasy black wings.

"It's tricky," Lonny says after he lands. He pulls a black plastic comb from his back pocket, slicks back his hair, and pats his ducktail back into place. "You got no place to land on the other side. So, once you start swinging, you got to hold onto the rope until you get back to the bales, so's you can land."

Lonny wipes his comb on the seat of his blue jeans and slides the comb back in his pocket. "If you can't touch your feet down on the bales, don't try to jump off or you're apt to hurt yourself. Just let 'er swing until I can get to you and pull you back over the loft floor. Give her a try, Spence."

Spence braces his insteps on the knot and grips the rope with his hands and elbows. Lonny hauls him up onto the hay bale launching pad and gives him a push off. Spence gives an imitation of Lonny's rebel yell, and swings out.

"Okay, Lissa. You're gonna catch your brother when he comes back," Lonny's voice roars at me as he picks me up and sets me down on the launching pad.

I try to grab Spence's heels, but I can't get a grasp.

"Higher up. You got to grab him higher up," Lonny yells.

"I hurt my hand."

"You do as I tell you, girl, and you won't get hurt. Now grab him higher up on his legs. Like this." Lonny catches hold of Spence and tells him, "Leggo the rope!" Spence flops down on the pile of bales.

"Now you swing on the rope, Lissa."

"No. My hand hurts."

"She's scared to," Spence says. "Lissa doesn't like to do scary things."

"Damn. Why, look. Ain't nothing to it. Just watch me." Lonny wraps the rope around one ankle and, standing on the rope knot, launches off. Ankles crossed tightly above the knot, he lets his whole body drop to swing full-length with his head dangling down.

I watch his face fill with blood and turn an ugly shade of purple. The cords of his neck jut out. The Olds isn't parked in the garage today—Jimmie took it out to do some grocery shopping at Sweeney's—so, by stretching out his arms, Lonny can trail his fingertips across the concrete floor and trace a trail of wiggly scrawls in the sifted straw. When the rope stops swinging, he reverses himself and drops easily onto the concrete floor. Then he climbs the wall ladder back up into the loft. "See how easy it is?"

"I don't want to do it," I whisper to Spence. I have what Jimmie calls a "stubborn streak" that she says can be "very provoking." But today I remember how my daddy always tells me not to hurt myself, and I put on that stubborn streak like a knight's coat of armor to protect myself from falling off and hurting myself.

"My sister doesn't want to," Spence tells Lonny. "And believe me, my sister won't do *anything* she doesn't want to."

"Well, listen." Lonny runs his fingers through his hair, picks at his teeth with a thumbnail, stares up at the roof beams, then down at me.

"Okay. Here's how we'll work it. You'll be the official circus catcher, Lissa. Spence and me'll be the flyers, and I'll be the ringmaster. That means I run the show." Lonny walks over to the back edge of the launching pad, squats down, and pulls out a carton of cigarettes that's wedged between two hay bales.

"Have a puff?" He lights a cigarette and holds it out to Spence, who swallows too much smoke and starts to cough.

"Listen, if you're going to be a circus performer, Lissa, you got to have you some costumes. Go look and see what you got tucked away in your bedroom drawers. Maybe you got something like a bathing suit or a nightie you can wear. But you mustn't tell your mother or she'll get real mad at you. Cross your heart and swear you won't tell."

I don't understand just why Lonny thinks Jimmie will be mad, but I'm too fearful of Lonny to ask him any questions. As scared as I am of Lonny, though, I'm even more afraid of disobeying my daddy.

"My daddy says ladies are not supposed to swear," I say to Lonny. Jimmie says that my daddy is the head of the household, and he is always right. I am not ever supposed to defy my daddy's wishes. If I do, it will make him cross. And I really don't want to make my daddy cross. The only time I've ever see him cross is when me or Spence make a sudden noise—like slamming a door—that makes Daddy drop a watch he is working on. Then he plucks the hairs out of his head, one strand at a time. And his eyes, which are usually a soft brown, seem to flash gold when he's riled. His mouth swims with ugly curses that terrify me because I understand them, but only partly.

Over the years, Daddy's spine has shortened and his once "straight as an arrow" neck and shoulders have begun to hunch; so, his face comes down close over me or Spence when he curses at us.

"I won't *swear* anything," I tell Lonny.

One Saturday, when it rains all afternoon, Lonny coaxes me to swing for the first time, sitting down on the rope knot. At first, I am trembly all over, but then I sail out through the air and it feels like I am flying on a trapeze in a real circus. Then I practice swinging again and again, until Lonny shouts at me from behind a pile of hay bales, "Come back here with me, and I'll show you how to do something else."

I crawl behind Lonny through a tunnel in the hay bales that opens into a small space in a corner of the loft. Lonny has been calling this little place my "dressing room," and this is where I have been changing my "costumes" in privacy between circus acts. Today is the first time Lonny comes with me into the dressing room, and he surprises me by pulling down his jeans and underpants. Then he orders me to "pull down your panties." I am wearing my favorite lace-trimmed baby-doll pajamas, printed with pink rosebuds, as a circus costume.

"I don't want to."

"You have to because I say so. I'm the ringmaster. And if you don't do what I say, I'll tell your mother on you."

I shake my head. I feel my eyes sting and fill with tears.

"Come on and I'll show you what me and my girlfriend, Cordella, do. Come on now. Pull your pants down."

I have seen Lonny's girlfriend once or twice in Lonny's car. Her hair is the color of straw and she teases it up high it like a miniature haystack piled up on top of her head. She wears white lipstick that makes her mouth look like a tiny powdered donut. She chews gum and pops it in time to the rock 'n' roll music on Lonny's car radio. According to Jimmie, Cordella is a "bad" girl.

I am afraid to disobey Lonny. My fingers fumble at the elastic waistband of my pajama bottoms. My nervous thumb slips; the elastic snaps back and stings my waist. Above my head, I hear rain beating against the loft window, beating hard and rattling the window frame like a wild animal trying to get in.

At the same time, I hear Lonny's voice, repeating, "Don't you dare tell your mother or she'll be real mad at you."

The two sounds blend together and become muffled as Lonny squats opposite me and scoots me farther and farther back into a corner of the loft until my head scrunches up against a hay bale. My feet slip out from under me on loose chaff and straw. The straw smells moldy, and it scratches my arms and legs. I close my eyes. I draw into myself, rigid and tight. I try to be so small no one can see me.

Lonny pushes my legs apart, shifts his weight, and keeps rubbing up against me, trying to push into me. I'm not sure exactly what he's trying to do. But after a while, he moves away from me, and I open my eyes. There is Lonny, towering over me, zipping up his pants. When he sees me looking up at him, he shifts his eyes away and turns his back on me. Then he is gone, and I know he has not been able to do what he wants to do.

I don't want to play circus anymore. I think something bad and wrong must be going on here. But I don't know for sure what is wrong or what I should do. I don't feel safe. I count to twenty-four over and over in my head.

———

"You children spend an awful lot of time in that barn. What do you do in there?" Jimmie asks when Spence and me are sitting at the kitchen table, eating fresh pea soup and dumplings. Daddy has already finished his meal and has gone back to work in his shop.

"Nothing," Spence mumbles and walks outside. I finish my soup and run out after him. "Why did you say 'nothing' just now?"

"Lonny said not to tell."

"But you lied to Jimmie."

Spence lowers his eyes and walks away from me.

I go around to the front of the house and sit in the tire swing, dangling my feet, scuffing up the dirt. I watch a tractor in the field. It carries a long side blade like a scythe and mows down timothy, clover, chicory. In the distance, I hear chainsaws whine. Then I see they are cutting their teeth on a grove of poplars but sparing the dogwoods.

After a while I go back to the kitchen where Jimmie sits peeling green cooking apples into a blue earthenware bowl. She has taken to wearing eyeglasses these days—cheap eyeglasses from the drugstore. She looks up from her work to stare out the window, out at the field; her hands keep the paring knife moving over the fruit.

"What are you staring at?" I ask her.

"Your old mother is just gazing into the future, honey."

I pull my chair up close to Jimmie at the table. "Mommy," I say.

Jimmie looks at me, surprised. "You called me Mommy!"

I am surprised at myself. For some reason, I need her to be my mommy now. My voice sounds funny, thick and furry. I squirm in my seat and begin to eat the apple peels as they drop from Jimmie's paring knife onto the oilcloth. "Remember when you asked Spence what we'd been doing in the barn?"

"Yes."

From the kitchen window, Jimmie and I can see a well-drilling machine going up and down, digging a deep hole in the ground. Behind us on the kitchen wall, the brass pendulum of the Regulator clock marks heavy strokes of time. A drop of water plops sluggishly into the sink.

Jimmie stops her work and gives me her full attention. "What *has* been going on in that barn?"

I pick up two long, coiling peels and dangle one from behind each ear. "How do you like my earrings?"

She puts her hand over mine. It's a strong hand, rough from farm work.

"You can tell Mommy, honey."

"Lonny said...not to tell."

The two wrinkles between Jimmie's eyes seem to etch deeper than usual. "He doesn't try to...to hurt you, does he, honey?"

I stare at the floor. "He tried to stick his...*thing* into me."

I peek up to see pink splotches form on Jimmie's cheeks. She swallows hard and says, "He could have hurt you, honey."

She picks up her paring knife from the table and an apple from the basket and continues at her work. "Don't you *ever* let Lonny do that to you again."

I am staring down, counting the cracks in the linoleum, when I hear Jimmie's chair grate across the floor. I look up to see her go to the black wall phone that hangs under the hall staircase. My mother repeats her sister's phone number to the operator, bites her lips, and fidgets with the telephone cord while she waits for the call to go through.

"Hello, Essie. This is Jimmie." I listen to my story being blurted out. Then I hear, "He ought to be ashamed of himself…he could have injured her for life…well, you just better *make* yourself deal with him. You don't, I *will*…I don't think so, but I'm going to look her over, just to be on the safe side.

"Honey, I'm going to take a look at you. And then, maybe this evening, I'll just take you for a ride over to Doctor Doc's. I want to make sure my little girl's all right." She pauses, looks sharply at me as if she is trying to size up my understanding of the situation. "We won't worry your father with this, will we? He'd be hurt for life."

I nod. I understand enough to know that my father would go crazy mad if he were ever to find out that Lonny tried to tamper with Daddy's most perfect creation. And somehow, I feel guilty, guilty, guilty—I must have done something really bad!

That evening, I am lying on my stomach in the tall weeds underneath our grape arbor. It's like being in a leafy green tunnel. The archway of dark leaves makes a hushing sound all around me like a lullaby. I am almost asleep.

I am just back from seeing the doctor. I'm here in the arbor filling my belly with grapes and my mind with forgetfulness. The doctor pronounced me good as new, and he gave me a tongue depressor and a hot cinnamon fireball for being a brave girl. But I don't feel brave. I feel guilty.

Through the grapevines, I see my daddy coming out of his shop behind the house. He locks the shop door behind him, and eases himself down on the wooden bench underneath the shop window.

When I part the vines like a curtain, Daddy spots me and beckons. I run across the lawn and huddle close to him on the bench. He takes my hand and holds it on his lap.

The bench faces the south field where a green truck, loaded with harvested bales, looms large, mid-field. Daddy seems to look beyond the truck. He clears his throat to speak and makes a sweeping gesture with his free hand, indicating the entire field.

"Nature," he begins hoarsely, but has to hawk and spit into his pocket handkerchief. After working in the shop, his throat is usually coated with fine sawdust.

He begins again. "Mother Nature provides for her own," he says. "See those discarded bales?" He points to a stretch of stubble-covered field littered with broken bales.

"You see a few of those bales left behind after every harvest. Nature always reclaims a portion of her yield. Those discarded bales are straw houses that Mother Nature gives back to her grasshoppers. Each un-gathered bale shelters a multitude of hoppers, whose offspring will continue to fiddle their wings and sing long after man's world has come to an end."

It has grown dark now, and a heavy dew is falling. Jimmie hurries out the back door and lopes across the yard to the clothesline. She takes down some sheets and pillowcases, folds them, and carries them inside in a large wicker basket so they won't get damp and mildew.

A few yards from the house, Spence is squatting between the gas pump and the kerosene barrels, digging for ants he's collecting for an ant colony he plans to observe.

Jupy wags his tail and snuffs at a rabbit hole beside the barn.

Daddy gestures toward Jupy. "Humans are a lot like animals. They go running from one rabbit hole to another, sticking their noses down into the dirt, trying to pick up the scent, sniff out the truth, digging even deeper when they think they've found it. But the truth can be an elusive thing."

Daddy lifts his work cap, scratches his scalp, and puts his cap back so it's looser on his head. He stares at the hay truck; its windshield is glossed with dew.

"You know, Lissa, all my life I've invented and loved and made a living by all kinds of machinery. When I was just a little tacker, not much bigger than you, steam was the coming thing. I saw a steam engine for the first time at an exhibition when I was eight years old.

"Well, I went straight home and made myself a miniature engine that worked on my Mammy's cookstove. And when I was a young buck, still wet behind the ears, I bought myself my first automobile, an R&V Knight. We had moved to the city by then.

"In those days, there were so few cars on the city streets I could park wherever I pleased, right in front of any restaurant or place of business I chose to go into. But soon, there got to be too many people and too many cars; there were traffic jams and road accidents; and there was noise like you never used to hear when there were only horse-drawn wagons and buggies on the roads.

"And then the whole world went to war—twice!" Here, Daddy pauses and seems to be watching a scene playing out across the field in front of him.

"For the First World War, the United States had three draft registrations. First, they called up men between twenty-one and thirty-one. Then, a year later, they registered the young men who had just turned twenty-one. Finally, in September 1918, they extended the age up through forty-five. Well, I was just about to turn forty then, so I signed up. The war ended in November, before they got to me. I was sixty-three when we got into the Second World War, too old for the draft, but I did work as a trouble-shooter in the government machine shops. I kept the drill presses and the metal lathes and shapers running, turning out weapon parts so men could kill one another faster and more efficiently.

"After the war, I made myself a vow that I would never again use machines for the purpose of destruction. I use my machinery now to create things that are beautiful to look at, smooth to the touch, and soothing to the soul.

"But man is still busy inventing bigger and better machines to kill with: A-bombs and H-bombs! And now he's working on rocket-powered engines, so he can invade other planets and create chaos in the universe. Chaos!"

My daddy's eyes look like they have a cloud passing over them. He lets go of my hand and raises his arms out toward the electric wires that run above the empty clothesline from the barn to the shop. A wren perches on the top wire, and way past the tenant farm across the road, I can hear doves cooing in the woods.

My daddy cups his hands, palms up. He whispers, *"Adveniat regnum tuum.* Thy Kingdom come," to the wren.

Then slowly, very slowly, he lowers his hands, looks at me, and says, "Pray, always pray to the Blessed Virgin Mother whenever you're in trouble, Lissa."

I clamp my mouth shut tight and stare at my daddy. I'm not sure what a virgin is, but from what I've learned in Sunday school, God likes Mary because she is a virgin, and some things girls do with boys make girls bad and not virgins. I'm not sure, but I think I might not be a virgin anymore. I am glad Daddy will never know about Lonny's circus. I whisper to myself, over and over, *"Mea culpa, mea culpa, mea maxima culpa!"*

CHAPTER SEVEN

THE END OF JIMMIE'S WORLD

THE battered old trailer where Lonny lived is locked, and the windows boarded up. He has moved away to I don't know where. I don't see him around anywhere anymore. Spence gets a mechanical drawing kit for his birthday and spends hours locked in his room. When I ask him what he's doing in there, he tells me he's drawing detailed plans for a spaceship that will take him to the moon.

"Can I see them, Spence?"

"No! It's top secret."

I dig out the composition notebook and read my moon launch story, up to where it ends in the middle of Chapter Three. I can't figure out what will come next, so I start a different story that seems to come into my head from nowhere—from the far end of nowhere. It goes like this:

> I live in a black house. It is very dirty. The chairs and tables—what few we have—are covered with dust. We don't have a carpet. At night, I wrap myself in a few worn blankets and try to get to sleep on the bare wooden floor. It is very cold at night. Sometimes, I hear the wind moaning outside the window, "Ah, me. Ah, me."
>
> I get up very early in the morning and give feed and water to the few chickens we have. We do not have a house for them. They sleep in the trees at night and wander loose in the yard by day.

I bring in some wood and start a fire in the cookstove. I scoop meal from the bin and make meal cakes. I wake up my two younger brothers and my baby sister. I feed her some soft mush made from the meal.

My father is too old to get up early. I stop by his bed to check that he is still breathing. I leave some meal cakes for him on the warming shelf above the cookstove. I get water from the spring and wash the few cracked dishes. I put my baby sister in a wooden pen with some blankets in it, where she can stay safe while I'm gone. I give her empty pots and pans and a spoon to play with. I tell my brothers to be good, and I go to school.

In the afternoons, I come home and take care of the chickens. I fix more meal cakes and make mush for the baby. I wrap the baby in some blankets, put her in a wicker basket, and carry her with me to our small garden. I bring in some vegetables for dinner tomorrow, which I do not get to eat except on Saturday and Sunday.

I pull, pick, or dig up more vegetables to take to the store. I sell them for meal, which is all I can get for them. I go back home and do my homework by candlelight. I go to bed and let the wind sing me to sleep. "Ah, me. Ah, me." The End.

It's spring when I first notice the strange man in our south field. I am swinging on the tire swing out front. Far across the hayfield by the wood's edge, where the pink and white dogwoods are blooming, a pickup truck moves slowly forward. When the truck stops, a man—far away and tiny—gets out. He walks to the back of the truck, pulls out a gadget that flashes like silver in the sunlight. He unfolds the tool into a tiny three-legged toy that looks something like Spence's telescope.

I run into the house to tell Jimmie about the strange goings-on in our field. Jimmie raises the kitchen window and sticks her head out for a good look. She calls the man's tool a surveyor's tripod.

"Your daddy," she explains, "decided to sell the land, all but two acres, to George Clay. George wants to add it on to his dairy farm.

"The property taxes are getting to be too much for us," Jimmie says. "I'm just thankful George promised to farm the land, and not parcel it into building lots."

Several weeks later, I sit on my daddy's varnished oak tool chest in the shop. I keep very quiet. Daddy lets me stay and watch him work—just so long as I don't distract him. Daddy stands at his woodworking lathe and turns a lamp. Sawdust is powdered all over his long work coat. Myshkin, the one-eyed tomcat, perches on the windowsill. As Daddy works, Myshkin's tail switches back and forth like a metronome.

Suddenly, Daddy shuts down the lathe and turns to me.

"I've made a mistake," he says. His face looks very tired.

"Did you ruin it?" I think he's talking about his lamp.

"It was a mistake to sell that land to old man Clay."

"Why, Daddy?"

"I had a premonition today about old man Clay falling from a great height and being swallowed up by the universe. He won't be around much longer. And when that son of his—what's his name? Cory?—gets ahold of that land, he's going to turn it over to the first building contractor that comes along. Mark my words, young Cory Clay is not cut out to be a farmer. Got his head in the clouds, that one. He's a dreamer boy. Out to make a fast buck. And that silly blonde wife of his—what's her name? Faye? Always puttin' on airs. And, in my humble opinion, that woman has a screw loose. The farm means a lot to your mother. She's a country girl at heart. Won't be country for long now.

"I lost most of my business," says Daddy, "when I agreed to move out to this godforsaken neck of the woods. But it's what you children and your mother wanted. You outvoted me, and I could see what our old neighborhood was coming to. I didn't want you children growing up there.

"Your mother wants to help out. She wants to go back to nursing. I was against it all these years. No self-respecting man depends on his wife to pay the bills. I didn't mind when she wanted to keep on with her father's chicken-and-egg route to make a little pin money, but now she's lost most of her customers to all the new supermarkets."

Before she got married, my mother was nurse. She wanted to be a registered nurse, but Grandma Magda made her drop out of school when she was only in the eighth grade so she could work on the farm. Without a high school diploma, she could only be a licensed practical nurse, but she's a good one. Probably the best, I think.

Now, because money is so tight, my daddy lets Jimmie take on private nursing jobs from clients who live on My Lady's Manor—on land that used to belong to Lord Baltimore. From nighttime to morning, Jimmie keeps charts on an old lady who is bedridden. Sometimes, she gets called in to clean up an old man who is senile and tries to poop everywhere, including on his daughter-in-law's fancy dining room table.

Sometimes, she takes cleaning jobs. When she cleans the local dentist's office, she brings home his discarded waiting room magazines—*Look, Life, The Saturday Evening Post*—for me and Spence to read and use for our school projects.

When she cleans the local churches, I help her dust the pews. They have curlicues and notches that are hard to get to, and they seem to go on—row after row—forever. In the wintertime, my hands get cold dusting when the church isn't heated.

One time, Jimmie finds a pretty pair of red gloves in a church's lost and found box. She gives them to me. The next week, a girl in my class at school sees me wearing them on the playground. Her name is Linda Willard.

"Hey, you're wearing my gloves. Where did you get those?"

"My mother found them."

"Well, they're mine." She grabs my hand and turns down the wristband on one of the gloves. "See." She points to the initials LW printed in indelible black ink on the inside. "I lost those gloves a couple of weeks ago."

I just take them off and give them to her. I don't say anything or even look at her. I feel guilty. I feel like a thief.

I repeat, "Thou shalt not steal, thou shalt not steal," over and over to myself all day. If I say it enough times, I will be safe. I will be safe, even though my fingers are frozen.

Sometime toward the end of August, George Clay falls down into his silo. He struggles for many hours in a quagmire of field corn, treading yellow kernels that give way like quicksand under his feet. Eventually, he is rescued. The fire department ambulance arrives, siren blaring, red lights blinking, and rushes Mr. Clay off to the hospital. On the way, he has a heart attack and dies.

Jimmie grew up with George Clay's sister, so she goes to his funeral, wearing an out-of-fashion black straw hat with faded cloth flowers and a skimpy net veil. Daddy stays home to keep an eye on me and Spence.

"I've seen too much of death already," he tells us. "And I'm too old to need reminding."

Just as Daddy predicted, Cory Clay inherits his father's land, which now includes the ten acres that used to be our east and south fields. First thing he does is build a brand-new brick house for his wife, Faye, over at the far end of the south field at the edge of the woods.

On a cold January afternoon, I hop off the school bus after Spence. We race each other up the driveway and burst into the kitchen, breathless.

"Go upstairs and change your clothes, children. Then I'll give you some of my lentil soup." We hurry to put on flannel shirts and old dungarees. Mine are hand-me-downs from Spence. Spence's are hand-me-downs from one of our cousins.

We return to find Jimmie ladling up some steaming lentil soup she's kept warm on our big cast-iron kerosene cookstove.

"This will warm you up," she says. "It's good luck to eat lentil soup in January, brings you luck in the new year."

Spence gulps down his soup in a hurry, grabs his work coat, and rushes out to take care of the chickens before it gets dark. "You stay warm in here with Mommy, Liss. It's too cold out there for girls."

While I finish my soup, Jimmie shows me a thick envelope with an opened gold seal.

"Look what came for me in the mailbox today, Lissa. Pretty fancy, huh? It's an invitation from Faye Clay to a housewarming." Housewarming is spelled out in swirly pink and gray lettering.

"What's a housewarming?"

"A party to celebrate a new house. You're supposed to bring a gift for the house. It's this Saturday evening. You want to come with me?"

"Oh, can I? Yes! Yes!" I always love to go places with Jimmie.

Jimmie grew up during the Great Depression, so she's very frugal. Nothing goes to waste. Worn-out sheets become dust rags or handkerchiefs. Socks are darned, shoes repaired, dungarees patched, torn shirts and dresses mended. Besides, we really don't have a lot of extra money to spend these days. To find a housewarming gift, Jimmie sorts through the big cedar chest—her hope chest—in her bedroom. The farmhouse has four bedrooms, and because Daddy has to get up so much at night, Jimmie and Daddy sleep in separate bedrooms.

Jimmie goes through gift boxes and tissue paper, sorting through presents she was given years ago at her bridal shower, gifts that have never been used. She says she's saving them for a rainy day, or to give to me when I grow up and get married. Finally, she selects a set of twelve linen dish towels, each embroidered with a different flower, tucks them back into their original bed of tissue, seals the box with tape, and covers it with pale blue wrapping paper—from the box of remnants she keeps in the closet.

On Saturday evening, Jimmie and I walk across the south field. It seems strange that this is not our land anymore. A square of bright light glares at us from the new picture window. Jimmie raps the shiny brass knocker. Faye answers the door. She looks tiny standing next to Jimmie, but she's all dolled up like a TV house-wife—like Lucille Ball in *I Love Lucy*, or *Leave It to Beaver*'s mom, June Cleaver—in a hostess outfit: a belted dress with rolled sleeves, turned-up collar, full skirt, high heels, bright red lipstick. Her hair is done in a sleek French roll. Jimmie towers over her in a plain cotton housedress and chunky, sensible shoes, her hair pulled back in its usual tight bun, no makeup.

Zora Clay, Faye's mother-in-law, a short, plump farm woman with a gold tooth, takes our coats, and we follow Faye as she flounces across her new living room with its split-level floor and gestures grandly at the table piled high with gifts. Jimmie places her gift on the table. It looks kind of plain and small next to the other brightly wrapped and ribboned gift boxes. I feel embarrassed for Jimmie, and tag along close behind her to the buffet table.

I sit on a sofa in the corner next to Jimmie, sip fruit punch, nibble pastel butter mints and cashews, munch on potato chips, and watch and listen to the grownups. Jimmie shushes me when I announce that I don't like the taste of the garlic sour cream dip. Faye is starting to open her presents. She gushes over the deluxe electric Mixmaster and a set of crystal wine glasses. When Faye picks up Jimmie's gift, she seems to inspect the blue wrapping paper (which, I now notice, looks faded next to the other presents), hesitates a moment, then rips off the wrapper, tears open the box, and shears the tissue apart with her red-polished fingernails. She lifts out the linen towels, stares at them, pulls them up to her nose, sniffs at them. Almost immediately, she squishes up her nose, pushes them away from her, and stuffs them back in the box.

"These things smell funny. And this box looks *old*. These towels are *used*, aren't they? I can't accept these." And she thrusts the gift back at Jimmie.

I feel like crying out that they've never been used, that they are beautiful. "No!" I hear myself screaming. Jimmie taps her forefinger to her closed lips, signaling me to be silent.

"Time to go," she whispers to me, taking my hand and leading me back out the way we came in. She carries the rejected gift—almost hidden—under her arm.

Zora Clay rushes up behind us, carrying our coats, murmuring and tut-tutting back toward Faye.

"I'm so sorry, Jimmie. Please don't mind, Faye. Girl's a silly romantic fool. Has bats in the belfry, if you ask me."

I hold tight to Jimmie's free hand and try to keep up with her as she takes long, powerful steps back across the field toward our house, which now looks bleak and tired and dingy and *oh so very old*. I feel like crying for Jimmie's shame. I remember what Daddy said about Jimmie and Spence, that they don't go too deep into their feelings. And I wish Jimmie could yell or curse to let her feelings out the way Daddy does. But she doesn't. Jimmie *never* does. And neither does Spence.

Later this year, in the spring, a siren wails across the south field and we see an ambulance pull into Cory and Faye's new driveway. After things quiet down, Jimmie hears through the grapevine, probably from Zora Clay, who is known to be a gossip, that Faye is pregnant and thought she was having a miscarriage when she had some stomach pain. False alarm. Probably something she ate griping her bowels. A few weeks later, another siren comes at us from across the south field. Faye has more gripes, and this time, she accuses the Cloverland milkman of putting poison in her milk. Jimmie says that pregnant women sometimes go off a little because of all the changes in their bodies. Daddy just circles a finger around one ear and says, "Cuckoo! Cuckoo! Cuckoo!" We all have to laugh at that.

But the peculiarity of Faye Clay is not all we have to worry about. It's 1960. Everyone is getting more and more scared that the Russians will drop a nuclear bomb on us. We are nervous about the behavior of a pudgy, funny-looking, bald-headed man named Nikita Khrushchev. We remember him saying, just a few years back, "We will bury you." Now, in October, the news shows pictures of him at the United Nations, banging his fists on the table, banging a shoe in protest.

"The Cold War," Daddy says, "is heating up!"

Winter and spring pass. Then, in the summer, I am sitting on the front-porch steps. Jupy is lying next to me. A building crew is clearing away the last of what used to be our south woods. I watch now as the scoop of a noisy yellow bulldozer digs holes where our wheat used to grow. The east field, out back, already has one finished house, and three more are going up where the cornfield used to be. I'm petting Jupy and smoothing his black and white head. Jupy lifts his nose. His ears perk up. His eyes are fixed on a two-tone car—white and aqua blue—as it speeds along the road in front of our house, flashing its chrome grill. The greyhound part of him cannot resist. He pulls out from under my hand and takes off after the car. His long, elegant legs gain on the competition.

Jupy catches up with the car just as it passes Aunt Essie's house. Now he's stretching out, almost even with the front bumper. In true racing form, Jupy holds close to the car's right front tire. The driver tries to negotiate a sharp curve to the right. The right front fender strikes Jupy's flank, throwing him off his stride. The rear tire runs over him, crushes him.

After the accident, I walk solemnly beside Jimmie as she carries Jupy back home. I touch our dog's once-powerful hind legs; they dangle limply from Jimmie's arms.

Side by side, my mother and I walk across muddy ground and buried corn stubble, careful to skirt the large gaping holes where rectangular foundations have been carved out for the eastern section of Cory Clay's housing development. He's calling it Cory's Ridge. We pass the one new house that is finished. A newly installed swimming pool has replaced a section of what old Mr. Clay had temporarily fenced in and was using for a cow pasture. The new homeowner emerges—gleaming wet, glittering like fool's gold as he walks. He stares at Jimmie, a farm woman in bib overalls, toting a large mangled dog who whimpers like a puppy.

After the vet puts Jupy to sleep and Jimmie brings his body home, Daddy builds a coffin of knotty pine and makes a cross of the finest rosewood. Jimmie digs a deep hole and buries Jupy on the sheltered side of the grape arbor. I get out the mother-of-pearl and silver rosary I found one day in a red velvet box in my grandmother Lovenia's trunk in the attic—Daddy said I could have it—and I recite the beads all the way around, as Daddy has taught me, and kiss the crucifix.

Spence looks like he wants to cry, but can't. The sight of Jimmie, swinging the shovel, dropping heavy loads of sod into the grave with the easy tempo of a laborer, stays with me because it is the last time I see the real Jimmie, the strong and healthy Jimmie.

At the end of summer, my daddy, Jimmie, me, and Spence make our annual visit to Timonium Fair. We only go on a few rides this year.

"The rides are getting to be expensive," Jimmie says.

So, we do things that are free—like looking at and climbing on the latest farm equipment, watching the sheep judging, and taking a tour up and down aisles of prize-winning jellies and quilts and pumpkins and squash. We are admiring the blue-ribbon eggplant—amazingly large and shiny and purple—when a girl I know from school runs over to me, tugging her mother along with her. Her mother is pale, with faded red hair. She reminds me of a tall, thin, withered carrot. Her daughter, Tishia, always bursting with wild ideas and brimming with self-confidence, likes me because I am quiet and let her do most of the talking.

"Hi, Lissa. Want to come see the sideshow with me? It's really cool!"

Daddy has gone to the car to get away from the noise and the crowds, smoke a cigar, and take a nap. I convince Jimmie to let me go off with my friend. Jimmie stays with Spence to see some of the 4-H exhibits. I promise to meet them back at the exhibition hall in an hour.

I have never been to a sideshow. A brassy huckster, wearing a bright bowtie that matches the band on his straw hat, bawls out a steady stream of bizarre sideshow attractions.

"Come one, come all. See them here. See them live. See them up close—the Two-Headed Man, the Snake Woman, and more. One-of-a-kind, unique freaks of nature. Step right up and get your tickets here. The chance of a lifetime! Come one, come all. See it here!"

The price of a single ticket is twice what it costs for the most expensive ride at the fair. It costs most of what Jimmie gave me to spend for the rest of the afternoon. I can hear Jimmie cautioning me, saying, "Lissa, don't throw your money away."

"Come on, Lissa. We've got to see this." Tishia locks arms with me, pulls me toward the ticket line.

I can't resist. I buy the ticket. We go inside the front part of the tent. Here, we are allowed to peer through a small hole in a covered box labeled *Dancing Fleas*. It's dark, and I can't see much of anything. A glass display case exhibits what looks like a short lumpy body wrapped in strips of yellowed white cloth. The sign says *Authentic Egyptian Mummy*. It doesn't move or do anything.

A man at a podium tells us that for just an extra fifty cents, we can go through a curtain and see the Two-Headed Man and the Snake Woman—live and up close.

We pay our money and file, in a line, through an even darker part of the tent. The Two-Headed Man lurks in the shadows at the back of a small cage. I can see two heads sticking out and I can hear his heavy breathing, but I can't make out his body. In another darkened cage labeled *Snake Woman, Daughter of Eve*, a woman writhes in a snake costume. Her face is painted a wicked green. She dances up close to the bars of the cage and hisses at me as I pass by. It's as if she's taunting me, calling me "SSSLissa, SSSLissa."

And then I hear Daddy's voice, as clearly as if he were standing right next to the Snake Woman in her cage, yelling at her, "How could you? How could you?"

By the time we get out of the sideshow, it's getting late. I say goodbye to Tishia and go back to find Jimmie and Spence in the 4-H pavilion. Daddy's with them, and he's pretty worried and upset. He's lecturing Jimmie, telling her he would *never* have let his little girl go to something as cheap and tawdry and depraved as a sideshow. He tells me he was just about ready to send a security guard after me. Jimmie just looks tired and sad. Spence doesn't say anything.

We go back to school, and this fall, in October 1961, President Kennedy gives a speech on civil defense. He advises American families to build bomb shelters to protect themselves in case we get attacked by the Soviet Union. Daddy reads articles in the newspaper about how to build a concrete fallout shelter in the basement. Spence clips out the instructions and saves them, but Daddy says, "Even if we could build a shelter under this old house strong enough for us to survive a nuclear attack, we would have to come out eventually. And the radiation would poison the soil and the air and the water, and all of us along with it."

Daddy and I have a special bond, but so do Spence and Jimmie. Jimmie is as curious and excited about science and medicine as Spence is. Sometimes, I can really see this connection, like one weekend when Spence is, at the last minute, trying to pull together a notebook on germ theory, microbiology, and vaccines for science class. Spence reads aloud to Jimmie sections of Paul de Kruif's *Microbe Hunters*. Then I see Jimmie and Spence put their heads together over the set of Compton's encyclopedias that one of Jimmie's patients left for us when he died. Red-bound volumes with gold lettering on their covers are spread open on Spence's bed. Jimmie helps him pick out key points to include in his notebook.

I hear Jimmie tell Spence, "Don't be like me, and put off your studying. I regret not getting my high school diploma. Maybe you can be the first one in our family to go to college."

When Spence gets the notebook back from his teacher, the cover is marked with a big red "A." Inside, on the title page, I notice that Spence has written a dedication:

Heroes in Medicine
by Spencer Power
For My Beloved Mother

I've never seen Spence express so much emotion before.

One morning when I am eleven, my mother feels a lump under her arm while she's brushing out her hair. Our family doctor examines her and tells her she needs to go to the hospital. "You're a nurse," he says. "You ought to know better than to miss something like that. That lump feels as big as an orange!" She has the lump removed at University Hospital.

The doctors find other tumors, and they remove her breast. We hope they got all the cancer out.

But the head surgeon tells Jimmie that because the tumors he removed were so large, he would like her permission to do all that is possible to halt this disease. Jimmie agrees to be his "guinea pig." Over the next months, the doctors give Jimmie a hysterectomy. They burn her skin red with cobalt treatments. Because she has been such a good, brave patient, the head surgeon arranges to have all her medical expenses waived.

In seventh grade, I meet a girl named Paloma. At first, I think she is kind of weird. She's so different from me. She's the same age as me, but talks to the high school teachers as if she's equal to them. Sometimes, she uses sophisticated medical terms—like cardiovascular and pulmonary, or hypertension, or hemorrhage and hematoma—when she talks to the science teacher. She even debates some teachers in class when she doesn't agree with a point they are trying to make.

Paloma and I are in the same homeroom, and one day, she comes over to me, introduces herself, and walks along with me to our next class.

"That's a pretty smart answer you gave in English class yesterday, Lissa," she tells me. "I like the way you wear your hair in a pigtail down the back, by the way. You don't seem snotty the way some of the kids are."

I like Paloma; she's not afraid to speak her mind. She likes to make fun of people who take themselves too seriously. She makes me laugh, and she thinks I have a good sense of humor, too. She says she likes me because I'm down-to-earth and not stuck on myself.

Sometimes, Paloma's a little hard on me, though. In Home Economics, for a sewing class, we have to go into a dressing room to measure each other's bust size for a blouse pattern. When Paloma wraps the tape measure around my small chest, she laughs so hard her face gets red and tears roll down her cheeks. "Bust size? What bust? You don't have a bust!" Paloma is pretty well-endowed herself. She makes me feel self-conscious about my flat chest.

I accidentally embarrass Paloma when I pull a sanitary napkin from her purse one day at lunch. I hold it up and ask her what it is. She pulls it away from me, hides it back in her handbag, and says, "I can't believe you don't know what that is." But I honestly don't know what it is, or what it's for. I'm not even sure why Paloma's embarrassed about it.

But Paloma is really impressed with me when she sees how well I do on IQ tests. And when Paloma finds out my mother has cancer, she gets really concerned about me. "You're way too thin, Lissa. You look malnourished. Are you getting enough protein in your diet?" Sometimes I think Paloma likes me because I let her be in charge and tell me what to do. Paloma has lots of pet animals—horses and burros and a monkey from her father's lab at Johns Hopkins. Sometimes I think Paloma treats me like one of her pets. Paloma says she likes animals better than people. So maybe, for Paloma, I'm like a stray animal that she can tame and groom. Anyway, I like animals, too. That's something we have in common. I've always had lots of pets around the farm.

In October, I hear Spence talking to his friend, Mark, on the way home on the school bus. Mark is all excited about something he calls the Cuban Missile Crisis.

Mark is skinny, with a crewcut and thick black-framed glasses. Paloma calls him a nerd. "Did you hear about those U-2 spy plane photos?" Mark says. "They prove that the commies have nuclear missiles in Cuba that could hit most of the U.S. We talked about it in current events today, and Mr. Burns says this just might be the start of World War III!" But I don't pay much attention, and eventually this crisis seems to fade away.

Anyway, I'm more worried right now about Jimmie.

For a while, Jimmie is still able to get around. When I am twelve, I have a toothache, and Jimmie takes me to an old-fashioned dentist downtown. Daddy drops us off where the bus stops at the Crossroads Inn parking lot, and we take the number eight bus. When we get on to pay the fare, the bus driver asks Jimmie how old I am.

"She's eleven," Jimmie says.

When we go back and take a seat, I ask Jimmie, "Why did you say I'm only eleven?"

"The bus fare goes up when you turn twelve. And we need to save every penny."

"But you lied, Jimmie."

Jimmie looks embarrassed. "Just a little white lie."

"What's a little white lie?"

"It's when you stretch the truth a little, but you do it for a good reason. Like when you tell somebody they look pretty when they really don't—so you won't hurt their feelings."

I think about this all the way downtown. I don't really understand how lying to save money is really a white lie. But I can see that my question has made Jimmie feel bad, so I don't say any more about it.

At the dentist's office, I am so scared that I shiver and my knees clap together. The dentist is an old man with a missing finger. He tells me he lost his finger because it got exposed to too much radiation from his X-ray machine. He pulls out my six-year molar.

Jimmie tells me, "You need to start brushing your teeth." I promise to do that. I don't want to lose any more teeth, and I don't want my teeth to look like Daddy's.

In February 1963, Jimmie comes home from her latest radiation session looking very, very tired. She seems to collapse into her chair at the kitchen table. Doesn't even take off her coat.

"What's wrong, Jimmie?"

She doesn't look at me. Instead, she stares straight ahead. "I was on the table getting my treatment." She seems to be talking to the wall across the room. "I couldn't read the time on the clock across the room. I couldn't see anything out of my right eye. The doctors say I have a tumor behind my eye, and my system can't stand any more radiation. All they can do is remove my eye." Jimmie's lips are quivering so much she can hardly get the words out. And then her tears come, and the rest explodes out of her mouth. "That's just too much! Too much to bear! I am not a vain woman, but I won't let them take out my eye." She buries her head in her arms on the kitchen table. I stand beside her, try to smooth her hair. She takes my hand. Finally, she raises her head from the table and peers deep into my eyes. "I've always liked being a nurse and taking care of people. The last thing I want, Lissa, is to be a burden."

One cold winter afternoon, Jimmie is kneeling down to help Daddy bleed the dining room radiators. All of a sudden, she collapses on the floor. She cries out a sound I have never heard her make before, a deep, wrenching groan filled with pain.

Jimmie prepares me to take over some of her responsibilities around the house. Daddy, she tells me, has a habit of sitting on the toilet for what she calls his "morning meditation." If he's smoking a cigar, he spits tobacco juice into the tub. So now Jimmie teaches me how to clean the toilet and how to scrub the yellow tobacco stains off the tub.

Jimmie spends the last of her own money on some home improvements she thinks will make our lives easier when she's gone. She gets Uncle Frantz to install storm windows upstairs, and she buys us a large freezer to keep in the cellar so we won't have to run over to use Aunt Essie's freezer—the freezer in our Frigidaire is very small, and doesn't keep things frozen. Daddy lets Jimmie get my hair cut short so it will be easier for me to manage.

Almost as an afterthought, Jimmie gives me a pamphlet to read about menstruation. She doesn't want me to be surprised by it, the way she was when she was thirteen and thought she was bleeding to death.

By the end of summer, the strong, sturdy woman, Jimmie—who used to be my mother— seems to have slipped away and vanished down some long hospital corridor. The woman who comes home for the last time is emaciated, her remaining breast just a flap of skin. This woman's voice is meek; her eyes glisten with the dull glow of pain masked by morphine. Aunt Essie comes over every day to tend to her sister and bathe her, leaving her body smelling of a tainted rose fragrance.

Some days, when Jimmie is too sick, I'm not allowed to go into her sick room. "Your mother doesn't want you to see her the way she is today," Aunt Essie tells me.

The last time I get to talk with Jimmie, she is propped up in bed. She has a weak smile today. Her arm, stretching out to me across the sheets, is so thin now. But when her hand grips mine, it is strong. "There are so many things I want to tell you, Lissa. I'm so sad I won't get to see you grow up. I'm so proud of you and Spence."

I'm crying now, but very softly. "I love you, Mommy. I will miss you."

"And, Lissa, always take care of your daddy and your brother."

I nod, and say, "Mommy, if I talk to you after you die, and if you can hear me, will you answer me back?"

"Yes, I will," she says. Those are the last words I hear her say.

One quiet Sunday evening near the end of August, when I am still twelve, right before I start eighth grade, a shadow lady who used to be my mother fades into a coma and dies of heart failure in her own mother's bed upstairs.

Daddy picks out a beautiful mahogany coffin for Jimmie. It's the most expensive one, but Daddy says, "Nothing but the finest for Jimmie."

The funeral is held at the local Methodist church. Jimmie is just fifty years old. She is the youngest sibling, and the first to die. Her brothers bear her casket, and she is buried in her family's plot, right next to Grandma Magda and Granddaddy Friedrich.

Jimmie's relatives and friends come up to me and tell me how sorry they are for me. I know I will miss Jimmie, but I'm not sure why they are so sorry for me.

I ask Daddy if he is going to be buried next to Jimmie, and he says, "No. There's not enough room there. I'd have to be stacked—one coffin on top of the other, and I don't want to be stacked."

The day after Jimmie's funeral, Zora Clay comes knocking at our back door. She's carrying a baking dish covered with a striped dish towel. It's raining, and she wears one of those fold-out plastic rain hats tied under her chin.

"Hello there, Lissa. I was doing my baking this morning, and figured you folks might like a nice fresh peach cobbler, what with your mother gone now and all. How are you making out here? I reckon this is right hard on your father, being so old and all." Zora is a plain farm woman, with coarse skin and a mole beside her nose. I stare at her gold tooth when she smiles, take the dish from her, and say thank you to be polite, as Jimmie has taught me to do whenever somebody gives me something. Zora seems to be trying to peep around me to see inside the house, but I stand my ground. I don't let her in, even though it's raining outside. Daddy doesn't like me to let anybody into the house, and he's warned me before that Zora Clay is a gossip, with a nose too much in other people's business. I am also worried that I'm not keeping the house clean enough. I don't want her to see this morning's dirty dishes, which are still sitting, unwashed, in the kitchen sink.

"How's your little brother taking all this?"

"He's okay." I don't correct her and say that Spence is my big brother. A lot of people make that mistake.

"Well, I hope you enjoy the cobbler. I'll come back sometime and get the dish."

"Okay. Thank you." And I shut the door in her face.

A few days later, Zora comes back.

"Did you like that cobbler? Just stopped by to get my dish back."

She's caught me by surprise. "Oh! I'll be right back." I close the door in her face and run into the pantry. The last piece of cobbler is still sitting on a shelf in the dish cabinet. I grab the baking dish, dump out that last piece on a clean plate, and give the baking dish a quick wash.

"Here's your dish." I can see Zora looking at the dish, and I'm embarrassed it's still sticky around the edges with baked-on pieces of peach. But Zora doesn't say anything about the dirty dish. Instead, she starts talking to me all in a rush about her daughter-in-law, Faye.

"You know, that woman is never satisfied. Crazy as a loon, and keeps pushing Cory to build and sell more houses so he can spend more money on her. Spends all afternoon watching old movies on TV. Saw *The Bishop's Wife* with Loretta Young and Cary Grant, and now she wants my son to build her an ice skating rink behind the house so they can ice skate together this winter in the moonlight. Cory says to me the other day, 'Mom, old man Brenner's putting that tenant farm of his up for sale. It's an opportunity I can't pass up. Going to take out a loan and buy that place. Seize the day! I have a feeling it's meant to be. Going to build high-end houses that'll attract professionals from the city, who want to move out near horse country and don't mind spending some money to do it. Going to call it Country Manor Estates after My Lady's Manor. And the roads that run through it will all have horse-country names, like Equestrian Way and Fox Hunt Lane.'"

Finally, Zora just shakes her head, saying, "I'm worried about that boy," and heads back home across Cory's Ridge.

Paloma calls me when she finds out that Jimmie died. School starts this week. "I guess you won't be coming back to school right away," Paloma says.

"Why not? No, I'm coming. I have to start school on time, don't I?"

"Well, sometimes people take a little time off after things like this happen."

"No, I won't be taking any days off." I'm surprised. I didn't think I was supposed to miss school unless I was really sick.

"You're very brave, Lissa," Paloma tells me, "to come back to school and all—right after your mother died."

"No. It doesn't mean I'm brave," I tell Paloma. "This is just what happened. It's the way things are. I don't have any other choice, do I?"

When I start back to school on the first day, Paloma looks me up and down, and asks me, "Who's fixing your meals now that your mother's gone?"

"I am," I say.

"Yeah?" She looks a little skeptical. "What did you have for dinner last night?"

"Oh, you mean supper. Muffins."

"Just muffins?"

"Yes. I like muffins. They're pretty easy to fix."

"What about vegetables and meat? Are you getting enough protein? Do you drink milk?"

"Sometimes we have bacon for breakfast on the weekend, and I put milk in my coffee."

"Coffee! Why do you drink coffee?"

"I love the taste of coffee. I've been drinking coffee since I was four. I never did like the taste of milk. My mother got me to drink milk by flavoring it with coffee. And over the years, the coffee got more and more, and the milk got less and less."

"Well, what about orange juice? You should drink orange juice every day with your breakfast. If you don't get enough vitamin C, you can get scurvy. If you don't get enough protein, you can get kwashiorkor. If you don't get enough calcium and vitamin D, you can get rickets and osteomalacia. You look malnourished to me."

I am pretty skinny. And it's embarrassing when the science teacher posts all our weights on a chart in the front of class. I'm the lowest-weight girl in eighth grade, except for one other girl, who is very short. I look up malnutrition in the encyclopedia, and I don't like the pictures it shows. I try to take some of Paloma's advice. I do the best I can.

That fall, after school, I begin to spend long hours alone on the tire swing, clinging to the familiar old rubber. I watch as two more new houses go up, on what used to be Mr. Brenner's tenant farm across the road. A new builder has started work on Cory Clay's second housing project. The Country Manor Estates sign looms large just about a hundred feet from the front of our house. It casts a shadow across our mailbox. Foxtail grass and chicory push through the bluestone gravel in our driveway, untended by Jimmie's sickle.

One day, I wind the tire swing tight on its rope, tuck my feet up inside the rim, close my eyes, and let the tire spin quickly down. I open my eyes mid-spin to see Spence, blurred as he comes down the front steps toward me.

I imagine I hear my brother saying, "You told Mommy, didn't you? Lonny's going to be mad." But really, he says nothing at all. I'm hearing echoes of something Spence said a long time ago.

Suddenly, I want to go very far away, to run across an open field, grow tiny in the distance, and disappear forever into dark and silent woods, into once upon a time. I cling more tightly to the tire's warm black rubber, kick off my tennis shoes, push hard with my feet, and swing high.

I curl my toes, then stretch them out toward the maple branches. Even though I keep my eyes shut, the vision comes back, long past, but vivid.

In between circus acts, on one of those washed-out summer afternoons when I am seven, lucky seven, Spence, my own brother, succumbs to Lonny's threats and bullying. Squatting opposite me behind the disc harrow, Spence touches—just barely touches—his most private self to mine, while Lonny watches through a peephole in the barn wall.

I never told my mother. At the time, it seemed too awful to tell. And I must never tell my daddy.

Later, much later, I will come to understand that more than the act itself, the reactions I feared from those around me made it all seem worse, much worse, than it actually was.

But for now, I feel the swing going higher and higher. Spence is pushing me. I open my eyes just in time to see him running under me, pushing and lifting the swing over his head. He gives a blood-curdling rebel yell.

I scream, "Don't!" just as my feet strike a branch. Down comes a shower of maple leaves, as bright and golden as the new moon that, in my innocence, I had wanted to look for; but these leaves are fallen, and they will soon be dead.

Spence runs off, up behind the corn crib, where he habitually goes to think. He paces vigorously around and around an oval path he has worn in the grass, talking aloud to himself from time to time, gesturing with bursts of energy as he ponders ways to conquer outer space.

By dragging my feet, I bring the swing to a halt. I put my shoes back on, run to catch up with Spence, and begin to pace behind him on his "thinking" path.

"What are you thinking about, Spence?"

"Why don't you make like a tree—and leave?" says Spence. He likes to be alone when he's thinking.

I give up trying to talk with Spence and run into the house.

"Daddy, is there such a thing as a new moon?" He's sitting in his armchair, nodding in front of the TV set, which is blaring at full-volume.

"Daddy," I repeat a little louder, and climb onto his lap. He wakes with a start, runs his tongue over his lips to moisten them, and hugs me close to him.

He tugs at my ears and says, "There's my little squirrel-ears, come home to her nest."

"Is there such a thing as a new moon?"

"A what?" he asks me, and cups his hand behind his left ear. He's told me the story many times of how the doctor gave him quinine as a child to treat malaria, how it left him hard of hearing.

"A new moon," I shout into his ear. His eyes have begun to water and he dabs at them with his dirty white handkerchief.

"There's only one moon," he tells me. "The same old moon. And there's a man in the moon. They talk of going to the moon someday with their rocket ships. But they oughtn't to do it. They oughtn't to go shooting their missiles and their Sputniks into that old man in the moon. He never did anybody any harm. Leave him alone. That's what I say."

Tears run down both of Daddy's cheeks, and some of them spill onto my face. I snuggle closer to him. I run my fingernails lightly up and down over his stubbly chin whiskers, the way I did when I was little. And here I stay for a while, believing that my daddy is crying for all of us, and for the moon.

The weeds grow high in Jimmie's vegetable gardens until the frost hits. The house is quieter now, without Jimmie in it. Aunt Essie doesn't come over any more. None of Jimmie's relatives are invited over anymore. Daddy doesn't like visitors or strangers—other than customers—coming into our house. And the customers he lets into his office directly through the side door.

Jimmie was friendly, and she always liked people. But now, Daddy tells me, "I used to like people too, Lissa. But when you get to be as old as I am, and you've seen as many things as I have, you might not like people, either. The older I get, the less faith I have in human nature. I don't trust people anymore."

For a while, every night before I go to sleep, I try to talk to Jimmie about all this. "Hello, Jimmie. Mommy? Are you there? Can you hear me?" I say.

I do this night after night, week after week, but Jimmie never answers back. And then, one night, when I try to picture Jimmie in my mind, I can't do it. I can't see her face anymore. It makes me want to cry.

I miss her so! I panic. I go up to the attic, where Jimmie's clothes and most of her things are stored, and dig out an old framed photo of her. Grandma Magda's black metal dress form appears to rise from the shadows under the steep slope of the roof, looming over me, terrorizing me.

Years ago, I drew Grandma's face with crayon on a brown paper lunch bag, and stuck the bag, like a head, on the neck of her dress form in the attic. Now, I give Grandma's form a strong spin and race down the attic stairs, clutching Jimmie's photo. If I can make it down the stairs, turn off the light, and close the attic door before Grandma Magda stops spinning, I will be safe!

I put Jimmie's photo on the dresser across from my bed, and look at it every day to keep my memory of her alive.

A couple of times, I dream that Jimmie didn't really die, and that she is still alive somewhere—sick and dying in a hospice. In the dream, I am so sorry that she's been there all this time, and I didn't even know it. She must think I have forgotten her; that thought makes me frantic! I search and search for the phone number for her room. Finally, I find the number and try to call her at the hospice, but I'm never able to get through to her. It's a wrong number, or I get a busy signal, or the phone just keeps ringing, and no one answers.

After that, the weeks seem to blur on for a while. Spence draws into himself more and more. Daddy looks so sad and lonely.

Then on Friday, November 22, 1963, an act of violence jars me and leaves a permanent scar on the whole world's consciousness. It's just six days before Thanksgiving when the brown wooden PA box at the top of the classroom wall switches on for an announcement. John F. Kennedy has been assassinated in Dallas, Texas. Our handsome young president is dead. Teachers gather in the hallway. My French teacher is crying.

Then come days of TV images that never fade—a pillbox hat, a bloodstained pink suit, a black-veiled widow leaning down, whispering to her three-year-old son. A little boy's farewell salute to his father. Throngs of mourners, a flag-draped casket rolling past, and a riderless horse with back-facing boots in the stirrups. Even when the TVs are silenced for the night, that primal presidential drumbeat goes on, marking time.

Not long after that comes a time when, right across the road, construction ceases mid-house at Country Manor Estates, where the sun still sets behind the pointed hemlocks. We hear through the Grangerville grapevine that Cory Clay, deep in debt, has put a bullet through his head. Faye has to be sedated, and is taken to Sheppard Pratt. Around here, Country Manor Estates comes to be known as Faye's Folly.

CHAPTER EIGHT

PUBERTY INTERRUPTED

In eighth grade, when I begin to read Pearl Buck's *The Good Earth* with the rest of my class, I come across a passage that describes what happens in bed on a wedding night. At our house, sex has never been spoken about openly—either before or after Jimmie dies. This passage startles me, and I make the mistake of reading it out loud to Daddy. He grabs the book from my hands, goes out back by the grape arbor, tosses the paperback on the trash heap, and lights it with a match. Watching from the pantry window, I see flames like obscene orange tongues licking at *The Good Earth*. Soon, it is just a smoldering heap of ashes.

Daddy writes a note to my teacher:

Dear Mrs. Comey,

I do not condone my daughter reading *The Good Earth*. It is a filthy novel.

Yours truly,

Stouten R. Power

The next day, I wait until the end of class to give the note to Mrs. Comey. I thrust it at her across her desk and rush out of the classroom, too embarrassed to look at her.

Later that week, Mrs. Comey asks me to stay for a few minutes after class. She gives me a different book to read, a collection of classic short stories.

"Lissa, I'm going to have you read this book while the other students read *The Good Earth*. You will be expected to listen to the class discussions on *The Good Earth*, but I won't ask you to participate in them. I will be giving you a separate exam on the stories in this collection. Your exam will include questions about the short stories you read, plus one or two essay questions on *The Good Earth*. You should be able to grasp what you need to know for the exam by reading all the stories in this book and by listening to the class discussions."

None of the other kids seem to pick up on what is going on. I just follow my separate path, and try not to call any attention to myself. From the discussions, I learn about the struggles of a Chinese peasant farmer in a time of change. At the same time, I am allowed to venture into the realm of the short story. I read Jack London's "To Build a Fire," Richard Connell's "The Most Dangerous Game," Willa Cather's "Paul's Case," O. Henry's "The Gift of the Magi," Henry Sydnor Harrison's "Miss Hinch," and Saki's "The Open Window." Here, linguistic elements—like the delicate escapement of a watch—engage, release, engage, release, carrying the reader forward at a measured pace. Tick, tock, tick, tock. These writers, like master watchmakers, have perfected their skills, and are meticulous in executing them. Rather than grinding and shaping and turning stainless steel, gold plate, gold, and platinum to produce elegant timepieces, these writers place, arrange, rearrange, conjugate, manipulate, craft, and polish language to create jewels of irony, intrigue, and humor. Like mainsprings, their narratives unwind, pulsing with flashes of setting, wisps of unforgettable character, quick-moving twists of plot, heart-opening epiphanies. The mechanism of the short story is as satisfying for me as the precision of a watch is for Daddy.

To catch the high school bus, we have to walk seven-tenths of a mile to the nearest intersection. Following behind Spence on the road's narrow shoulder, trying to keep up with his long strides, I glance at the new tribe of children, elementary school kids from the modern suburban houses, gathered at the end of the communal driveway for Cory's Ridge, waiting for their school bus—kids dressed, every day, in the latest styles that Spence and I could never afford to wear, not even on Sunday. Blithely, these children swing shiny new lunchboxes; the boys indulge in lighthearted tussling; the little girls trade self-satisfied giggles.

One of the older girls calls out to me, "Hey, you! Is your house haunted?" I try to be a brave soldier. I just keep on walking.

As I hurry past, I overhear her tell another little girl, "My mother thinks *her* house is an eyesore. It ought to be torn down." I just keep on walking.

Sometimes, the Cory's Ridge kids poke fun at Daddy. They think he's my grandfather. When I tell them he's my father, a little red-headed boy pipes up, "You're a liar. My parents say he's too old be your father." I try to shut my ears, go inside myself, and just keep on walking.

One of the friendlier mothers stops by Daddy's workshop to ooh and aah over his craftsmanship—his inlaid lamps and wooden plates and jewelry boxes—but she isn't willing to pay for the time and effort he put into them.

A year of un-ironed clothes, burnt bacon, and too many macaroni and cheese suppers passes. I find out the hard way, in winter, that if you hang wet clothes on the line when the temperature goes down below freezing, the clothes will freeze solid—so solid that a pair of pants can stand up on its own—and you will have to thaw them out on the radiators. Gradually, as spring and summer come and go, I learn to do the things Jimmie didn't have time to teach me—cooking ham, potatoes, and string beans in a pressure cooker without having the top blow off; spritzing clothes with water to make them easier to iron; separating colors from whites in the washing machine so Spence doesn't wind up with pink underpants.

Daddy's most reliable source of income has always been making cams for the gas and electric company. When the order comes in, he gets to work on the special machine he invented. He turns the cams, makes the brass bushings, and gets Spence or me to help him operate the small mechanical presser that pushes the bushings into the centers of the cams. Daddy makes us wash our hands after handling the freshly worked brass. He says it's toxic. Spence just runs a little water over his hands and wipes them on his pants, but I want to be safe. I do what Daddy does after handling the bushings. I wash and scrub, really scrub, my hands and under my fingernails, over and over again with Daddy's Boraxo powdered hand soap.

Daddy inspects each cam to make sure it is perfect, and that the bushing is flush with the cam's surface; but this year, something goes wrong, and Daddy gets the cams sent back to him in the mail. The enclosed letter says the cams are "eccentric," and that the gas and electric company will be doing their business elsewhere in the future.

Daddy's hand shakes as he holds out the rejection letter. Then he goes off by himself to work on something else in his woodshop. A half hour later, he comes rushing back inside, his finger bleeding. "Get me a Band-Aid, Lissa! I've cut myself."

I wash his hand in the kitchen sink and watch the diluted blood run down the drain. It's not a bad cut. I've seen Daddy cut his hand many times before. It's part of the kind of work he does. But this time, Daddy looks forlorn and bewildered in a way I've never seen him before.

Daddy says we need to "economize." He has us turn off any lights we're not using to save electricity; he turns the thermostat back to conserve fuel oil; we chink the cracks in the downstairs doors and windows with folded newspaper. When wind blows through the newspaper, it fills the house with an eerie whistling. At least we have the storm windows upstairs that Jimmie got Uncle Frantz to install about a month before she died. Daddy teaches us to warm ourselves on cold winter evenings by jumping up and down and slapping ourselves. "Keeps the circulation going," he tells us.

Daddy starts to worry again about keeping up with the property taxes and taking care of Spence and me. Finally, on the first warm day, he swallows his pride, overcomes his shyness, and walks from door to door, carrying a clock he made years ago, a clock shaped like a French cathedral. Its walls and flying buttresses are varnished mahogany, its spires intricately carved on the jigsaw.

I can see how hard this is for him. In preparation, he puts on his only suit, his blue wool wedding suit—now frayed, shiny, and crusted black at the wrists and elbows. He has shrunk over the years, so the suit is way too big for him. The pants droop, and the hems drag on the floor at the backs of his shoe heels.

At the bathroom sink, he shaves, practices smiling at the mirror with his lips pressed together so as not to show his yellowed, rotting teeth. He ties on his best red-striped silk tie, which has a grease stain near the bottom. He dons his downtown fedora, sets the brim just so, and walks door to door.

He tries to get one of the new homeowners to buy the cathedral clock, or perhaps place an order for another of his wooden "creations." He pulls from his pocket photos he's taken of his inlaid plates and jewelry boxes, a lighthouse lamp, a wooden cigarette box—pull one of the four plastic knobs at the front of the box, and out comes a cigarette from one of four holes.

Word gets back to me at church that some of our new neighbors are complaining at the bank and at Sweeney's store about an unkempt old peddler. One of the kids brags that his father, who is a lawyer, might just have the old man prosecuted for soliciting.

School starts again. Spence and I are both in high school. I'm in junior high (ninth grade); Spence is in senior high (eleventh grade). Negotiating high school without a mother is tricky for Spence and me. Daddy keeps insisting that we need to economize. He buys us a seven-piece haircut kit at the local five-and-dime—an electric clipper, barber scissors, comb, and four comb-like attachments to vary the length of the cut.

Spence is definitely in need of a haircut. His hair, black like Jimmie's but straight like Daddy's, is thick and unruly. It has grown over his ears and way too far down his neck.

I get Spence to straddle a backward-turned kitchen chair. Then I tie a bathroom towel around his neck, drape it down his shirtfront, and attempt my first haircut. Standing and facing my unsuspecting victim, I snap on the clipper's longest attachment (to be on the safe side), and switch on our new money-saving gadget. At first, Spence sits patiently, lightly grasping the chair back in front of him, as I propel the first cuts from front to back. Moving around the chair, I sheer up the right side, up the back side, then up the left side, comb out the entire head of hair, and inspect my work. Then I hand Spence the ornate handheld mirror, retrieved from Jimmie's old vanity set. "What do you think?"

"It looks the same to me. Did you cut anything off?"

"Sure. Look at the floor. There's a pile of your hair."

"Well, maybe cut a little more off."

"Okay." This time, I go to town with the medium-length attachment, gaining confidence and enthusiasm. "I think I need to taper it some." I apply the shortest attachment, then take that off to achieve an even shorter, razored layer at the neckline. I finish up by adding a few creative clips directly with the barber scissors.

"Ow!" Spence jumps. "You cut me."

"Just a little nick. Sit still, you're making me cut steps in your hair. Now I have to even it out."

But the more I try to fix the mis-cut hair and even it out, the worse it gets. I have to admit that the next day, Spence is pretty good about going to school with hair that looks as if it had been chewed on by a dog with dull teeth. Before we set out on our walk to the bus stop, he does a quick comb-over to cover some of the rough spots. Of course, he can't see all the jagged chops and bald spots in the back the way I can when I walk behind him to the school bus.

I seem to live in a world apart from my high school classmates—an old-fashioned world that adheres to Daddy's rules. No bathing or shampooing in cold weather—it would, according to Daddy, give me a catarrh. Daddy doesn't want me to wear makeup or shave my legs. According to Daddy, those are not things that ladies do.

"You must always be a lady, Lissa," Daddy says. "Not like those women who primp and preen and try to get men to fight over them like those saloon girls on the TV." Daddy gets upset when he sees cowboys getting into a fistfight over one of Miss Kitty's girls at the Long Branch Saloon on *Gunsmoke*.

I'm not allowed to go to school dances or participate in after-school activities. Because he's a boy, Spence does get to spend the night at his friend Mark's house sometimes. But I'm a girl, and according to Daddy, girls are supposed to stay at home, especially at night, and be protected.

"You need to stay home and take care of me," Daddy tells me.

I still do have my one friend at school: my best friend, Paloma. We are still in most of the same classes. More and more, she sees how shy I am, how serious, how I have to deal with lots of things most of the other kids in our class don't even think about.

Paloma decides I need to get out more. She invites me to spend the night at her house.

"I don't think my father will let me do that," I tell her.

"Where do you live?" she asks me. "What's your address? I think my mom would like to meet your dad."

I tell Paloma my address, and the next weekend, she and her mom pull up in our driveway in her mom's Volkswagen bus. Paloma's mom has brought my daddy a knife with a broken handle to repair. She's very polite to Daddy, and she smiles a lot. Daddy warms up to her right away. He even shows her around his woodshop.

"I sure do admire your craftsmanship, Mr. Power," she says. "My dad was a cabinetmaker, so I can appreciate the skill and care you put into your work. And, you know, Paloma just can't say enough good things about Lissa."

"Lissa is my best friend," Paloma tells Daddy. Her words come out, as usual, in a rapid burst of feeling. "Lissa has a brain, and she's a good listener, and she doesn't fit in with the other girls any more than I do."

"Well, any friend of my little girl is a friend of mine," Daddy says, and he shakes Paloma's hand.

After that, Daddy surprises Paloma's mom by making her a whole new rosewood knife handle. He winds up letting me spend the weekend at Paloma's, and her mom kind of takes me under her wing.

Paloma's father is a professor and researcher at Johns Hopkins, and her mother comes from an old Ruxton family. Paloma lives with her parents and siblings on a big horse farm in the northern part of the county, not too far from where I live. We have dinner at a long table. It's very formal and elegant. The china has gold trim, and there are more forks and knives and spoons than I know what to do with. Paloma's older sister, Phoebe, sits across from me and just stares at me as I fumble with the silverware. Paloma's father presides at the head of the table, dominating the conversation, booming out strong opinions, telling razor-edged jokes that I don't get, laughing harshly and raising his eyebrows at the punchlines. With dessert, Paloma's mom distributes fingerbowls, and Paloma has to show me how to use them.

After dinner, Paloma's mom clears the table, Phoebe goes off to her room to do homework, and Paloma and I follow her dad into the living room. Here, the walls are lined with bookcases, and a baby grand piano dominates one corner of the room. There's no TV. Paloma tells me later that they don't own a television. "Dad says only idiots watch TV!"

"Paloma tells me you play the piano," her dad says to me. "Play something for us."

I'm only just learning, and I don't really want to perform in front of Paloma's dad, but he insists. I play Beethoven's *Für Elise*, the only thing I know from memory. Paloma's dad is standing right behind me, so close I can feel him breathing and smell the smoke that's coming off his pipe. He is a huge presence, and seems to give off some kind of menacing power there behind me. I'm so nervous, I lose my place, but I keep repeating the opening passage until I find my way forward, and finish with a strong chord.

"Not bad," he says, between puffs at his pipe. "Do you play chess?"

"Well, my brother taught me how to move the pieces."

"Fantastic!" He sets up a chessboard at a small round table. "Here. You can challenge Paloma." Paloma's dad hides a pawn in each hand and holds out his fists to me. "Pick one." I tap his right hand, and he opens it to reveal a white pawn. That means I get white, and get to move first.

I don't really want to challenge Paloma, but there's no escaping her father's wishes here. He towers over us, breathing heavily, watching each move. I don't know what I'm doing. I just start playing. After a few moves, I look up at Paloma. Her face is flushed, her lips pressed so tightly together they are white, her chin clenched in a knot. I realize that Paloma is scared. The one who always stands up to everyone at school is scared of her own father!

"I don't want to play anymore," I say, and lay my king on its side.

"You can't resign," Paloma's dad growls. "You were winning!" Paloma bursts into tears and runs out of the room. Her father doesn't say anything. He just folds his arms across his chest and watches her leave. He has a funny kind of crooked smile on his face.

I follow Paloma up to her bedroom and hug her. "I wasn't winning, Paloma. I didn't even know what I was doing."

"I know," she says. She tugs on my pigtails, and her sobs start to subside. "My dad is very competitive with me. He loves to see me lose. He tells me I'm clumsy and ugly and stupid. And did you notice? He had a white pawn in both hands. He rigged it so you would have the advantage."

"Oh, no!" I say. "I'm so sorry, Paloma."

"It's not your fault, Lissa. You just don't know how lucky you are to have a dad who loves you."

On Saturday, Paloma lets me get on one of her horses—a nervous young thoroughbred filly. "She'll let you mount her. You're skinny and light like a jockey. That's what she's used to." Paloma gives me a boost into the saddle. I've never been on a horse before. I didn't realize how high up they are. I don't really know how to ride, so I get off after a few minutes. "Next time you come over, I'll teach you how to ride. You look good up there, Lissa!"

After that weekend, Paloma and I start to talk for hours on the phone.

Daddy just teases me and says, "You teenagers. Always on the phone. Just like Penny Pringle in the funny papers."

CHAPTER NINE

UNWITTING VICTIMS OF FALLEN ANGEL SWAMP

DADDY and I spend a lot of time together in the evenings, now, after supper. We both miss Jimmie. To escape the sadness, Daddy tells me stories about his childhood in Southern Maryland.

Tonight, I start by saying, "Tell me what it was like when you were a little boy, Daddy." And he goes on to tell me about a time when there were no cars, no electric lights, a time when folks moved more slowly, with the rhythm of nature. A much quieter time, but not an idyllic one.

"You remember me telling you about my Cousin Urchie, Lissa?"

I nod, and he continues.

"Many generations ago, my cousin Urchie's family settled on a small parcel of land in what the locals called Fallen Angel Swamp, a wetland in the Potomac River Basin that ran the length of Charles County, more than twenty miles along a braided stream, and eventually emptied into the Loco Moco River. Even though their property—a mosquito-laden strip of land rising only a few feet above the wetland—was not much good for farming, it belonged to Urchie's family, free and clear—or so they thought.

"And so, generation after generation, Urchie's progenitors were born breathing the fetid swamp gasses. Some died in childhood. Some lived long enough to reproduce. Some died giving birth. Eventually, all of them fell mysteriously and terribly ill, and died.

"Now, while the local doctor—who was not much more than a pill peddler—dispensed his new-fangled patent medicines, the swamp kept on nurturing hordes of mosquitoes. And they went about breeding and biting and spreading an inventory of diseases as long as your arm. Fouled, stagnant water. No electricity. No indoor plumbing. All this worked in cahoots with people's ignorance of the simplest tenets of sanitation and personal hygiene to unleash furious demons. Cholera. Dysentery.

"After we learned of Urchie's death, my mammy, Lovenia, went to care for her sister—Urchie's mother, Aunt Cealanne. I drove Mammy over there in the wooden oxcart I built myself. I had a team of oxen named Pilot and Lively—trained them myself to pull that cart. Pilot was the steady one. He kept the cart on track. Lively was the spirited one. He kept the cart moving at a good pace, even through the boggy stretches.

"Pilot and Lively drew the cart, as far as its wheels would turn, deep into Fallen Angel Swamp, jouncing precariously along that dirt road's narrow ruts. My mammy sat beside me, balancing a big wicker basket chock-full of covered dishes and clean linens for our stricken relatives.

"About a hundred yards from our destination, a bog cut through the road. Oh, Lively made valiant efforts to keep that cart moving! But finally, he gave in to Pilot's better judgment, and the cart came to a halt, up to its axles in mud.

"Mammy and I were forced to abandon the wagon. I unhitched the team and tied them to a chestnut tree. I toted the basket of provisions and slogged alongside my mammy the rest of the way, through the murkiest water I'm ever likely to see, toward a careening slab-board house. As we got closer, I could see that the house was built on a finger of soil that pushed out just a few feet above the far edge of the bog. The closer we got, the more that house seemed to back away and cower in the shadows of a dark hardwood forest. A small chicken coop huddled near one side of the house. As we crossed the narrow front yard, we passed Urchie's grave—newly dug and filled.

"When we got inside the house, it smelled so bad I nearly passed out. But I followed my mammy up those steep, narrow stairs to the only bedroom in that house. It was right under the roof. The ceiling was so low I had to duck my head.

"Come to find out, Urchie's father, my Uncle Willie, was away on a shooting trip, and the rest of the family members were all there, sick in just one bed. Urchie was survived by a younger sister, a scrawny girl they called Tickintit. She was in that bed fretting, trying to sleep beside her mother underneath a vomit-soaked quilt.

"Aunt Cealanne was in a family way, and she had herself propped up on one elbow, moaning and puking over the side of the bed. Excrement was smeared on the bedsheets. Chamber pots were poking out from under the bed and spilling over onto the floor. In one corner, a wooden commode was overflowing.

"My Cousin Tickintit was thought be 'tetched,' that is, not quite right in the head. When she was just a little girl, no more than seven, she learned that the fried chicken drumstick she had just eaten for supper was none other than her favorite hen, Magnolia!

"Well, now, Tickintit was overcome with sadness. Her father swore to her that Magnolia had been ailing, otherwise he would never have grabbed her off the eggs she was nesting.

"So, on that stagnant spring evening, driven by a fierce, albeit somewhat unnatural, maternal instinct for those motherless eggs, Tickintit climbed the wooden ramp to the henhouse, gently removed Magnolia's four eggs from the nest, and carried them in the skirt of her dress to the upstairs bedroom.

"She took the eggs to bed with her, nestled in her underpants. Cousin Tickintit clucked like a mother hen, and vowed she would hatch those chicks herself. For weeks, she refused to leave the bed and abandon those eggs. Aunt Cealanne accommodated her daughter by bringing her food in bed.

"When word of this behavior spread, some of the more self-important parishioners at St. Ignatius got together to beseech Father Martin to call on and counsel my dim-witted cousin and my weak-willed Aunt Cealanne.

"Though Father Martin declined to set foot on what he called 'the devil's own doorstep,' he did consent to hold an expiatory novena for the cursed family.

"As for Tickintit, she stayed in that bed with those eggs until they had turned rotten and started to stink.

"One muggy afternoon in late spring, Tickintit got up, went to the outhouse, and tossed those foul eggs into the pit latrine. Then she resumed her customary occupations as if nothing strange had happened. She came back to our one-room schoolhouse, where she sat next to me. And she whispered out loud, repeating voices that spoke to her in Latin, 'Cave, cave, Deus videt.' Beware, beware, God sees! 'Ad maiorem Matris Glorium.' For the great glory of the Mother."

There, side by side, in that one-room country schoolhouse, we heard the voices of angels and saints and prophets. But no one besides Tickintit and me seemed to hear them."

For some reason, hearing old-time stories from my daddy is comforting to me, grounding.

"Tell me the story about Moses Queen, Daddy."

I've heard this story many times before, and Daddy tells it a little bit differently every time. But that's what's so beautiful about stories. They take you to a space somewhere beyond right or wrong, correct or incorrect, accurate or inaccurate. A place that's free and clear and pure, somehow. That's why I like words better than numbers. Words give you room to escape, to pretend, to imagine *what if...*

"So, Lissa," Daddy begins.

"Once upon a very long time ago, I knew an old, old black man, a former slave by the name of Moses Queen. Some folks said he must be older than Methuselah. Said he was a young man in Civil War times.

"Well, now, Moses Queen lived in a cabin deep in Fallen Angel Swamp. My Pappy's tobacco farm at Tulip Hill butted right up onto the swamp near the mouth of the Loco Moco River, and sometimes, Moses Queen helped us crop tobacco.

"I loved to listen to that old black man telling his stories. So sometimes, coming home from school, I would purposely take a detour over to Moses Queen's place.

"One afternoon, I came upon Moses splitting logs outside his cabin. Soon as he saw me, he dropped his axe, sat on the chopping block, and patted a spot on the ground next to him.

"I took my customary place, sitting cross-legged on the dark, clammy earth.

"Now, Moses Queen had the blackest, most wrinkled face I have ever seen. Deep creases and crevices etched across it like bottomless furrows plowed into fertile black soil. When he strained at his work, the skin on his cheekbones flushed a dusky purple, but the rest of his body was taut and shiny. His muscles, when he flexed them and worked up a sweat, rippled with hints of chestnut and gold. A dark, irregular weave—like grain running through the finest cocobolo heartwood—traced through his tendons, and glinted as if it had been polished to a sheen.

"Moses picked up a stick of wood, began to whittle it, and embarked on his story about the fine white gentleman who had crossed his path.

"'You know, boy,' says Moses, 'it was just about this time of day, just before sunset, when I was making my way home through Fallen Angel Swamp. And what should I spy but a horse come galloping along like a bat out of Hades, carrying a handsome young gentleman, riding alongside another white man. Now, this gentleman in all his finery looked right bad, pale as a ghost and tormented-like. He pulled up sharp in front of me, leaned toward me from his saddle, and said in the most graceful of tones, "Boy, could you help me out. I'm lost in this godforsaken bog."

"'I looked him up and down, and well, his leg looked like it was busted and had been patched up, and his face looked so pitiful and twisted, like his soul was in the deepest of turmoil.

"'Well, you know, the pathways through that swamp is laid out like a puzzle with false leads and cutoffs and undergrowth that blocks your way. Course, I know Fallen Angel like the back of my old black hand. So, I guided him and his companion, used my homemade machete to bushwhack through them laurel and rhododendron thickets.

"'Guided him and his friend safe and sound through that swamp, and delivered him to a Confederate safe house he knew of, just outside the swamp. The hurt man's friend rapped on the door, and the fine gentleman made a case for himself. By and by, the owner came out on his front porch. I overheard them all talking, and it seemed like them two men was in need of help to get across the Potomac and into Virginia.

"'The handsome white gentleman gave me some money for my trouble, for which I thanked him very kindly. Then I bade them all farewell, and made my way back home in the moonlight.

"'Well, it turned out to be a right funny situation, after all. Come to find out, by and by, I had played a bit part in the chronicles of time.

"'The newspapers was reporting different stories about where this man was, and who it was helping him. And there was talk about how a black man—some said a former slave, some said a half-breed or a We-Sort, you know, we-sorts-of people (mixed black, Piscataway, white)—came to the aid of an actor named John Wilkes Booth who broke his leg escaping from the Ford Theater in Washington, D.C., after assassinating President Abraham Lincoln.

"'Seems this Mr. Booth was making his escape through our own Fallen Angel Swamp here in Charles County. In fact, it was a local doctor, one Samuel Mudd, who patched up that actor's leg.

"'Turns out he had left Mudd's place and was trying to outmaneuver the Union soldiers who were swarming like bloodhounds over the countryside, hunting him down. To elude them, he wound up having to cross through Fallen Angel Swamp, which was foreign territory to him.

"'That plantation I guided him to was home to a Confederate sympathizer, who helped that handsome play actor—the very man who felled our President Lincoln—make the rest of his way to safety—across the Potomac, in a hired flatboat, to Virginia.'

"'But why did you help that man, Mr. Moses?'

"'Well, first I must confess to you that I was downright enchanted by him. This Booth was the most beautiful white man I had ever seen—countenance like a porcelain doll baby, raven black hair, flowing mustache,' Moses Queen replied.

"'And he spoke his words so fine and melodious. He *was* quite an actor! It was like he was puttin' on the voice of the Angel Gabriel. Or maybe he could have been the devil, playacting his part in history.

"'But it seemed to me at the time,' Moses added, smiling a most glorious smile, 'that I was just helping one of God's lost children. Now, you remember that, young Stouten. Always remember that we are all, after all, God's own children.'"

Daddy stops speaking and gives me a look to see how I'm reacting. Then he stands up and acts out the rest of the story.

"Now remember, Lissa, Moses Queen was a tall, lean man with a powerful, sinewy build. And at this point in his narrative, Mr. Queen would always pause for effect. Then he would stand and draw himself up to his full height, expand his powerful chest, and hold forth like a preacher.

"'Besides,' Moses Queen concluded, 'I figure Mr. Booth has either gone to hell or is destined to spend quite some time a-struttin' and a-frettin' upon that fiery stage in purgatory.'

"And with that, Moses would slap his thighs and bust out laughing so hard, it echoed as far as it could go before being swallowed up forever in the dark abysses of that infernal swamp."

Hearing Daddy's tale about Moses Queen makes me wonder what Daddy really thinks about black people. When he uses the n-word, I think he must be prejudiced. But when he talks about Moses Queen, he seems to make Moses the hero of the story. I think this must be what my teacher Mrs. Comey means in English class when she talks about ambiguity in the stories we read. She says that, sometimes, words allow a writer to convey an "uncertainty of meaning." It explains how my daddy can be prejudiced and not prejudiced at the same time. Mrs. Comey says that understanding human nature requires us to come to terms with contradiction, and creative language allows us to waltz with ambiguity. All of this helps me deal with my own struggle with *maybe, maybe not.*

CHAPTER TEN

CHARLIE BROWN CHRISTMAS TREE

This Christmas, when I am fourteen, is a sad one for Daddy and Spence and me. Thick snow begins to fall the day before Christmas Eve, slowing, impeding—and finally stopping—traffic. Northern Baltimore County succumbs to a profound silence, buried beneath a shroud of white. Snowdrifts form along fences; dirt and gravel driveways disappear. The county plows priority-one roadways and designated snow routes first. Our narrow, less-trafficked, country roads must wait. And we must clear—or pay to have cleared—our own driveway. By morning, we are snowbound at the farmhouse.

As the snow tapers off, Spence borrows one of Daddy's saws, and together, we trudge toward the narrow strip of trees that still stands beyond the new houses. These few remaining trees stand like weary sentinels along the steep ridge that used to divide our fields from those of George Clay's neighboring farm. Now, like remnants of a defeated army, they stand watch between the eastern and southern sections of Cory's Ridge.

Spence and I tread cautiously now, fearful that we might be caught trespassing. Between mongrel evergreens and inbred deciduous specimens, we spy a small scraggly fir—short in stature, thin of branch, but definitely a Christmas tree. Spence cuts it down, and I follow as he drags it home across the snow.

We call it our Charlie Brown Christmas tree, and decorate it with a few of the ornaments kept stored in the attic. A single string of lights is almost too much for the fragile tree to bear, and the larger Christmas balls bob and dangle precariously from the puny branches. The angel, whose feathers are molting, is too heavy for the little tree, so we prop her up on top of the old upright piano Daddy bought me a few years ago from his old German piano-tuner friend, Mr. Spiegel, for two hundred dollars.

Mr. Spiegel comes to visit annually to tune the piano for free. He drives an ancient-looking car with running boards, and always wears the same old-school suit and wide tie, with a fresh rosebud set just so in one of its wide lapels. Invariably, Mr. Spiegel greets me with a courtly handshake, presents me with a two-pound box of chocolates, and presses a five-dollar bill into my palm.

We try to carry on as usual and celebrate a normal Christmas, but for the first time in my life, no presents are waiting under the tree, and our Christmas stockings hang empty. The snow stops us from getting out to buy anything.

I boil chestnuts and bake a ham for Christmas dinner. Then Spence and I try to amuse ourselves, and pass the afternoon playing board games—Monopoly and Clue—and card games like gin rummy and I Declare War. Daddy joins us in playing Authors, giving funny names to the famous writers depicted on the cards. He dubs Charles Dickens "Old Snaggly Puss." Henry Wadsworth Longfellow becomes "Old White Beard," Robert Louis Stevenson is "Mr. Droopy Whiskers," and Louisa May Alcott is christened "Miss Ruffles." I end the day by playing a few carols on the piano and reading the Christmas story out loud to Daddy and Spence from the Book of Luke.

On the day after Christmas, Spence retreats to his bedroom to sleep and read science fiction. Daddy and I occupy our usual spots in the dining/living room—me on the sofa, Daddy in his threadbare gray armchair. Daddy pulls out his worn leather wallet and shows me, for the umpteenth time, the blurry antique photo of a baby squirrel he carries with him, always, and begins a rambling story about cold winters and pets and Christmases on Tulip Hill.

"One Christmas morning when I was about your age, Lissa, it was so cold that all the chamber pots were frozen solid. We children all ran downstairs to find the oranges and hard candy and chocolates and firecrackers that old Santa Claus had left in our Christmas stockings. After breakfast, I went out with my brothers to set off the firecrackers in the lane. John, my oldest brother, dared me to go out to the barn and lick a wagon wheel. Well, I did, but, of course, the saliva froze, leaving my tongue stuck fast to the wheel. When I pulled my tongue free, I could see a little piece of pink skin stuck to the cast-iron rim. After that, I learned that John was not a brother I should take a dare from.

"Later that same day, I went walking through the woods. Found a baby red squirrel abandoned in a leaf nest, fallen to the ground at the foot of a big oak tree. I rescued that little fella, named him Chicoree. Carried him around in my pocket for days. Built him a little wooden cage and carved and glued some sticks to make a tiny wheel for him to play on."

Daddy leans over from his armchair and strokes my arm.

"You must always take care of your pets, Lissa. When you make an animal into a pet, it forgets how to take care of itself. I loved my little Chicoree. I loved him so much that the night before I went back to school, I fed him candy from my Christmas stocking.

"In the morning, I found my little Chicoree dead in his cage. That goes to show you, Lissa, that the wrong kind of love, no matter how well-intended, can be poison."

I listen, nod in agreement, and hold Daddy's hand. I have always made pets of orphaned animals—baby chicks, a baby duck dropped by a hawk on our property, a gray lamb whose mother wouldn't nurse him, plenty of stray cats and dogs.

"You know," Daddy tells me, "my pappy loved animals. And it nearly broke his heart when he accidentally killed his favorite guinea keet. That little keet would eat cracked corn right out of my pappy's hand, followed him everywhere. Then one day, when Pappy was working in his toolshed, he stepped back, not thinking, not knowing the keet was there. Stepped back hard and killed that innocent little creature. My pappy sat right down and cried."

I can see that Daddy is fighting back a few tears himself, and plucking at his hair.

"Stop pulling the hair out of your head, Daddy!" I grab his wrist and pull his hand away from his scalp. "I love you, Daddy. Don't do that."

Two days past Christmas, the snow plows make it through the drifts, and I help Spence shovel our driveway. Finally, we venture out to buy each other belated Christmas gifts. Daddy drives a 1964 maroon Corvair Monza, a replacement for the 1950 Olds that gave out not long after we lost Jimmie. This new car has its engine in the rear. The Corvair is much lighter than the Olds, and it skids easily on the icy roads. After a slow and treacherous eight-mile drive, we make it to the nearest local discount store. There's not much money to spare for Christmas gifts this year.

Spence and I split up to shop for each other, while Daddy waits in the car with the engine running to keep warm. As we drive back home, I sit in the back seat and try to keep the parakeet I bought for Spence quiet in its cardboard box. Even though I pet its head through one of the holes in the box, occasionally, it lets out a chirp, which I try to disguise by coughing loudly or bursting into "I Want a Hippopotamus for Christmas," my very favorite Christmas song. Apparently, this ruse works—or maybe Spence and Daddy are just pretending they don't hear the bird's cries.

Daddy drops us off at the house and goes back out to Sweeney's.

"I'll be right back," he says. "Just need to pick up a few things."

Spence and I go to our separate rooms to wrap the gifts, then pile them under our Charlie Brown tree. I don't try to wrap the parakeet. I'm afraid he might smother in there, sealed up in wrapping paper.

The shape of Spence's gift to me gives it away. Long and thin, with a hooked handle poking through the top of the wrapping, it is obviously an umbrella. We give Daddy his perennial Christmas gifts—the *Hagers-Town Almanack* and a package each of dried figs and dates. Daddy calls them "figs and digs."

When he thinks we're not looking, Daddy stuffs each of our Christmas stockings. He puts an orange in the toe, then pours in nuts and chocolate malted milk balls (we call them "moth balls") just the way Jimmie used to.

Spence names his new parakeet Asimov after his favorite science fiction writer. We put Asimov in Spence's bedroom, in an old metal cage we find in the attic. I spend the long afternoons near the cage, keeping the parakeet company and reading a library book called *Winter Wheat* by Mildred Walker. I begin to identify with the heroine, a farm girl growing up in the 1940s in the wheat fields of Montana.

I count each day of Christmas vacation, marking how much time I have left to be safe, to be at home, to read and dream in peace. But then, as always, it arrives. Sooner than soon, it's six A.M., time to get up for the first day back at school.

I get dressed, fix breakfast, bang on Spence's bedroom door. "Time to get up for school!" Then I pack our lunches.

At 7:25 A.M., Spence and I put on our coats and say goodbye to Daddy, who is still eating his breakfast. Then I remember Asimov, and run to give him more birdseed and fresh water. I find him lying stiff in the bottom of his cage, yellow and green plumage still bright, even in death. I yell for Spence, who comes running. We see a large dry wound at the parakeet's throat. His cage is littered with mouse droppings. He has been bitten to death by a vagrant mouse!

Spence and I place Asimov gently on an old dish towel in the bottom of a shoebox, and place the box high on a back-porch shelf. No time now. We will bury Asimov later. His body will stay cool here. We have taped the shoebox lid shut so the cats can't get to him.

Spence and I race the seven-tenths of a mile to catch the bus at the intersection. I take my seat in the school bus, my heart still racing from the sprint. As the yellow bus crawls over narrow winding passageways between steep banks of plowed snow, I can see before me, as clear as day, the vibrant small soul of a parakeet named Asimov flying past the limits of time to meet another loved one, the soul of a baby red squirrel named Chicoree. I know surely now that animals do have souls. Is it our human love for them that has given them souls? Or is it the surrender of their own wild spirits to us that has grown our human souls?

CHAPTER ELEVEN

TRYING TO FIT IN

CHANGING clothes in the girls' locker room is a real education for me. Here, I can see that all the other girls wear bras. I don't really need a bra yet. I'm flat-chested, and still wear an undershirt under my slip. Also, I see the other girls using underarm deodorant on their shaved armpits, pulling on nylon stockings over shaved legs, fastening their nylons to garter belts.

I want to fit in. It would be nice to be popular. I begin to take some steps on my own. I buy a couple of "trainer bras" (the kind with flat cups that stretch), find some old nylons and garters in Jimmie's dresser drawer, and begin my inside-out transformation. A couple of problems: Jimmie's stockings are way too long for me, and her garters are too big around for my skinny thighs. I get a needle and thread from Jimmie's sewing basket, stitch gathers in the garters so they fit more snugly, pull the nylons up as far as they will stretch, and wrap the tops, roll upon roll, around the garters. When the stockings are finally on, I notice how hairy my legs look through the tight taupe fabric.

I borrow Daddy's razor and shaving cream, sit on the edge of the bathtub, wet and slather my legs in the tub, and run the razor up and down each leg to a couple of inches above each knee. That seems to be how far up the other girls shave.

I know Daddy won't approve, so I keep the bathroom door locked while I shave. I finish off by doing my armpits, and putting a Band-Aid on the nick I've cut into the back of one ankle. I clean up the hair and Daddy's razor, and put everything back the way it was.

The next day, I wear a bra and nylons for the first time at school. The bra works out fine, but as the day wears on, the nylons begin to work their way out of the garters, and start to sag down around my legs. Whenever I stand up and walk through the halls to change classes, the stockings work their way a bit more out of the garters, farther and farther down my legs, bagging and settling in ever-thickening coils around my ankles. Every chance I get, I duck into the girls' room to tug them back up and reroll them in the garters, but the elastic in Jimmie's garters is worn out, and just won't hold those stockings up for more than a few steps.

Some of the girls begin to titter at me. Paloma pulls me aside and tells me I need a garter belt and smaller stockings.

When I get home, Daddy greets me in the kitchen, razor in hand.

"Lissa, have you been using my razor? Spence says it wasn't him. He's got his own razor."

I have to think fast. "I borrowed it for Home Economics, for my sewing project. I use it to cut fabric."

"You shouldn't use my razor on fabric, Lissa. It makes the razor dull, and I'll wind up cutting myself."

The next day, Paloma hands me a Hutzler's bag. "Here. My mom got these for you. I think they'll fit." In the bag, I find two pairs of nylons and a pink garter belt.

Another day, Paloma pulls me aside and tells me, "Your hair is dirty. It's greasy. You should shampoo every night when you take your shower." The next day, she brings me a tube of concentrated green shampoo and a small portable hair dryer that has a plastic hood and a hose that attaches the hood to the dryer. I tote them home in my book bag and, feeling like a criminal, smuggle them into the house.

Well, we don't have a shower at home, just the bathroom sink and the tub. So that afternoon, as soon as I get home, I lock myself in the bathroom and shampoo my hair in the bathroom sink. The shampoo from Paloma smells really good. Afterward, I lock myself in my bedroom and dry my hair. The plastic hood balloons out around my head. The dryer is kind of loud, but Daddy is out working in his woodshop. He won't hear it running.

About an hour later, I emerge from my room and start to fix supper. Daddy comes in and stares at me. I glance in the kitchen mirror. My face is bright pink from the heat of the hair dryer, and there is a line on my forehead where the plastic band of the dryer has left its mark.

"Why is your face so red, Lissa? What have you been doing up there in your bedroom?" His voice is stern, disapproving. He continues to glare at me.

"Have you been drinking?" Daddy's voice is suspicious and accusing. Daddy doesn't approve of drinking. Alcohol is forbidden in the house, except for an old, nearly empty bottle of Four Roses whiskey at the back of the dish cabinet in the pantry. I think it belonged to my grandfather. Once, Daddy poured a little bit of it into a teacup and made a hot toddy for Jimmie when she got back home from walking through snowdrifts to see a patient during a blizzard, half frozen to death.

"No," I say. I can't look him in the eye. I just get started fixing our supper.

The next day, Daddy has a surprise for me as soon as I get home from school. He's made a special tool for me. "Here, Lissa. Now you won't need to borrow my razor for your sewing projects." The tool has a delicate silver handle and two screws at the top that clamp a razor into position so that both edges are set for cutting.

Paloma tells me I should bathe every day so I won't stink. I start getting up very early in the morning, while Daddy is still asleep. I push the stopper down in the tub and start running the water. The tub is set in the wall right opposite the headboard of Daddy's bed in the next room. Even though I try to be very quiet—I even put a washcloth in the tub directly under the faucet, to muffle the sound of the water—sometimes, Daddy wakes up.

"Lissa, is that you?" Daddy calls from his bed. "Is that water I hear running?"

"It's raining," I say. I don't dare keep the water running too long, for fear Daddy will get out of bed and come to the bathroom to see what's up. When the water rises to just a few inches, I turn off the faucet, sit in the tub, and take a very quick and shallow bath. Jimmie used to take what she called "sponge baths" standing at the sink, but I like the idea of immersing myself as much as I can. I feel cleaner that way.

In ninth grade, I begin to notice the makeup the other girls wear at school. Jimmie never wore makeup, and I've heard Daddy say bad things about what he calls "painted women."

"They're just trying to get men to fight over them," he says.

But I really do want to fit in and be attractive, so I use some of the birthday money I've been saving. I buy foundation, eyeliner, and mascara at the drugstore. Locked in the bathroom, I put on the makeup last thing before I leave the house to catch the school bus.

Transformed, I rush out the door before Daddy can get a good look at my "painted" face. I soon learn that Daddy's eyesight is so bad, he doesn't notice the makeup.

Daddy trusts Paloma's mom so much that he lets her take me along with Paloma to our class dance, the Eight Ball. Paloma's mom buys me a blue and white (our class colors) dress for the dance, and I have fun watching the other kids do the twist. A bunch of us learn to do the Freddie together. It's easy to do. All you have to do is stand there and move with the music. It's like you're doing jumping jacks. First, you stick out your left leg and raise your arms. Then you stick out your right leg and raise both arms again. You just keep doing this until the song is over. It's so much fun!

When I'm near the end of the ninth grade, Spence tells me, "Hey, Lissa, my friend Mark says I have a good-looking sister." Spence seems proud of me, the way he was a long time ago when I won that bubblegum bubble-blowing contest. It makes me feel good about myself, but it's a revelation to me. No one—other than Daddy—has ever told me I'm pretty.

Men are starting to act differently toward me. A girl at church pulls me aside and tells me her dad says I'm one of the prettiest girls he's ever seen. "And he should know," she says, "because he travels for his business, and he sees lots of women."

Another man at church, the greeter who welcomes people when they enter the sanctuary, has started to pinch me on the butt whenever he shakes my hand. Right hand, handshake; left hand, butt pinch. I'm too confused to know what to think about this, and too embarrassed to say anything. Is this a good thing or a bad thing?

One day, the greeter's nephew, who is about my age, pulls me aside after he sees his uncle pinch me and says, "Why do you let him do that to you?" I don't have an answer for him. I guess this pinching must be a bad thing. Spence doesn't seem to notice or have an opinion about it. Daddy doesn't know anything about it; he doesn't go to our Methodist church.

This growing up seems to be a pretty mixed-up thing. On the one hand, I do like boys to think I'm pretty. And most girls I know seem to be intent on dating and eventually getting married and having kids. But I'm not sure what I really want to do with my life.

Paloma fills me in on what's going on at the weekend parties at the other kids' houses. Who is dating, and who is breaking up. Who is drinking, and who is taking drugs. Nobody invites me to these parties. I guess it's just as well. I'm pretty sure Daddy wouldn't let me go. Paloma tells me I'm not really missing anything.

I like to get good grades. English and French are my favorite subjects. Jimmie always seemed to want me to be a nurse, but I think I'm smart enough to be a doctor. So why just be a nurse? I admire some of my women teachers. I guess they are my role models, now that Jimmie is dead. I think I'd like to go to college after high school, but Daddy seems to expect me to stay around and take care of him.

In the summer when I'm fourteen, going on fifteen, I see an ad on our church bulletin board about summer jobs as counselors for inner-city kids at a Methodist summer camp. I tell Daddy I'd like to sign up for this. I explain to him that it's a voluntary position, but it does pay a stipend for expenses, and it would be good work experience.

"Who's going to fix my meals and make my bed while you're away?"

"Spence can help you with those things while I'm gone. It's just for two weeks."

Spence seems okay with the idea, and Daddy reluctantly agrees to let me go. It helps that it's a camp that the church sent Spence to when he was twelve—not as a counselor, but as a kid.

I get a work permit and pack my clothes. Daddy drives me about a mile to the nearest bus stop. I kiss him on the cheek goodbye, and promise to call him as soon as I can to let him know I'm okay.

The Methodist minister who runs Operation Open Air meets me at the terminal. He's easy to spot—clerical collar, typical clergyman's wire-rimmed glasses.

"Hi, I'm Pastor Dan. You must be Lissa. Welcome." He greets me with a strong handshake and an easy grin. He must be in his sixties; his hair is mostly gray. But he is tanned, fit, and relaxed.

The waiting room is roiling with noisy, restless midsummer travelers. Most of the folks here don't own cars and can't afford more expensive means of transport, so they take buses.

Pastor Dan grabs my suitcase, and with supreme confidence and long strides, parts the sea of agitated voyagers and shepherds me across to his Jeep in the parking lot. Something about him puts me immediately at ease as we drive through the downtown traffic.

I'm signed up for two weeks as a camp counselor. I'll be spending weekends with the other counselors at the former Norwegian Seaman's Home in Baltimore—a rambling old house that now serves special mission groups like Operation Open Air and Head Start.

As soon as I've deposited my suitcase in the dorm room I'm to share with one other counselor, I call Daddy from the roomy wooden phone booth that's built in beneath the wide front staircase.

"Hello, Daddy. I got here safely."

"You take care of yourself, Lissa. Come back to me safe and sound."

"Yes. Everything's fine. I'll call you next weekend."

Pastor Dan holds the first meeting on Friday evening. I meet the nine other counselors I'll be working with. Apparently, I'm the youngest, and probably the least experienced among them. I learn that the first week, I'll be overseeing six elementary-school age girls in my cabin. The second week, with more experience, I'll be bumped up to working with six kids in junior high.

After the meeting, we gather around a grand piano, sing some Methodist hymns, and receive a prayer and blessings from Pastor Dan. Then we're free to spend the rest of the evening as we choose. I head up to my room with my roommate, Toni. She's just finished her freshman year at college, and plans to major in psychology. Toni has been doing an internship, working with some of the girls who'll be staying at camp with us.

"Pastor Dan's philosophy," Toni says, "is to get kids out of the inner city, away from the brick and mortar and asphalt, out into a more natural setting. Most of these kids have never been close to nature.

"I'm doing a paper on one of your girls. Her name's Wanda. She's nine years old and has a twin sister, Anna. Wanda is very bright. She tests much higher than her sister, but she gets worse grades than Anna. I'm trying to understand what's going on here. I'd be interested to hear what you think of Wanda."

Toni goes on to give me the lowdown on the other counselors. Michael is a nice guy. David is a playboy. Sally always wears cheap clothes and carries a battered suitcase to disguise the fact that she's from a wealthy Baltimore family.

"She's almost ashamed to have so much money," Toni says.

On Sunday afternoon, the day before the first group of kids arrive, Pastor Dan takes his colleague Pastor Bob, Toni, and me out for a sail on West River. The boat is just about big enough to seat the four of us. Pastor Dan calls it a daysailer.

This is my first time in a sailboat. Pastor Dan shows Toni how to operate the tiller. The wind catches; the sail billows; the boat leans over the water and picks up speed. I am on the low side of the boat, so close to the water I can trace my fingers in it. Surprisingly cold, it sends an unfamiliar tingle up my arm. An overwhelming sense of exhilaration and untamed freedom flows over me.

As the wind speeds us along the river, the two ministers begin to discuss theology. They debate concepts I've always assumed preachers agree on: the virgin birth, the Trinity, the existence of heaven and hell, the meaning of sin.

At one point, Pastor Dan says, "You don't still believe in all that original sin, passed down from Adam and Eve, do you, Bob?"

"Well, I do believe that story is a wonderful allegory of man's disobedience and his subsequent loss of innocence. The snake and the apple resonate as universal symbols of evil and its temptation," says Pastor Bob.

"Well, Bob, have you ever wondered why God would want to deny man the knowledge of good and evil, that crucial ability to discern right from wrong? Do you really think He wants us to remain ignorant, gullible, clinging children? That doesn't sound to me like a very loving Heavenly Father. Have you ever considered that sin is purely the separation of an individual soul from the universal oneness of all beings?"

"Hold on, Dan. Sounds like you're straying into Spinoza and maybe some Hindu philosophy, here."

Just then, a gust of wind strikes the sail, suddenly and at an unlikely angle, threatening the boat's balance. Pastor Dan calls out, "Bob, I hope you're prepared to teach us all how to walk on water!" as he makes some quick maneuvers to keep us on an even keel.

I give Pastor Dan a startled look. He chuckles softly. "Sacrilegious?"

"No," I say. "I've just never heard a minister talk this way before."

"Fair enough," he says, gently. "Fair enough."

This first week of camp flashes past on waves of frustration, adventure, and unexpected tenderness. I'm assigned to a cabin with six girls from Baltimore City's elementary schools, a rainbow of colors and ethnicities. Most of them are seven, eight, and nine years old. One chubby little girl named Mary Lou is about to turn six, so she's really too young for this group. She tends to overeat, get homesick, and cry easily. As expected, Toni's Wanda is part of my group. Wanda is very talkative, and calls me "Teacher."

On our first night in the cabin, Mary Lou begins to fret. Her mother forgot to pack a pillow, so I give her my pillow and try to calm her down. I fall asleep in my upper bunk, exhausted after a day of crafts, swimming, canoeing, and singing around a campfire. In the middle of the night, I wake to feel a soft prodding under my head. It's Wanda on tiptoe, pushing her pillow under my head. Toward morning, I wake up to Wanda's snoring, Mary Lou's farting, and moist, chilly air puffing up from the river through the wide-screened cabin windows.

The first week goes pretty smoothly. My girls are all sweet-tempered. Wanda turns out to be a natural teacher. She shows Mary Lou how to swim, and by midweek, Mary Lou has gained so much confidence, she forgets to cry for her mother at night.

The toilet and shower facilities are a short walk from my cabin. If the girls need to pee at night, I have to go with them. To cut down on the nighttime walks to the toilets, I get my girls to limit the amount of bug juice (the camp's name for Kool-Aid) they drink at the evening meal.

At bedtime, I tell the girls stories about what it's like to live out in the country. Most of them have never seen a farm.

On the last evening, three of the girls—Wanda, Mary Lou, and a doe-eyed girl of Puerto Rican descent named Dolores—get my address on scraps of stationery and promise to write. We are treated to a final bonfire, and a display of fireworks set off from a pier across the river. The small girls compete to walk next to me and hold my hand. As the final fusillade peppers the night sky with light and color and sound, and the faint smell of gunpowder lingers over the river, Dolores squeezes my hand and tells me of the night she saw her uncle gunned down in the street beneath her bedroom window.

Week two is more of a challenge. I share my cabin with six junior high school girls from impoverished Baltimore neighborhoods. Two cabins are reserved for a dozen "troubled juveniles"—six girls, six boys, charged with an assortment of offenses—petty theft, shoplifting, indecent exposure, possession of illegal drugs, assault. One girl, we are told, is a kleptomaniac and compulsive liar. These troubled youths are assigned specially trained counselors.

Before long, I run into Jamal, a thirteen-year-old from a broken home, who, we have been warned, is a troublemaker who bears watching. On the first afternoon, I return to our cabin with my girls after an unsuccessful attempt at rowing. Initially, when I told the girls I had never rowed a boat before, Patty, the oldest and most athletic-looking of my brood—and a bit of a loudmouth—swore she knew how to row. But soon it became obvious that Patty had no more experience at rowing than I did. We got stuck mid-river, with Patty rowing in circles, and the other girls freaking out with fear. Finally, Todd, the camp maintenance guy, came roaring across the water in his motorboat to haul us back to the dock.

"I thought you said you knew how to row," I say to Patty.

Patty giggles back at me. "I lied. I just wanted to go rowing."

Feeling humiliated and sorry for myself, excruciatingly aware that I am the youngest and least-experienced counselor, I trudge up my cabin steps late that afternoon, my girls in tow. And there's Jamal, squatting under the farthest bunk, rifling through one of our suitcases!

Just then, Jim, Jamal's counselor, comes searching for him, and Jamal takes off, sprinting down the lane back to his cabin.

"I'll have a word with Jamal," Jim tells me. "Just make sure you're not missing anything."

It turns out to be a difficult and, in some ways, illuminating second week. On Tuesday, one of my girls, Belinda, emerges from the pool red-eyed and screaming, "I can't see! I can't see!" and is rushed to the hospital to have her eyes flushed. The rest of us are banished for the day from the pool while it is drained and cleared of excess chlorine. We try to amuse the kids with crafts and a sing-along, and Jamal persists in substituting the foulest lyrics he can come up with to get our attention and try to shock us.

On Wednesday, it rains, and we continue halfheartedly with camp songs and crafts.

On Thursday, we take a long hike through the woods. Later that night, as the sky begins to darken, I start to change into my pajamas for bed. Behind me, just as I unhook my bra, I hear branches scratching against the cabin wall, just beneath one of the large cabin windows. I turn to look and spot Jamal, hiding outside in the bushes, his face pressed against the window screen, spying on me. Unintentionally, I present this precocious Peeping Tom with a full-frontal view of my bare breasts. Jamal's mouth falls open. For a moment he stares, and then—I'm convinced this "bad" little teen is embarrassed at seeing more than he planned to—Jamal blushes, snaps his head away, and runs off to find security among the lengthening shadows. Jamal's vulnerability and innocence are so striking, so endearing, that for the moment I forget to be self-conscious about my own nakedness.

On Friday I wake with a bad case of poison ivy crawling up both legs, and realize I neglected to wear my long pants for yesterday's hike.

Ted, a good-looking blond counselor who is studying to be a doctor, insists on having a look at my legs, but his obsessive fascination with the ugly pink rash and oozing yellow pustules makes me feel more like a specimen than an attractive girl.

On Saturday, when Pastor Dan drops me off at the bus terminal, I am more than ready to go home. Pastor Dan hands me my stipend, extends a firm handshake, and says, "Is this enough to cover your expenses?"

"Yes." I stuff the money into the pocket of my shorts and start to board the bus, feeling a bit defeated.

Pastor Dan lays his hand gently on my shoulder and gives it a firm squeeze. I turn and look up at his face. He seems to be studying me, reading me like a book. Finally, he says, "Would you be willing to come back again next summer?"

"Yes." I nod and beam up at him. An irresistible feeling of pride and strength and burgeoning self-confidence washes over me as I find a seat on the bus.

Daddy is waiting at the Crossroads bus stop in our maroon Corvair, smoking a cigar. "I missed you, my little squirrel ears."

"I missed you, too, Daddy." I flip down the mirror on the windshield visor and take a good look at myself for the first time in two weeks. I'm tanner than I've ever been, and my teeth look extra white. I feel healthy.

Before school starts, Paloma insists on taking me shopping for a new school dress at Hutzler's. I gawk at the magnificent gray stone palace storefront on Howard Street, craning my neck to take in the building's intricately carved arabesques. I feel like a poor kid standing on the pavement outside, pressing my face against one of the store's huge display windows.

"Come on, Lissa," Paloma calls to me, and I rush over to follow her and her mom through one of the revolving doors. At one point, we board an elegant elevator operated by a uniformed woman. Seated on a stool that's pulled out from the wall of the elevator, she announces the floors and the names of the departments. I am intrigued by a department called Notions.

As we shop in one of the junior dress sections, a lady comes over to help me find the right size. I am just home from my stint as a camp counselor, so I'm fit and tanned. After looking me up and down, the store lady says, "I'll bet you're a perfect junior size eleven." She pulls several outfits off the rack, and shows me to the fitting rooms. When I come out modeling a bright orange and yellow patterned jacket and matching skirt, she smiles.

"I'm a fashion director here. I run the teen fashion shows," she says. Let me know if you ever want a job here as a model."

Paloma and her mom buy the orange and yellow outfit for me. They won't take no for an answer.

CHAPTER TWELVE

ESCAPING TO "FLORIDA" ON SUNDAY AFTERNOONS

IT turns out the shopping trip to Hutzler's for the new outfit was a kind of farewell gift to me from Paloma and her mom. The day before I start tenth grade, I get a phone call from Paloma.

"I won't be seeing you for a while, Lissa. My dad is forcing me to go to Bryn Mawr. It's kind of a status thing with him." I learn that Bryn Mawr is a girls' prep school in Roland Park. It's a private school in a wealthy Baltimore neighborhood.

I miss Paloma, and as autumn withdraws into gloomy winter, I find myself clinging to the safety of the past. On Sunday afternoons, I retreat with Daddy into a comforting ritual. After church, I change into my everyday clothes, fix lunch for the three of us. We used to call it Sunday *dinner* when Jimmie was still around, and it was a much more sumptuous meal.

After lunch, I clear the dishes, and Spence paces around the kitchen table, "thinking" and wearing off the linoleum in a black oval path. If the afternoon is sunny, I escape with Daddy to the sun parlor to soak in the bright light and warmth coming through the broad banks of windows that Granddaddy Friedrich salvaged from a nearby mill town back in the 1920s, when it was razed and flooded to supply drinking water for Baltimore City. Daddy calls it "going to Florida." Here, Daddy relaxes on a Craftsman-style wooden rocker and puffs a cigar. I perch on Daddy's antique watchmaker's stool, finding comfort on its curved oak seat. Resting the balls of my feet on the stool's cast-iron frame beneath me, I can walk the seat around to face any angle of the room.

I open the first of Jimmie's two five-year diaries, the ones she kept when she worked as a licensed practical nurse at Harford Memorial Hospital in Havre de Grace and lived in the nurses' quarters. That was when Daddy was "courting" her. The diaries were kept regularly, from the beginning of 1936 to almost the end of July 1942, when Jimmie's writing abruptly ends.

Jimmie used to tell me, "The diaries will be there for you to read, Lissa, when I'm gone. I've never written anything there I wouldn't want you to know." There are five entries per page, so each passage is very short.

Wed, January 1: Beautiful day—Snow. Am in charge on Emergency Shift III. Miss Linganore very sick. Spent quiet evening in room.

Thurs, January 2: Raining very bad underfoot and overhead! Business picking up on Emergency III. Broke connecting nozzle. Visited Heinricks and received letter from pastor. Morning hours.

Fri, January 3: Beautiful warm sunshiny day. Visited Anna. Had a P.M. with Essie. Was home for supper. Visited Heinricks when returned. Received invitation to Helen Petersen's party Saturday.

Sat, January 4: Cloudy day. Rained tonight. Miss Linganore, aged 75, passed away at 6:58 P.M. Was with her. Went to Helen Petersen's party (17 young people).

Had the best time "Cheating the Lawyer" (game). All night leave. Stayed home.

Sun, January 5: Beautiful warm day. Miss Craymore and I worked. Went to M.E. Church with Essie and Scottie. Took down Xmas tree. Had morning hours.

Mon, January 6: Snowing turned to rain (had P.M. off). Went to see Shirley Temple in *Littlest Rebel* with Stouten and to Virginia Dare for dinner. Received leather gloves and 1-lb box of candy. Had lovely evening. Learned a lot about Catholic beliefs.

Tues, January 7: Lovely day. Stayed in. Lived over pleasant memories.

When I look up from Jimmie's diary I see that Daddy has leaned his head back on the chair's headrest. His eyes are closed, but I can tell he's not asleep. The tip of his cigar smolders in his hand on the armrest.

"Daddy, do you remember going to see that Shirley Temple movie with Jimmie?"

He nods. "In those days, you could go to see a new movie every night of the week." He sits up straighter and leans toward me.

"You know," he tells me, "your mother was a good woman. I saw her for the first time at the old Allison place out in Harford County. She was running in the field, chasing turkeys. Only thirteen years old. Black curly hair. Dark brown eyes. I knew right then and there I would marry that girl one day, and sure enough, I did.

"When she was a little older, I took her to the circus, and we started up a correspondence. 'Dear Stoutie,' she would write. And she'd end each letter with, 'Your little pal, Jimmie.'

"Course, I thought such a young woman would outlive me. When she trained to be a nurse, I thought she'd learn how to take care of me in my old age. Life takes some funny twists and turns." Daddy shakes his head and takes a long draw on his cigar. Its tip glows red like a fiery red eye, opening.

One Sunday, as I read from the diary, Daddy and I learn about a mysterious player in Jimmie's life, a navy pilot referred to only as ESB. We've progressed to March 1937.

> Sun, March 14: N.D. [Jimmie's shorthand for night duty] Snow to rain all day (4 inches). Took Levine to church. Had emergency appendectomy at 8 A.M. with Dr. Stebbins. Went for walk with Levine this evening in snow. Met ESB. Walked back with us. (Forgot to call me for church.)

> Mon, March 15: N.D. Snow and rain all day (6 inches). Levine and I walked to bank this A.M. Had my duty shoes reheeled. Saw ESB in truck. On maternity ward. Everything quiet.

> Tues, March 16: N.D. Beautiful. Cold. Levine and I walked out on errand for Miss Craymore. Met ESB on way back. Have date for Friday night.

"Who's this ESB?" I ask Daddy.
"Don't know."
"I thought you were courting Jimmie then."
"I was." Daddy starts to pluck at his hair. He does that sometimes, when he's tense and thinking hard. I found out from the encyclopedia that this habit is something called trichotillomania. "Thought I was the *only* one."

> Wed, March 17: N.D. Clear, warm, snow melting. Levine ½ night off. Took her to bus terminal. Wrote

letters and stitched fine seams. Got up at 4 P.M. Went out for walk. Beautiful.

Thurs, March 18. Rain to cloudy warm. Levine, Hendricks, and I walked to post office. Called ESB at 6:30 P.M. Quiet evening. Girls went to St. Patrick's service at M.E. Church.

Fri, March 19: Beautiful, warm. ½ night off. Levine relieved. Drove home at 8 A.M. Got Struggle stuck in snow. Had to be pulled out by horse and wagon. Went to Baltimore to Stouten's to pick up watch. Had date with ESB at 7 P.M. Went to ESB's home to meet his mother.

"What does Jimmie mean when she says, "Got Struggle stuck in snow"?

"Struggle was Jimmie's car. Her father and brothers didn't think a woman needed to know how to drive a car, and refused to teach her. Well, she could already drive a tractor, so I taught her to drive my car. She got her license, and eventually saved enough money to buy herself a sporty little roadster. She named it Struggle." Daddy chuckles softly, then leans forward and gestures with his cigar.

"What I want to know is, who is this ESB fellow? Jimmie never mentioned him to me."

I skim through Jimmie's entries now, searching for more information about ESB.

Sun, May 23: ESB and I went to Mt. Zion M.E. Church tonight. Wore blue crepe dress with flowered jacket and yellow picture hat. Lovely evening.

Sun, June 6: Went to Children's Day at M.E. Church. Had date with ESB at 7:30 P.M. Went for drive. Talked of future. Came in at 10:30 P.M.

Gleaning these tidbits and reading between the lines, I pull together the following scenario. ESB works at Willow Grove, an airfield in Pennsylvania where they design, construct, and test aircraft. He helps build planes, falls in love with flying, and joins the navy, hoping one day to become a pilot. On leave, he meets Jimmie at a Methodist Episcopal Church service and invites her home to dinner with his family. Soon, she becomes good friends with ESB's mother and sister. When Jimmie visits her parents, ESB often comes along for meals, and becomes friends with Jimmie's brother Ray, who is in the Coast Guard. In February 1937, Jimmie goes ice skating with ESB on his family's pond, and when she falls through thin ice, ESB rescues her, carries her into the house, wraps her in a warm blanket, and makes her a hot toddy.

Later in February, ESB seems always available to lend a hand when Jimmie's car, Struggle, has a flat tire or needs a wash, an oil change, or a grease job.

In March 1937, Jimmie and ESB begin to date. Jimmie's diary mentions phone calls, moonlight drives, visits to nearby towns, seeing the movie *Waikiki Wedding*, listening to the radio together, having long talks on his family's front porch that result in confessions and revelations. "ESB told me of an accident he had as a child."

Jimmie's entries are mostly in black or blue fountain pen ink. Occasionally, a few days are recorded in pencil, as if no pen was at hand when Jimmie wrote them. In some places, the ink is faded or blurred, or the script becomes so small it is illegible. The pencil entries have become dim, but still, the diary gives me glimpses of a youthful love, the pendulum of emotions as their hearts open and close: "lovely time," "ESB very tired," "misunderstanding," "cross words," "parted as friends."

In May, Jimmie gives ESB a military set—two silver-plated, monogrammed boar-hair-bristle brushes—for his birthday. He is eleven months older than she is. Their dates become more frequent, and they continue to "talk of future." In June, while driving Struggle, Jimmie hits another car, breaks her radiator, and bends both front fenders. ESB brings a truck and tows Struggle home. ESB gives Jimmie a gold necklace with a cross. Three days later, she loses the cross.

And all the while, Jimmie records her ongoing relationship with Stouten. She drops off friends' watches for him to repair, and then picks them up; he showers her with gifts—a mirrored music box shaped like a grand piano, bouquets of roses and sweet peas, a gold lavalier necklace with a diamond, opal, and sapphire (her April birthstones) pendant, a Shirley Temple doll. Stouten takes her bowling, and on a fishing trip. Jimmie refuses a kiss.

On night duty, Jimmie serves trays and assists with patients in the maternity ward. She cares for a patient with an ectopic pregnancy, is "showered with amniotic fluid," and "cuts the cord."

Several doctors routinely ask her to be their instrument nurse. Jimmie knows that "Dr. Stein likes to have the instruments slapped firmly in his palm. Dr. Cooper likes a gentler approach." On a busy night in July, Jimmie scrubs for and assists with eleven surgeries, including a ruptured appendix and multiple accident cases that expose her to a panoply of injuries—fractured pelvis, ruptured bladder, concussion, punctured lung, extensive laceration of tongue, fractured skull, fractured leg, fractured patella. Some nights, Jimmie says there is a "full house" at the hospital, and they have to use "the last bed." On one particularly busy night, she deals with "45 patients, 8 babies, cots everywhere."

One night in September, a patient with the DTs gets out of bed and has to be put in a straitjacket. On another night, an accident case is dead on arrival, and a young woman dies from eclampsia. The next day's dairy entry: "Wanted to resign. Very much upset. Slept all day."

She returns to night duty, scrubs for Dr. Stein, and assists with an emergency repair of a ruptured gastric ulcer. She continues night after night, dealing with pneumonia, a chartered plane accident, emergency appendectomies, stillbirths, premature delivery of an infant with spina bifida. She is busy one night with five compresses "to keep up with." She has "a run-in" with a head nurse.

On December 3, 1937, ESB meets Jimmie and her mother in Elkton. "License passed." Jimmie is "unable to sleep" that afternoon before going on night duty. On December 4, ESB calls at 7:15 P.M. His "last call before ceremony." On December 5, ESB does not show up for the "ceremony." Could this be a wedding ceremony? Jimmie goes home with ESB's mother and sister. They are "very lovely to me." Again, Jimmie is "unable to sleep."

Jimmie's next entries about ESB occur in 1938, and speak of a separation. He is leaving for Florida, for the Pensacola Naval Air Station, to begin training as a navy pilot.

> Fri, Feb 4: ESB called tonight at 8 P.M. Coming home Sunday.

> Wed, March 9: ESB called at 9 P.M. Separation last night. Moved out completely today.

These messages send me searching for a framed photo I came across one day, not long after Jimmie died, in her dressing table's bottom drawer. I rummage through layers of Jimmie's white nursing hosiery. It's still there, in black and white—an eight-by-ten-inch photo of a handsome young man in a navy pilot's uniform, cap tilted back jauntily on his head, dark features like Jimmie's, his wide smile brimming with good humor and self-confidence. A trace of despondency is beginning to show in his eyes. It's signed, "Only Forever, Eddie." This must be ESB! I don't show the photo to Daddy—that would betray Jimmie, pierce Daddy's heart, and shatter an old man's fragile memories.

I stop reading the diaries to Daddy, but continue to search their yellowing pages for clues and innuendos. I am searching for myself, for the adult conversations I will never have with my mother. I remember a brief comment I once heard Jimmie make to another woman. They were talking about what it was like being married to a much older man. "It's a deeper, more mature kind of love," Jimmie said.

No more mention of ESB until 1941, when Jimmie corresponds with him in Pensacola. On November 13, Jimmie drives to Baltimore, goes to the bus terminal to get rates for a ticket to Florida. That same evening, she dines with Stouten; their discussion on the future is "undecided."

> Dec 8, 1941: Simon girl delivered with low forceps, 9-lb boy at noon. Scrubbed for Dr. Stein, appendix. War declared with Japan at 4:10 P.M., USA.

With the war, Jimmie's workload at the hospital picks up night after night. Two soldiers from Fort Meade come in after a brawl needing sutures for ear and jaw injuries. Jimmie helps suture a woman who has been slashed with a razor blade across the buttocks. Six soldiers are involved in a car accident on a toll bridge. One dies on the table; the others are transferred to Walter Reed.

Jimmie continues to dine and go to the movies with Stouten while corresponding with ESB in Pensacola. For Christmas 1941, Stouten has a radio installed in her car and showers her with gifts—an inlaid lamp, wooden salt and pepper shakers, cut flowers with roses, two pairs of kid gloves (red and blue), six linen hankies, two pairs of nylon hose, and a wine-colored turban. ESB sends her a Christmas card. In January, Jimmies receives a letter from ESB telling her he has "just taken exams."

Stouten continues to take Jimmie to dine at the Pickwick Inn, the Log Cabin Tea Room, the Oriole. They see many movies together—at the Hippodrome, Howard, New, Keith's, Little, Mayfair—often several in one week—and snack on fruit and popcorn. After seeing Jimmy Stewart and Hedy Lamarr in *Come Live with Me*, Stouten mentions the "future in a casual way."

On Valentine's Day 1942, ESB sends Jimmie a two-pound box of chocolates and a card. On February 19, she drives to the blood bank, gives a pint of blood to the Red Cross, and gets a parking ticket.

On April 12, 1942, Jimmie learns that ESB "made rating," and will be having a fifteen-day leave. On the same day, Jimmie shops downtown with Stouten. They buy sheets and material for a suit. Jimmie's mother will be making a suit for Stouten.

In the next weeks, airmail missives soar past each other on parallel flight paths between Havre de Grace and Pensacola, as plans are made. In April, Jimmie receives a "Birthday Anniversary" telegram from ESB; Stouten gives Jimmie a three-drawer glass candy box for her birthday. In May, Jimmie sends a birthday card to ESB.

On June 5, Jimmie dines with Stouten at the Oriole. She buys four new dresses for her Florida trip. On June 9, she sends an airmail letter to Pensacola and buys two bathing suits. On June 23, she comes off duty for vacation at 7:30 A.M., has her car greased, and goes home to the farm "for dinner, a good night's sleep, and a fond farewell."

She leaves next morning at 7:30 A.M., drives 440 miles through intermittent showers, and stops at a hotel in Florence, South Carolina, for the night. On the way, she runs out of gas, and a truck driver comes to her rescue. "Everything is fine thus far," she writes.

On June 25, she drives through showers to Savannah, Georgia, where she has dinner. As she continues her trip, Struggle stalls out on train tracks, but she manages to get the car started and makes it to Jacksonville, Florida, at 8:05 P.M., where she checks into the Hotel Burbridge. She has Struggle's gas line cleaned and tires checked, and calls Pensacola, but ESB can't be located.

Jimmie's cursory diary notations, like the blank pages of a coloring book, trace only the perimeters of her trip. I long for more vibrant images of Jimmie's Florida adventure, so I rely on a Florida atlas and tour guide I've borrowed from the school library to bring Jimmie's story to life.

On June 26, Jimmie leaves Jacksonville at 10:20 A.M. She drives through rolling fields of citrus, traverses a lush garden and a bird sanctuary. Here, at the summit of Iron Mountain, on one of the highest points of Florida's peninsula, rises a 205-foot tower of pink and gray marble and coquina stone, the Singing Tower, its full length mirrored in a reflection pool. Jimmie must marvel at the sight of it. She is caught in the rain and waits it out in the ticket booth, perhaps serenaded by the tower's sixty-bell carillon, then continues on her way.

Coming into Canal Point, she has a flat, gets it fixed at a gas station, and arrives at Pahokee at 9:30 P.M. She hooks up with an old friend from nursing school, and the next day, they drive up between sugar cane fields to Canal Point, overlooking Lake Okeechobee. They chat for most of the evening.

On Sunday, June 28, she goes with her friend to early Mass. In the afternoon, her friend's brother takes them both for a drive, and they go to a Methodist church service. On June 29, Jimmie drives on to West Palm Beach, buys two new tires for $17.50, and spends the night at her friend's home.

The next day, she drives 172 miles, stays one night at a cabin, and continues on to Pensacola. She arrives at 6:30 P.M. and calls ESB. He meets her at the naval post gates; they go out to dinner, and chat until one A.M. "ESB is glad to see me," Jimmie writes.

She "puts up at a tourist home." The next day, she leaves ESB behind to take a side trip to Mobile, Alabama; Gulfport, Mississippi; and New Orleans, Louisiana. She passes back through Mississippi, bathes in the Gulf of Mexico, and is "nearly eaten up by mosquitoes." Again, she stays at a tourist home.

The next day, she leaves Mississippi and meets ESB in Pensacola at 2:35 P.M., dines with him; they drive on, arrive in Jacksonville at 12:10 A.M., and spend the night at cabins for three dollars a cabin. On July 4, they drive around Jacksonville until noon. Jimmie bids ESB "a fond farewell" and begins her trip home, stopping at Myrtle Beach to see the ocean. Then she drives all night, arrives in Baltimore at nine A.M., breakfasts with some nurse friends, goes back to the farm, and tells her mother "all about the trip, etc." The next day, the airmails between Jimmie and ESB resume.

On July 19, 1942, ESB arrives home in Harford County, and spends the next week in Maryland. On July 21, Jimmie and ESB go to visit her mother, who is in Maryland General Hospital for the removal of kidney stones. On July 23, Jimmie goes with ESB to buy tickets for Florida. On July 25, she has dinner with ESB and his family. She and ESB go out for a drive until midnight. She sleeps until 2:30 A.M., then drives ESB to Baltimore's Penn Station, in time for the 4:52 A.M. train on July 26. She sleeps all day, writes a letter to ESB, and mails it the next morning. This is the last mention of ESB.

On some Sunday afternoons in our sun parlor, "Florida," Daddy puffs his cigar and tells me about how, after months and years of "courting," he finally "won" Jimmie.

"It was May 8, 1945, Victory Day. The war in Europe had just ended, and I thought it was time to go after a more personal victory. I unlocked my safe and pulled out the blue velvet ring box I'd been keeping there. That box held the finest diamond ring Regal's had to offer—only the best for Jimmie. Bought it years before from Irvin Weinstein, and stashed it away until the time was right. So, while the country celebrated, I asked Jimmie to be my wife.

"The next day, your mother went down to Regal Jewelers to take in some watches for me. She asked to see Mr. Weinstein. When the secretary told her she would need an appointment, your mother just flashed her new diamond engagement ring at her and said, 'But you don't know who I am. I'm engaged to marry Mr. Stouten R. Power.'

"After hearing that announcement, the secretary escorted Jimmie right in to see Irvin. He got on the phone with me to say, 'Congratulations! I just heard the good news.' I said, 'Yes, we finally put those Nazis in their place.' 'No,' Irwin said, 'I mean your engagement. I just met your lovely bride-to-be.' There was a long pause on the line, and then, both at the same time, old Irvin and I busted out laughing.

"I married your Mother on Christmas Day, 1945. And the rest, as they say, is history."

Daddy's cigar has burned to its end. Daylight is gone from the sun parlor. I shiver as evening shadows surround us, clinging like black webs on dusty windowpanes.

After a while, Daddy stands up, comes over to me, and strokes my hair. His voice is heavy with sadness and regret when he says, "And I thought I knew your mother so well. She never mentioned this ESB fellow to me. Just goes to show you, Lissa. Wisdom doesn't always come with age. There's no fool quite like an old fool."

"You're not a fool, Daddy," I say. "Jimmie loved you so much she gave me to you. Don't you remember?"

"How could I forget?" Daddy says, and we leave "Florida" together to find warmer havens in the farmhouse.

My "Florida" talks with Daddy leave me curious to know more. What actually drew this lively young nurse, at the age of thirty-two, to marry a sixty-seven-year-old man?

I go up to the attic and do some more digging. Far back in a dark corner, I find one of the "courting" gifts from Stouten that Jimmie described in her diary, a glass-paneled music box shaped like a baby grand. The miniature piano's blue and silver mirrored glass is blackened with grit sifted down through the asbestos roof tiles. I raise the piano lid. Inside, a thick stack of yellowed envelopes tied with a faded pink ribbon wait to be reopened, reread. As I unknot the ribbon, it falls apart, crumbles to dusty tatters in my hands. A handwritten gift card flutters loose: "Candy and music for a little girl for the wee hours. Stouten."

For a LITTLE GIRL? I'M his little girl. It sounds like something Daddy would write to me!

Sitting cross-legged on the attic floorboards, head bent, neck cramped under the low pitch of the roof, I read through each letter, searching, searching for clues. Most of the letters are from Amish Mennonite relatives in Kansas or from Jimmie's nursing buddies— congenial, folksy, newsy. But two letters, on heavyweight ivory stationery ornamented with a gold gothic capital "S," stand out. They are from Stouten.

> Baltimore, Md.
> July 14, 1937
> Dear Jimmie:
> Well I was over to see the radiator and fender people to-day but they didn't seem to be able to give me a very definite answer as to how long it would take to give your sick child a treatment. They said it might take two hours or two days they couldn't tell until they see it. Their place is under a different management since I was there, so I didn't know any of the bosses.
> Anyway, you bring it in as early as you can and we will take it over and get it fixed O.K. even if we have to stand by and supervise the job ourselves.
> "It Shall Be Done."
> Now don't you worry, we'll see that your little sick Struggle gets all cured and as good as new again.
> When a certain little girl has troubles with her sick child, and is worried and sad, it just simply has to be fixed and cured so that she will be glad.
> Now take care of yourself until then.
> Your Pal,
> Stouten

Did Daddy really treat Jimmie like a little girl? He obviously loved her and wanted to take care of her the way he takes care of me. But was there any adult passion concealed beneath this lovey-dovey baby talk? Could this adventurous young woman ever have been completely satisfied with an old man for a lover? I remember how she said it was a "different kind of love" they had. Was this what she meant? Maybe this explains those many early mornings I would come into the kitchen and find her, sitting all alone at the big round table, staring into space. Maybe it explains why, sometimes, she would start to cry for no apparent reason. I read the second letter.

Baltimore, Md.
June 24, 1942
Dear Jimmie:
After all, I let you get away and didn't get the size for that pretty little dress that you liked, the one in Brager's store window. So if you will just jot down the measurements of the correct size to fit a certain little girl and mail to me before you leave on your trip, we will have it all ready for the fishing trip when you return. So now don't forget, and take good care of yourself on your trip, and have a good time.
Your Pal,
Stouten

This, I realize, coincides with the date Jimmie leaves for Florida to meet up with ESB.

Inside this letter, there's a snapshot of Daddy and Jimmie. Jimmie stands at the edge of a pier, having just stepped out of a large rowboat. She looks like a buxom gypsy in a full-skirted striped and flowered dress, her black hair tied back with a matching scarf, her dark eyes fixed on what looks to be a catch of a least six fish, tied and dangling from the cord she holds. Daddy, slim and solemn and dapper in a suit and straw hat, stands opposite her on the pier and reaches across with slender, delicate fingers to touch, tentatively, one of the dead fish.

I find one other photo, tucked away at the bottom of the music box. Here, Jimmie and ESB stand side by side on our front lawn. There are no maples yet. Striped awnings shade the front porch. Tender young grapevines are just beginning to twine around bare wooden stakes to form the grape arbor. ESB, handsome in a three-piece suit, is caught mid-sentence, his hand blurred in a lively gesture. Jimmie, looking young and happy, is smiling, gazing directly into his eyes—with a different kind of love.

One afternoon in "Florida," I say to Daddy, "Once, Jimmie told me she always wanted four children, but she said she guessed that 'wasn't meant to be.'"

Daddy pauses for a moment, starts to pluck at his hair, stops himself, and says, "Well, you know, Lissa, your mother lost two babies before you and Spence were born. Made her very sad."

"Oh, maybe that's what she meant—about wanting four children."

"Could be." Daddy looks down at the backs of his hands, smiles a quick, embarrassed smile, and blurts out, "I was strong as a bull when I made you. Was taking hormones. Strong as a bull!"

I think that's the closest Daddy and I have ever come to talking about sex.

CHAPTER THIRTEEN

AT LOW EBB

THE old iron pipes corrode, rust deposits form on the white porcelain under the faucets, and the tap water runs red. When I try to wash the old sun parlor windows, the cracked putty comes loose and smears the glass. In midwinter, the old furnace clogs and puffs out black smoke that leaves a coating of soot on furniture, walls, and windowpanes. We are almost out of financial resources, and Daddy is desperate to earn a living so he can support Spence and me and pay for repairs to keep the house from falling down around us.

Daddy buys a Kelsey hand press and sets up a small printing business in the downstairs front room where he keeps his watchmaker's bench. He assembles the press, fastens it atop a two-drawer oak cabinet he's built, and fills the drawers below the printer with essential items he's ordered from the Kelsey catalog—extra printer parts, large tubes of ink, and special cuts (engraved images mounted on small wooden blocks for printing pictures).

He builds a separate cabinet to hold reams of blank stationery and boxes of business card stock of varying weights and finishes. He fills two tall wooden cabinets with fonts of type and puts an ad in the local paper, promising *Expert Printing. Business Cards. Wedding Announcements and Invitations. Greeting Cards. No Job Too Small. We*

Aim to Please. To his wooden business sign beside our roadside mailbox, he adds the words *Quality Printing* below what's been on the sign since we moved here: *Expert Watchmaking and Repairs. Woodworking.* His hammer rings with hope as he nails the metal letters onto the wood.

And then we wait for business to roll up our driveway and knock at the white side door with peeling paint that bears the sign *Office* in stenciled lettering. In the meantime, Daddy lets me help him design our first greeting card. From the printer's catalog, under Daddy's close supervision, I select a printer's cut—a bouquet of spring flowers—and a dainty, archaic type font called Edwardian Script. Then, all on my own, I write a short verse to display inside the card.

> When winter like an old man dies
> And pinkened April dawns arise
> With birds released from frozen wing—
> Then I my dappled freedom ride.

I read the verse aloud to myself and, before I show it to Daddy, change the first line from "When winter like an old man dies" to "When winter winds desist their sighs." I also revise the last line from "Then I my dappled freedom ride" to "Then Spring returns from Hades' side." I don't want to hurt Daddy's feelings.

In March, our first printing job arrives. The lady who runs the local chapter of the My Lady's Manor Equestrian Society, just north of us, wants us to print announcements for some of their upcoming events.

In the colder months, the radiator in the front room doesn't keep the room warm enough for printing. Daddy hangs a bare lightbulb just above the printer's ink table to keep the ink from hardening.

Daddy trains me to be his "printer's devil." I help him set the type in a heavy steel frame called a chase. He fills the empty spaces around the type with blocks of wood he calls "furniture." He uses quoins— pairs of wedges facing in opposite directions—to lock everything in place within the chase, and a quoin key to force them together. Then he sets the locked-up chase—the "forme"—into the chase bed.

Daddy teaches me to operate the printing press. It's done entirely by hand, slowly, mechanically, one sheet of paper at a time, one color at a time.

To print, I align—very precisely—a single sheet of paper within the paper guides on the open press. Then I grasp the smooth wooden handgrip at the end of the long cast-iron handle, which is attached at the side of the printer. As I pull the handle steadily down toward me, it brings the soft roller down and over the ink plate at the top of the press, allowing the inked roller to pass over the type and causing the platen—a sturdy metal plate—to press the paper against the type and transfer the image as the press closes.

As I operate the press over a stretch of time, I fall into a soothing rhythm, my arm moving in sync with—and powering—the mechanical parts. I begin to feel the satisfying symbiosis of human and machine that Daddy must have thrived on for years.

Daddy relies on me to search the floor for any dropped pieces of type. "You are my eyes, Lissa," Daddy says. "I used to have eyes like a hawk, but now I rely on your young eyesight."

For every job, when the first good print is ready, Daddy calls me in to proof it for him. I learn to detect the smallest of errors in spelling, punctuation, grammar. If I find a mistake, that page is reset and I proof it once again, assuring him that everything is exactly as it should be.

I also learn to distribute each piece of type, after it is cleaned of ink, back into the correct compartment of the correct wooden type case, then insert the case back into the correct drawer in the type cabinet.

"Try not to make a *pie*," Daddy teases me.

"Make a pie?"

"A *pie*," Daddy explains, "is what printers call the mess you make when you spill a case of type on the floor. All the spilled type pieces are a *squabble* and need to be sorted out all over again, inspected for any broken edges, and redistributed in the case."

"I will only make apple and pumpkin pies, I promise. No printer's *pies*."

"Better not, or I may be *out of sorts*. In the printer's world, that means I won't have enough of the pieces I need to fill the type case."

Even though we both laugh at Daddy's play on words, I take my job, as I do all jobs, very seriously. I try very hard to do everything perfectly—to please Daddy, and, I'm realizing, to feel okay about myself.

It is 1966. Spence is a senior in high school. I am in the tenth grade. I am good in English and French; Spence excels in science and math. He's so good, the math teachers get him to tutor other kids in the Advanced Calculus class. When he's offered the math award for the Class of '66, Spence refuses to attend the graduation ceremony, so he doesn't receive the award. He also refuses to have his picture taken for the school yearbook. When asked why, Spence's only response is, "I prefer not to."

Spence's classmates have begun to call him Bartleby after Herman Melville's curious character in "Bartleby the Scrivener." Initially, Melville's Bartleby, hired to copy legal documents by hand for a Manhattan law office, works efficiently and produces a large quantity of excellent work. But when asked to proofread a document, Bartleby responds, "I would prefer not to." Soon, this becomes his response to every request: "I would prefer not to."

I begin to worry about Spence's reclusive behavior. I wonder if he is going through something like my "maybe, maybe not" phase. Whenever I try to ask Spence, "What's wrong?" or "Are you okay?" he rebuffs me.

Finally, I get so frustrated with him, I say, "You're driving me crazy, Spence!"

He just says, "It's a short trip," and clams up.

One day, I decide to talk with Daddy about Spence. Daddy is in his front office, cleaning the press's roller and ink table after a round of printing. I pull up his watchmaker's stool and observe him for a bit. As usual, he performs every task with intensity, precision, and fierce concentration. I wait until he sets aside his tools and looks up at me from his work. Then, quietly, I broach the topic.

"Daddy, do you think Spence is acting a little weird these days?" Daddy is sitting in the cane-back swivel chair at his desk. He wipes his hands on an ink rag, and for a few moments, seems to be considering my question. Finally, he speaks.

"I have to admit, Lissa, that I've never understood that boy. The more I try to get him interested in my work, the more he resists. I used to think Spence would follow in my footsteps, get married one day, and have some sons to carry on the Power name."

"I can carry on the Power name for you, Daddy."

"No, Lissa. You can't. Only boys can carry on family names. All my brothers died without sons, so Spence is the only one left to do it after I'm gone."

"Well, that doesn't seem fair. What's wrong with girls?"

"Nothing. But that's just the way it is, Lissa."

"Hmmm." I decide to let that subject drop—for now.

"So, Daddy, do you think Spence is depressed? Giving up the math award is a pretty big deal."

"Well, Spence was always closer to his mother than to me. He was always Jimmie's boy. I don't think Spence has been the same since your mother died."

"I'll try to be extra nice to him, Daddy. I'll make him pork chops for supper. That's his favorite."

Daddy just shrugs and gives a little tilt of his head, as if approving my intentions.

Spence spends the summer caddying at a couple of local golf courses. He has to bum a ride with a friend, walk, or hitchhike to get there.

He saves his money, and at end of summer, he buys himself a 1940 Plymouth coupe for just eighty dollars.

One of his high school math teachers has kept in touch by phone, and insists that Spence enroll in college. Spence's first choice is the University of New Mexico. He's accepted there, and seems intrigued by its department of physics and astronomy, but daunted by the distance he will need to travel in his antiquated, slow-moving Plymouth.

Spence gets a part-time job at Sweeney's delivering groceries, and decides instead to attend the University of Maryland, where he has also been accepted. He drives off to the campus in the 1940 coupe. The car has two doors, two seats, a pull starter, two small windshields divided in the middle by a metal strip, and no defroster. Its small oval rear window doesn't give much of a view out over the car's stubby rear end, which rounds downward to its trunk in an awkward hump, like a squatting dinosaur's droopy hindquarters.

Spence returns late in the day, pale and shaken by the chaos of trying to enroll at the large campus—long lines, crowds of noisy, surging freshmen—and frustrated by his inability to coordinate the required courses with his work schedule.

"Don't think I could make that drive every day in the Plymouth. And if I stay on campus, they said I'd have to sleep, at least for the first semester, in one of their temporary prefab dorms. Eight guys in one dinky unit. Can't do it."

The next week, Spence tries to sign up for the navy, but he's found to have a heart condition, and doesn't qualify for service. He comes home looking defeated. Over the next few weeks, he drifts around the house, or shuts himself in his room for long periods. A sense of purposelessness steals the youthfulness from his step. His trademark excited pacing—around the kitchen table or in a circle behind the barn—has ceased. A suppressed anxiety daubs shadows under his eyes, and settles a look of permanent dejection around his mouth.

"How's your brother doing?" Mr. J. Winfred Walker asks me one Sunday after church. J. Winfred is a mover and shaker at my

Methodist church, a successful businessman and landowner, and, in some ways, the lord of the manor in our rural (and latently feudal) farm community. "Haven't seen him in church in a long while."

J. Winfred is an influential man who believes it is his Christian duty to look out for church members who are less fortunate, and apparently, at the moment, our family fits that description.

I'm somewhat tongue-tied around this important man, who projects a colossal presence in his impeccable three-piece suit. Before I come up with a response, this pillar of the church presses both my hands in his, gazes at me with deep, soulful brown eyes, and says, "I'm sure they could use someone like Spence at the bank. I'm on the board of trustees at Maryland National. Have Spence give this gentleman a call, and use me as a reference." Releasing my hands from his grasp, he slides a pen and business card from the silk lining of a clandestine inner coat pocket, and scribbles a name and phone number on the back of the card.

Spence is interviewed in the personnel office in the bank's downtown Baltimore headquarters at the corner of East Baltimore and Light Streets, an art deco giant that soars up beneath its copper-clad dome to dominate the city's skyline; but he is hired to work blocks and blocks away, at an entry-level job on the first floor of a much smaller building facing Calvert Street. His first "real" job is handling coins for Maryland National Bank.

I always have supper ready for Daddy and Spence when Spence gets home from work. And sometimes, when he's not too tired, I get Spence to tell me a little about his new job before he goes off to bed.

Each morning, he comes in the back of the building through the loading dock, punches in, and enters the first floor, which houses two work areas: the coin room and the dollar room. Though both rooms share a manager, they have discrete staff and functions. The coin room deals only with coins; the dollar room is reserved for paper money. Employees share a small kitchen and bathroom.

Spence has been assigned to the coin room, where machines that process metal money dominate the space. Bags, heavy with loose change of all denominations—collected from vending machines, pay phones, church collection plates—are dumped into the coin machines for sorting, counting, and weighing to verify the count. Day after day, Spence handles coins—sticky, grimy coins—as machines deposit them into rolls and seal the tops. The coins get hot in the machines, sometimes so hot they burn and blister my brother's hands. He foregoes wearing gloves, and builds up calluses.

Within the year, the bank administers a logic test. Spence aces the test, and is promoted to data processing. At first, he runs the check sorter; then he becomes a computer operator. The bank's senior programmers soon recognize my brother's prodigious skills. They lend him their programming manuals and groom him to become a computer programmer.

At home, Spence resumes his characteristic pacing around the kitchen table after supper. He spends hours in his room studying thick manuals, teaching himself computer languages—ALGOL, COBOL. He begins writing programs for the bank. On weekends, he sits for hours at a large wooden table, in the room we use as a combination dining/living room, poring over tall stacks of computer printouts.

Daddy and I come in here to chat and watch TV while Spence goes over his printouts. Sometimes, we call over to Spence to include him in the conversation, but often, he becomes so absorbed in the strings of computer code that he doesn't seem to hear us; he doesn't respond. Spence has entered, on the ground floor, a new world called the Information Age, a world that is alien to Daddy and me.

One Friday night, Daddy has gone up to bed, Spence is still poring over his printouts, and I'm standing in the kitchen doorway ironing, watching an old movie on TV. Then there's the sermonette and "The Star-Spangled Banner," and the station signs off. I click off the TV. The only sound now is the hollow, persistent ticking of the Regulator clock in the kitchen.

"Spence," I call over to my brother. Sometimes, very late at night is the best time to have a conversation. "Spence?" He looks up. "Why do you like computer stuff so much?"

Spence stares across the room for a while, at nothing—or at everything—and says, "If you make a mistake with something mechanical, like a watch or a clock, it's ruined, and you have to throw it away. But if there's an error in a program, you can always fix it, rewrite the code, make it work. A little time lost, but no material wasted." I remember what a perfectionist Daddy has been with Spence, and how angry Daddy used to get when Spence did something wrong in the shop. Now I get it. Now Spence has found something of his own, something that carries him beyond Daddy's criticisms. Before long, Spence is training other programmers, and fortunately for Daddy and me, his salary steadily increases. Our family's finances take a sharp turn upward. Spence begins to buy nice three-piece suits. I wash and iron his dress shirts every week, and when he goes out of town to do a training, I fold and pack his clothes neatly in his suitcase.

CHAPTER FOURTEEN

PICKUP TRUCK PICKUP

Now that Spence has graduated from high school and started to work, I have to walk by myself to catch the school bus at the intersection. Spence leaves for work too early in the morning for me to get a ride with him, and he doesn't get home until six P.M., in time for supper.

I really don't mind the walk itself, but waiting in the cold at the corner for the bus to arrive is not my favorite thing to do. Sometimes, my feet freeze so badly they throb with pain when they start to thaw out on the bus.

By now, I've learned to dress more like the other girls—makeup, hose, a conservative but fashionable dress length just above the knee. I'm kind of alone here at school now, with Paloma gone, but once in a while, we talk on the phone. She doesn't like the private school, and she's mad at her dad for making her go there.

I feel pretty good about myself, and am starting to think about college. Daddy still doesn't allow me to participate in after-school activities or go on dates, but I'm okay for now with romance novels like Daphne du Maurier's *Rebecca* and Victoria Holt's *Mistress of Mellyn* and old movies on TV like *Hold Back the Dawn* and *The Swan*, with heart-melting French actors like Charles Boyer and Louis

Jourdan to satisfy my longings. I don't think I'm ready for the real thing, yet, anyway.

I dig out my old writing notebook from the bottom of my desk and try to write my own version of a passionate romance novel, but revise as I might, the characters keep coming out two-dimensional, like paper dolls cut from flimsy paper. It's always about two vague young women vying for the love of one ill-defined man. One woman—the one I identify with—is quiet, shy, serious, intelligent, mousy. She dreams that the man will rescue her from her drab life. The other woman is her opposite—the one, in my heart of hearts, I'd like to be—beautiful, lively, daring, self-confident—maybe the way I imagine Jimmie was before she married Daddy. The man, of course, is handsome and troubled in a meaningless way. Because I've never had a boyfriend, my story inevitably shuts down, and never progresses beyond a paragraph or two.

It's a Monday morning in May, and the weather has turned warm enough to leave my jacket at home, hanging on the hallway coatrack. I get even warmer as I walk, so I take off my cardigan and tie it around my neck. I'm just past Cory's Ridge, moving under a fringe of old trees whose roots cling precariously to the road bank on either side, when a pickup truck, heading in the direction I'm walking, comes to a sudden stop alongside me.

The driver, a man who looks to be in his thirties, rolls down his window and calls out to me, "Hey! Where you going? Want a ride? Hop in."

Over the years, Spence and I have accepted lots of rides, especially when the weather's bad. After all, we grew up in Grangerville, a small farming community where everybody knew everybody. Even though I don't know this guy, he seems pretty friendly, so I cross over to the pickup's passenger side and climb in.

He looks over and smiles at me. "Hi, I'm Jake. What's your name?"

"Lissa," I say. "I'm just going to my bus stop at the intersection. Not far." As usual, I'm toting an armload of books. Jake has short-cropped reddish hair and a plump pink face. He drops me off at the stop sign beside my bus stop, smiles and waves, makes a right, and drives away.

Two mornings later, Jake stops for me again on my way to the bus stop. I climb in, and he starts up a conversation. "That's a lot of schoolbooks you got there, Lissa. What grade you in?"

I tell him I'm in eleventh grade. Again, he drops me off at my bus stop, waves, and drives off. He seems very pleasant. The next morning, his truck passes my house just at I'm coming down the driveway. He spots me, throws his truck in reverse, backs up, and waits for me at our mailbox at the end of the drive.

"We seem to be on the same schedule," Jake says. "I pass by here every morning on my way to work." He drives for a moment in silence, then reaches over to hold my hand and says "I'm married." Taken by surprise, I draw my hand away, feeling embarrassed. I don't know what to say. He releases my hand, and we continue on, in silence.

Then he looks at me and says, "You know, you're a pretty girl. Anybody ever tell you that?" I turn my face away. I can feel fear creeping up my spine like the thick mercury surging up a thermometer held to the radiator. As a kid, Spence used to warm up a thermometer that way when he wanted to play sick and stay home from school, but Spence could never fool Nurse Jimmie!

When Jake stops the truck at the bus stop, I jump out quickly and slam the door behind me. I don't look back, and am relieved to hear the pickup drive away.

I sit by myself on the school bus, scrunched up next to the window. I'm not sure what just happened, but it doesn't make me feel good about Jake or about myself. I don't feel safe. To soothe myself, I start counting the telephone and electric poles as the bus passes them along the winding roads to school.

All day, my mind goes over and over what Jake said and did in the pickup. I am miserable. In class, my focus on conjugating French verbs or listening to the English teacher lecture about Hawthorne's *The Scarlet Letter* is interrupted by the incessant, infernal echoing of Jake's words in my head. "I'm married. I'm married." The words continue with increasing intensity, like Poe's "tintinnabulation" of the "bells, bells, bells," throughout the day. "Married, married, married," pulses in my head, a broken record. I decide I must talk to Daddy this afternoon when I get home from school.

The words spill out quickly. "Daddy, there's this guy in a pickup truck who's been giving me rides to the school bus. But today he tried to hold my hand. He said he's married. What should I do?"

I watch as slowly, from somewhere deep inside Daddy, I see tension and anger mount. His lips begin to quiver, then move. At first, no sound emerges, but then, like molten lava from a volcano, the words erupt from Daddy's mouth. Obscenities, superlative expletives I've never heard him use before, spew out, vilifying Jake, a man he's never met. "I'd like to get my hands on that mother****ingest son of a b****."

Fuming, Daddy makes his way to the black wall phone in the hallway and calls the police. Within fifteen minutes, a county police car pulls into our driveway. Two uniformed officers rap on the back door, and Daddy lets them in through the back porch into the kitchen. Daddy tells them what I told him, adding in a few choice swearwords to convey what he thinks of this man Jake.

When I come into the kitchen, one of the police officers, who looks pretty young, is sitting at the kitchen table, writing up a report. The other officer looks older. He's overweight and balding, and stands facing Daddy. As I enter the room, the older policeman looks me over. I realize I'm still wearing my school clothes. I can feel his gaze sweep over me, top to bottom, bottom to top. It makes me self-conscious. I feel the makeup on my face exhibiting to him something unintentionally provocative. I feel betrayed by the tightness of my form-fitting dress as it follows the contours of my body, by the sheer hosiery clinging to my legs. I am ashamed of my appearance.

"Pete," he calls out to his partner and tilts his head sideways in my direction. The partner responds to the signal, takes a long look at me, snaps closed the notebook he's been writing in, stuffs it in his uniform pocket, and scrapes his chair back from the kitchen table.

"Not much we can do without a license plate number," says the senior partner. "Lots of men in pickup trucks around here." With that, both officers leave abruptly.

Friday passes, and no sign of Jake. I'm thinking maybe the police caught up with him. The weekend passes quietly, but on Monday morning, just as I leave the house, there's the pickup, rocking back and forth at the bottom of the driveway. Jake is gunning the engine. He rolls down his window all the way and rests his arm on the sill, his elbow sticking out.

"Mornin', Lissa. I saw you at your bedroom window a couple nights ago. You had your light on."

Now I'm really scared. Did he really see me at night? How does he know which room is my bedroom? Then, behind me, from the front porch, I hear a strange, loud bellowing sound. For some reason, it reminds me of the sound I once heard coming from a young bull while it was being clamped and emasculated on Mr. Clay's farm. The sound is coming from Daddy. He's at the front door.

Now Daddy's running down across the front lawn. He's flailing his arms, shaking both fists at Jake. I've never seen him look this angry. He stands right next to the truck, glaring at Jake. Daddy's face is red and contorted; the veins protrude on his neck. "You get the hell out of here, you son of a bitch. You stay away from my little girl."

Jake draws his arm back inside the truck, steps on the gas, and the pickup roars away and disappears around a bend in the road. That's the last I ever see Jake, and we hear nothing more from the police. But now, Daddy seems to watch me more carefully than ever. And I retreat again into the safety of his world.

In English class, I sit next to my friend Ben. Ben is a fullback on our high school football team. He's so big and heavy, his teammates call him Big Bad Ben, or BBB. But he's really a nice guy. He calls me a "soul sister" and makes me laugh. His smile spreads wide across this face, and his teeth flash white against his dark brown skin. During class, he sneaks candy bars from inside his desk.

Our English class is still studying *The Scarlet Letter.*

"The scarlet letter A that Hester Prynne wore, what did that scarlet letter stand for?" asks Miss Fogarty, our English teacher.

Ben's hand shoots up.

Miss Fogarty calls on him. "Ben?"

Ben chuckles. "It means," Ben pauses for effect, "she was *A-vailable.*"

The class erupts in laughter. I find myself laughing right along with them as Miss Fogarty struggles hard to keep a straight face.

CHAPTER FIFTEEN

ON THE VERGE

IT'S 1968, I'm a senior in high school, and the world is turning upside down.

At the end of January, communists launch the Tet Offensive. Televised footage of this initiative invades American living rooms night after night on the evening news. Spearheaded by Viet Cong elite forces, sapper-commandos, Tet is backed by wave upon wave of supporting troops that wage local battles in more than a hundred South Vietnamese cities and towns.

Tet is a human tragedy. It kills 37,000 of the Viet Cong troops deployed, leaving many more wounded or captured. It creates more than half a million civilian refugees. With Tet, America loses 2,500 of its men, and those of us who thought the Viet Cong guerillas were a weak opponent, an enemy we could drive back easily, begin to have our doubts about this war.

At the end of March, President Lyndon Johnson stuns the country with a televised speech from the White House, announcing, "I shall not seek, and I will not accept, the nomination of my party for another term as your president." He recoils from persisting with the war in Vietnam, predicting that "many men—on both sides of the struggle—will be lost." He warns Americans to "guard against divisiveness, and all of its ugly consequences."

On April 4, Dr. Martin Luther King, Jr. is shot in Memphis, Tennessee. He dies at 7:05 P.M., and shockwaves spread across the country in newspapers and on TV. I flip from channel to channel—we get three major channels here. I see a photo of him collapsed on that motel balcony. I hear excerpts of his sermons and speeches. There's something about him—a soft sadness in his eyes, a pulsing power in his voice, a ring of truth and prophecy—unlike anything I've seen or heard before. His people mourn for him.

Feelings run deep and raw. Unspeakable anger, suppressed far too long, erupts like a festering abscess in black communities across the country. In Baltimore, the riots rage for four days and three nights. Stores go up in flames, looting spreads like an epidemic along York Road, Harford Road, and Edmondson Avenue. Police and firemen are pelted with bottles and stones. Groups form on street corners, taunting each other, alienated by the color of their skin.

On North Avenue, kids run from store to store, setting off fires with lighted torches. Sidewalks become harsh passageways littered with broken glass. Buildings smolder. More than 1,000 city police officers, 400 state troopers, and more than 5,000 National Guardsmen are mobilized in Baltimore, some of them just startled kids behind their fearsome gas masks.

When the riots end, and the city rouses herself like a wound-weary beast, the reporters begin to compare her devastation to the Great Fire of 1904. Massive, unprecedented ransacking and arson, six dead, more than 700 injured, 5,800 arrested. More than 1,000 businesses looted, vandalized, or destroyed by fire.

It's not for some weeks after the riots that Daddy and I venture downtown on the number eight bus. The bus crawls south on York Road, groaning heavily as it stops to pick up passengers along the way. We pass 42nd Street, and York Road becomes Greenmount Avenue. We cross North Avenue and pass Greenmount Cemetery on our left.

Besides the driver, Daddy and I are the only white people on the bus. We pass block after block of boarded-up shop windows. A teenaged boy takes the seat across the aisle from me. I stare at him warily out of the corner of my eye. I guess he must be a couple of years younger than I am. I wonder what he's thinking. He stares straight ahead, his jaw set tight. I am afraid to smile at him. I feel so conspicuously white. Does he hate me for it? Even worse, does he have good reason to hate me?

Daddy sits beside me, leaning against the window. His breath leaves a smudge of white mist on the pane. With his pocket handkerchief, Daddy wipes the window clear, takes another look, then turns to me and whispers in my ear, "Destruction—block after block of it. As with Sodom and Gomorrah, God has delivered his divine judgment upon us."

As we approach the corner where we get off, the bus lurches to a stop. Daddy and I are thrown forward. Daddy has to clutch at the nearest seat handle to keep from falling. He's eighty-nine now, and loses his balance pretty easily.

In English class, my friend Ben smiles his big wide smile and asks me if I'm going to the senior prom.

"I don't know," I say.

"How would you feel about going with a soul brother?"

I look down at my desk and say, "I don't think I'll be going." I'm thinking that Daddy won't let me go. He's only let me go to one school dance, and that was back in ninth grade, when Paloma's mother convinced Daddy that everything would be okay, that she would take me and Paloma safely to and from the class dance. I'm also thinking about the black-white thing. There's no cross-racial dating at our high school. I just know Daddy would hit the roof if I went out with a black guy! I'm feeling more and more how different my world is from the world Daddy grew up in. I am sad and ashamed and confused—all at the same time.

Even though Paloma goes to a different school now, she and her mom keep an eye out for me. When I tell Paloma I really do want to go the senior prom, she tells me, "You don't want to miss your senior prom, Lissa. My mom says this could be a rite of passage for you. It's kind of like a coming-out party. Lissa, you gotta go!" I convince Daddy that this is a very important, one-time event. Daddy finally gives in, and I wind up accepting my friend Seth's invitation. Seth and I sit next to each other in Civics class. He's smart and funny, and has a way of making me laugh in spite of myself. Also, Seth is white, so going with him to the dance won't raise any eyebrows. Besides, rumor and innuendo have labeled him as "queer." Homosexuality is considered to be something shameful. It's not openly discussed, but I know I'll be safe with Seth.

On the afternoon of the prom, Paloma and her mom take me to a hairdresser where I have my hair teased, piled high, bobby-pinned, and lacquered with hairspray into a chic bouffant at the top of my head. I wear a sleek white satin dress with an empire waistline, lace bodice, puff sleeves, and long white gloves. Paloma's mom made the dress for me. I picked out the pattern and material myself. I want it to look like a gown Audrey Hepburn wore in *War and Peace*.

Seth doesn't have a driver's license, so his father picks us up in his huge white boat of a car. Seth and I sit apart in the roomy back seat. I see Daddy peering out the window of the back-porch door as the big car rolls down our gravel driveway. During the ride to the prom, Seth presents me with a purple orchid in a fancy box. He grins and watches, but he doesn't touch me as I fumble, trying to pin on the corsage.

When we enter the prom together, Seth says, "You look gorgeous!" I'm wearing my first high heels, white pumps. Now I'm pretending to be Audrey Hepburn making her entrance at the embassy ball in *My Fair Lady*, passing herself off as royalty. I really do start to feel like a princess. It's a heady feeling!

But in the middle of our first dance, Seth breaks away and wanders off, chatting with other friends. I stand alone, feeling abandoned on the dance floor.

The prom is held in the gym, and far across the room, I spot my friend Ben huddled with some of his black friends under a basketball hoop that's decorated with streamers in our class colors. Ben seems to be looking my way. Maybe he's even catching my eye. And suddenly, I don't feel like a princess anymore. In my imagination, Ben's face swims and blends with other faces, now memories. I see the defiant, yet innocent face of young Jamal at summer camp. I feel shamed by the firm set of the black teenager's jaw opposite me on the number eight bus. The truth comes to me—hard and real. I didn't go to the prom with Ben because he is black. I am prejudiced!

Then, suddenly, the gym begins to spin around me. I stand alone at the center of a whirling vortex. The band plays in slow motion, the streamers blur, the prom queen on her throne smiles as she and her court swirl past. Something vibrates up my spine, explodes in my head. I see a blazing red X, hear a voice saying, "We need more light about each other." Then I feel my knees buckle, and everything goes dark.

The next thing I hear is one of the chaperones, Miss Fogarty, saying, "She needs more air." At first, her voice seems to come from a distance, but then it's right here, and I can see Miss Fogarty bending over me, fanning me with a cardboard poster, offering me a glass of water and telling everyone to step back.

"Are you okay, Lissa?" I'm sitting on a metal folding chair now at the edge of the gym, sipping water. I nod, more embarrassed than anything.

Seth's dad picks us up after the dance, and I ride home in silence next to Seth.

Daddy's gone to bed, but I stop in to say goodnight and tell him about the vision I had when I passed out. "Clairvoyance," is all he says, and I remember his story about his cousin Urchie. "Urchie's dead."

I keep thinking about the red X and the voice saying, "We need more light about each other." What does it mean? Where did it come from? The next week at school, I search in the library for the quote and finally I find it, buried in a letter Malcolm X wrote in 1964 to the *Egyptian Gazette*, the year before he was assassinated. His letter opens by saying:

> . . . racism has rooted itself so deeply in the subconscious-ness of many American whites that they themselves oft-times are not even aware of its existence. . . .

Well, that hits home with me! But later in the letter, Malcolm X goes on to say:

> We need more light about each other. Light creates understanding, understanding creates love, love creates patience, and patience creates unity. . . .

I can only hope that Malcolm X and Ben and Jamal and all the rest of black America will not shut the door on me and other white Americans against the possibility of overcoming the prejudice we have been raised with.

In June, I graduate from the stage at our high school. Daddy sits proudly in the audience next to Aunt Essie. Daddy doesn't drive at night, and Spence says he prefers not to go back to his old high school. So, even though he still doesn't like Jimmie's sister, Daddy accepts a ride from her.

I stand onstage in my white cap and gown, accept my scholar-ships—a small gift for college textbooks from the PTA and a four-year senatorial scholarship—and my high school diploma. Afterward, Aunt Essie drops Daddy and me off at the house, and I go to sleep excited about the future.

The next morning, Daddy lets me sleep in and fixes his own break-fast. Finally, I make my way downstairs, still foggy and dreamy about my new status as a high school graduate. The first thing I do is turn on the TV. Instantly, my daydream is ruptured. The screen is flooded, on every channel, with reports of Bobby Kennedy's assassination shortly after midnight on June 5, 1968.

The weeks and months that follow are a tumble of world-changing, life-changing events. America's involvement in the Vietnam War continues to expand. Many of my male classmates become soldiers and deploy to Vietnam.

Paloma has graduated from Bryn Mawr, but she stays in touch. That summer, she sends me letters from Florida, where she's set to begin college in the fall. She fills me in on all her escapades—she's hanging out on the beach a lot, doing drugs, making out with some of the college professors, having a blast. She calls me her "sensible and serious, Wendy Darling"; she calls herself "just another Peter Pan, who won't grow up." Then, abruptly, the letters stop, and for months, I lose touch with her entirely.

Like many other guys his age, Spence lets his hair grow to shoulder length. He buys himself a green Plymouth Roadrunner and spends weekends away with a friend, watching stock car races in Pennsylvania or Ohio.

I begin to lose all sense of time. I stop going to church, stop paying much attention the news. When I'm not cooking, or cleaning the house, or doing laundry for Daddy and Spence, I pass the remainder of summer in other times and other places. I spread Lovenia's old handmade quilt beneath the red Japanese maple tree, and pass the long hot afternoons communing with some of my favorite muses.

I imagine what it might be like to be the overworked, exhausted young girl child in Anton Chekhov's "Sleepy," whose only respite is to smother the crying baby in her charge. What might it be like to be reincarnated as this same weary young girl in Katherine Mansfield's "The Child-Who-Was-Tired," and driven once again to suffocate the screaming infant who will not allow her to rest? Then I remember that once I nearly suffocated in the Oldsmobile, and I wonder how the tiny victim must feel. Am I tormented victimizer or innocent victim, worn-out girl child or murdered baby? For what purpose have I come around again?

When I read Leo Tolstoy's *Anna Karenina*, the scene of Levin's marriage proposal to Kitty jumps out at me. Seated at a table in the drawing room, these two communicate their deepest feelings for each other by writing, with chalk, just the first letters of each word. This magical clairvoyance found only in the closest of relationships is a mirror of what happens when Daddy and I read each other's mind.

I read on and on all summer, telling myself that plowed and harrowed, I'm lying fallow now, gathering strength for when the school year comes upon me once again.

CHAPTER SIXTEEN

SCHOLARSHIP INTERRUPTED

I BEGIN college with a full load of classes. To get there, I have to take the bus, then walk blocks and blocks to campus, carrying a satchel full of heavy books. I come home each evening too tired to study. When I do try to read my texts after supper, Daddy frets that I will ruin my eyesight with so much reading. I feel pressured. I know I won't be able to keep up with all these classes. I officially drop out of a few, but as the first semester is about to end and the first wave of exams arrive, I still feel overwhelmed. I fear I'm about to fail some of my classes. I panic.

Over the weekend, on a chilly November afternoon, I talk my situation over with Daddy.

Though the air outside is nippy, I find Daddy stretched out on his back on the red bench in front of his woodshop. Breathing deeply, his legs stretched up over the back of the bench, feet pressed firmly against the shop's white shingle wall, palms pressed together, and head hanging upside down, he appears to be performing a series of isometric exercises. Seeing me standing behind him, he finishes his current set of presses and releases, swings his legs around, sits up on the bench, and pats the space beside him, inviting me to sit there.

"A penny for your thoughts, my little squirrel ears."

I sit and button my jacket against the cold. "I'm worried, Daddy."

"What's wrong, Lissa?"

"My exams are all scheduled for next week. I've been studying, but I'm afraid I might not pass some of them. There are just too many things to read and memorize all at once. I'm okay with the French and English, but I'm not keeping up with the math and the science. I don't really want to give up my scholarships, and I sure don't want to flunk out." I look over toward the house and notice that the gutters, weighed down with leaves, are sagging, coming loose from the eaves. Nobody's taking care of these things anymore.

"Well, you know, Lissa, I've been worried about my little girl, too. I'm afraid you may be ruining your health with all this commuting back and forth in cold weather. I haven't said anything, but I've seen you go out in the morning with a wet head. You could come down with a bad catarrh if you keep doing that. I think that's what killed my brother William. For some reason, in the middle of winter, William loved to strip naked, dive into the river for a quick swim, then run around outside—with his wet hair and his bare feet—to dry himself. Said it was invigorating. Well, William died from a bad catarrh when he was just sixteen years old.

"Besides, I need you here during the day to take care of me. What if I should fall on the pavement here outside the shop, and hurt myself so bad I couldn't get up, or cut myself on one of my machines?"

On Monday, I go to the registrar's office and say I want to withdraw from college. A tiny old lady in a red suit searches my records, hands me some paperwork in a manila folder, and directs me to the office of the dean of students.

The dean is a black-suited, middle-aged man. He sits behind a formal desk in an old office with high ceilings and ancient radiators that ping as he gestures for me to take a seat. I sit there for cumbersome moments, nervous as he slowly peruses my paperwork. The silence is broken only by an erratic chorus of frantic pops and pings from the radiator. Finally, the dean looks up and peers across at me over the severe black rims of his glasses.

"So, Lissa. Why do you want to drop out of college?" The dean poses the question formally, with gravity. He leans in toward me, stretches his arms out to me across the desk, hands solemnly clasped.

I'm tired and *I'm not ready* are the answers that come to mind, but the dean's question has filled the room with a dark threat of impending fatality. I am confused, and fear the irrevocability of my response. All I can think to say is, "I'm not sure."

The dean withdraws his arms to the sides of his chair, rolls it back away from his desk, and says, "You realize, Lissa, that most women meet their future husbands in college."

His statement takes me by surprise. It makes no sense to me. The last thing I want to do right now is find a husband. That's *not* why I came to college.

"College is just not working out for me," I say.

The dean pulls his chair back up to his desk and signs my withdrawal papers. He comes around the desk, hands my folder back, and shakes my hand.

"Good luck, Lissa. You're leaving in good standing. Maybe you'll come back to us one day." I leave his office feeling relieved, but somehow doomed.

To keep me content after leaving college, Daddy buys me a subscription to a correspondence course, Benson Barrett's *How to Write for Money Right Away*. One of my assignments is to write up some recipes. I find my grandmother Magda's old recipe book on a shelf in the pantry. Tucked inside the cookbook's cover is a folded page of yellowed notepaper bearing a handwritten recipe for Sunshine Cake. I submit my grandmother's cake recipe, along with a recipe I've come across for making tortillas from scratch. Encouraged by the positive feedback I get about the tortilla recipe, I move along with my lessons.

"You see," Daddy says, sipping iced tea, "didn't I tell you? It's not real."

It's July 21, 1969. Yesterday evening, at 10:56 P.M. EDT, Neil Armstrong became the first man to walk on the moon. I haven't been paying much attention to the news for a while; it's usually pretty depressing. But today, the news channels are showing footage of what appears to be a major achievement.

Daddy and I are in the dining/living room, watching hazy images on TV. A man in a cumbersome-looking spacesuit seems to bounce across a pocked landscape. Daddy wears his watchmaker's loupe fastened on top of his regular glasses, moves up closer to the TV, and stares fixedly at a label at the bottom of the screen that says "simulation."

"You see," Daddy says, jabbing at the TV screen with his forefinger. "It says it's a sim-u-la-tion." He makes his point by pronouncing every syllable distinctly.

"I knew they couldn't put a man on the moon. And they shouldn't be messing around with the moon like that, anyway." For Daddy, the man in the moon is an old friend, a soft-faced, wise, luminous fellow who rises outside his bedroom window at night to comfort him. The moon helps him get through those sleepless nights when his prostate won't let him rest, when frequent, urgent, burning urination keeps him awake at night. He keeps a large tin can (formerly a fifteen-ounce can of Ann Page Bartlett pears) to pee in at night.

I refill Daddy's glass of iced tea and start fixing his supper. My mature side is telling me I know better—I know that this first moon landing is real. My child side—the part of me that's still lovingly entwined with, and obedient to, this old man's will—is inclined to believe that what Daddy is saying must be true.

Later, while Daddy, Spence, and I are having supper, Daddy says again that the whole moonwalk was a hoax. "It even said on TV that it was a simulation."

I look over at my brother. "Spence?"

Spence just shrugs and says, "Perhaps."

After supper, I ask Spence, "What did you mean by *perhaps*?"

"Well, I wasn't going to try to argue with Daddy. I was working late last night, so I didn't see any of the live coverage. But they probably used some mockups and simulations to fill in the details. I'm just wondering what they'll discover when they analyze those moon dust samples they collected. It's all pretty amazing."

After supper, with dishes cleared and the TV turned off, I sit hugging a pillow on the worn-out sofa next to Daddy's armchair. He rubs doggedly at the frayed arms of his chair, his fingers plucking obsessively at the chair's yellowed stuffing. From the opposite wall—which is papered with the remnants of a sad, faded, water-stained Victorian floral design—a large portrait of Daddy's father, Tommy, looks on.

My grandfather Tommy Power's dark hair and beard remind me of pictures I've seen in schoolbooks of Ulysses S. Grant. But Tommy Power's features are more handsomely arranged, and his demeanor reveals a certain gentleness not befitting a military man—though according to Daddy, Tommy signed up for the Confederate States Army in Virginia when he was just nineteen.

Gradually relaxing, Daddy leans back in his chair, closes his eyes, and takes me back with him to a time and place at the far end of nowhere, where everything begins.

I hug my pillow more tightly and close my eyes for the voyage back in time.

Here, the wind is ruffling trees, and it is snowing cherry blossoms. Places like Tulip Hill and Coffee Hill ride on dream clouds, and bear remembering. The wind of memory exhales deep whispers from people who also bear remembering. People like Fringe-a-Frock, a sawmill foreman—not a tailor—who exploded, and Urchie, the cousin who perished in childhood and alerted my young father to the notion that he was perhaps clairvoyant.

Daddy recounts to me his family's history for the umpteenth time—how he was born in 1878 on Coffee Hill in St. Mary's County, and grew up on Tulip Hill in Charles County in Southern Maryland. I never tire of hearing it. Daddy has the storyteller's gift of elaborating upon, embellishing, and carrying the narrative a little further forward with each telling.

"My pappy daddy—his first name was Virgil, but they always called him by his middle name, Tommy—he was born into a family in Virginia. They lived on a big spread, and had slaves. But then, during the Civil War, they lost everything, and my grandpappy wound up migrating to St. Mary's County to take up tenant farming. And it was here my pappy had the good fortune to meet up with my mother, Lovenia. Lovenia, you see, was a descendent of folks who sailed over, way back in the 1600s, on the Ark and its pinnace, the Dove. The first thing they did was plant a big cross on St. Clement Island, claim the land for the King of England, hold their first communal Roman Catholic mass, and settle in St. Mary's County. After Lovenia and Tommy were married, he moved in with Lovenia and her family on one hundred acres of bounty land her grandfather Jesse Thompson had been awarded for his service in the Revolutionary War. Lovenia's family had turned that land, with its loamy soil, into a thriving tobacco farm.

"When I was a very young boy, ideas for inventions just started to come to me like magic. I started to conjure up better and easier ways to get the work done. I hated to see my mother work so hard from sunup to sundown, and then, after a long day's work, have to wear out her hands shelling peas for our supper. For many a day, I sat opposite my mother in the kitchen and made a careful study of the motions of her hands, sizing up just what was required to strip those peas out of their pods.

"When the other boys were out playing baseball in the meadow after the farm work was done, I went out to the smokehouse to be alone. That's where I first started to come up with my inventions. I would pace around in a circle and think, and pace some more, and think some more, until I finally figured out just how a machine might do the same job my mother's hands did. I borrowed some tools from my pappy's toolshed and put together a wooden contraption that would shell those peas for my mother. That was my first real invention."

As the stories go on and on, night after night, after supper, I'm reminded over and over again how my father's soul was captured at an early age by the power of the steam engine, the beauty of a pocket watch's workings, and all the fascinating mechanisms that were ushering the country into the twentieth century. Ben Franklin, Thomas Edison—these were Daddy's childhood heroes.

Months slip by, and I spend most of my time at home with Daddy. I stopped going to church a while back. I started to feel like a liar every time I had to recite the Apostles' Creed during the service. I can't really believe anymore that Jesus "was conceived by the Holy Ghost, born of the Virgin Mary." I get out some library books on religion and philosophy, but the more reading I do, the more doubts I have. I do still love the Sermon on the Mount, but religion itself is beginning to seem more like self-hypnosis, a palliative measure at best. Just another fantasy, and not even always the best fantasy.

It's October of 1969 when I finally get another letter from Paloma. She's been living in a commune in California and has found her soulmate, a guy named Gary. She's coming to her mother's farm in Virginia for her wedding later this month. She wants me to be her maid of honor.

Daddy is worried about my being away so long in Virginia, but as a wedding gift for Paloma, he makes a mahogany lazy Susan turntable inlaid with roses.

Gary and Paloma pick me up in their GTO (they call it "The Goat") and drive me to her mom's Virginia farmhouse, a grand old place built in the 1700s. Remnants of the original family's graveyard are still visible in a field near the house.

Gary gives Paloma's mom a big hug. He calls her Hippie Momma, and she does look kind of like a hippie with her long straight hair, no bra, no makeup. She's very informal these days, seemingly laid back, and she still drives her vintage VW bus.

Paloma's mom and dad are recently divorced. Her dad walked out to marry his childhood sweetheart, a Texan oil heiress. When Paloma's dad arrives with his mother to attend the wedding, tensions in the old farmhouse run high. Paloma is furious with her father.

Gary, who grew up working-class and makes a living driving eighteen-wheelers across the country, popping uppers to stay awake, is as different as a man could be from Paloma's dad. Her dad is a well-heeled college professor with a PhD in Molecular Biophysics and Biochemistry from an Ivy League university. On our first night in Virginia, Gary sneaks out and paints over the VW logo on the front of the bus, transforming it into a peace sign.

Paloma has her mother put me up in the bedroom that served as the family nursery in American Colonial times. Paloma orients me to the room. She points to a shadowy corner near the fireplace, occupied by a child-sized wooden rocking horse and a small rocking chair.

"Those belonged to Sarah and Matthew, two of the original owner's children."

Paloma tells me this room is visited regularly by their diminutive ghosts—Sarah, a four-year-old with long blonde curls who comes back to rock in her old rocking chair, and her brother Matthew—six years old when he died—who loves to tickle guests who sleep in his old bed.

"I hope you don't mind, Lissa," Paloma tells me, "but you're going to have to share the room with Iris." Iris is Paloma's paternal grandmother, a wealthy woman from Texas who owns one quarter of an oil well. Paloma, who took her mother's side during and after the divorce, goes out of her way to poke fun at Iris.

"That rich old bag. She must put her makeup on with a trowel. I hope you don't gag when she chain-smokes and loads her hair with hairspray. She'll be in Matthew's bed. She'll probably have a cow when Matthew tickles her. I'd love to get a picture of that!"

I laugh at Paloma's depiction of Iris, and Paloma gives me a big hug. "So glad you could make it, Lissa."

I fall asleep wondering if Sarah or Matthew will pay us a visit tonight. In the middle of the night, I wake up. I hear something! I get up and take a quick look around the room. No movement from Sarah's rocker in the corner, but a curious grating sound is coming from Iris's bed. I tiptoe over. Nope. No Matthew in bed with Iris. Just Iris, grinding her teeth.

As soon as daylight wakes me, I make my way to the guest bathroom to take a shower. When I step out of the shower, I'm startled to see Paloma's dad standing in the bathroom doorway. I grab for my bathrobe, belt it around me, squeeze past him, and hurry down the hallway back to the guest bedroom. I figure he needed to use the bathroom and didn't realize anyone was in there. But when I mention this to Paloma, she's furious. "Oh, Jesus! That bastard! Dirty old man. Wanted to get a good look at you naked. You're lucky he didn't try to grope you."

The wedding is held in a large sitting room. The wide-plank colonial flooring is fastened with pegs. A local Unitarian minister officiates, expounding on a theme—selected by Paloma—that emphasizes universal love and peace. As maid of honor and the only bridesmaid, I process in first, to the strains of the theme song from Stanley Kubrick's *2001: A Space Odyssey* playing on a tape player on top of an antique baby grand piano. There is no pianist.

Paloma has picked out (and her mother has paid for) all the wedding outfits. Balancing a flower wreath on my head, I make my way carefully down the center aisle wearing a colorful floor-length hippie skirt and a white embroidered peasant blouse. The minister wears an ordinary suit, but Paloma has dressed Gary in a mango-colored East Indian tunic and baggy trousers. Paloma enters after me wearing a long, flowing dress, tie-dyed in rainbow colors and covered with block-printed peace signs. Daisy chains trail down her waist-length red hair, and she carries a bouquet of jaunty wildflowers. As she swaggers down the aisle at an exaggeratedly measured bridal pace, I can see she's having a hard time trying not to burst out laughing.

After the ceremony and a rushed reception with punch, cookies, coffee, and a many-tiered chocolate wedding cake topped with two white doves, Paloma and Gary drive off to a local motel to spend their wedding night.

The next morning, I get a phone call from Daddy. All the other guests have left except Paloma's older sister, Phoebe. Paloma's mom is in the kitchen, cooking our breakfast, when the phone rings.

"Lissa, it's your father." Paloma's mom motions me over to take the call.

"When are you coming home?" Daddy's voice sounds urgent, almost panicked.

"Paloma and her husband are going to drive me up to Maryland day after tomorrow, when they get back from their honeymoon."

"Lissa, I need you here. I fell the other day while Spence was at work. I'd like you to come back right away. I'm not feeling so good."

Now *I'm* panicking. I can't just abandon him. "I'm so sorry, Daddy. I'll come home as soon as I can."

I try to explain the situation to Paloma's mom and Phoebe. "I need to get home as soon as I can. Could someone drive me back to Maryland later today? Phoebe?"

"I think," Phoebe says, "that you ought to wait until they get back. Leaving without saying goodbye to Paloma would be pretty rude."

Overwhelmed by guilt about neglecting Daddy and wounded at the thought of being rude, I burst into tears. Paloma's mom, concerned about my father's health, calls Paloma at the motel. Paloma, who knows me very well, rushes back with Gary, and they drive me home that very afternoon.

CHAPTER SEVENTEEN

I AM THAT I AM

WHEN Paloma and Gary drop me off in Maryland, Paloma says, "I love you, Lissa," and gives me a strong hug at the back door. Gary backs the car around, ready to head back down the driveway, and honks. Paloma hops back in the car and waves, and they head back to Virginia. I guess they want to salvage as much of their honeymoon as they can.

I rush inside the house to make sure Daddy's okay. I find his bedroom door closed—unusual during daylight hours. I tap on the door. No response. I put my head against the door and hear a deep, solemn voice coming from inside. I enter the room slowly. The yellowed paper window shades at both bedroom windows are pulled down to shut out the fading afternoon light.

Daddy is reclining, propped up against the adjustable back support of his Morris lounge chair. A record turns on a portable record player, newly placed across from Daddy on his white marble dresser top. A droning voice intones, at regular intervals, "I am that I am, I am that I am...." From his chair, Daddy repeats those words.

Though I am standing behind Daddy, I can see his reflection in the large mirror that rises nearly ceiling-high, a looking glass opening the narrow bedroom into a duplicate world in another dimension. Daddy's eyes are half-closed. His hands are relaxed, palms up, on the chair's broad cherrywood arms. I tiptoe over to the dressing table and read the label on the record jacket: *Overcome All Pain with Self-Hypnosis.*

"I am that I…Lissa! I'm so glad you're home. I was worried about you." Daddy grabs my hand and squeezes it tight in his as I walk back past his chair. "What are you going to make for supper? I sure did miss your cooking."

I shrug. "Guess I'll have to take a look and see what's in the pantry."

"You'll find a new recipe book on the top shelf. Adelle Davis. Maybe you could try one of her recipes for supper."

"Okay, Daddy. I'll see what I can do."

"You know, Lissa…." Daddy grabs me by the arm as I start to leave the room. "I'll be ninety-one at the end of this month. So, if I eat right, I could live another nine years. I could live to be a hundred. I'm determined to do that, Lissa, so I can be around long enough to see you and Spence grow up and get a good start in life. I don't know what I'd do without my little girl to take care of me. I had to make my own bed while you were gone."

As I head downstairs to start supper, I feel a weariness like old age bearing down on my shoulders, threatening to collapse my spine. I make a grocery list for the missing ingredients in Adelle's stew recipe. She's big on adding yeast as a nutritional supplement.

As winter approaches, Daddy invests more heavily in health foods. He buys a juicer. He takes me with him to visit an old Greek man who makes a special fermented yogurt health drink and bottles it himself. The drink is called *lozak*, and the man who makes it has a disheveled mane of white hair and an ageless face. Thick black nose hairs bristle in his nostrils, and very long, curly gray hairs protrude from both his ears.

Wednesday becomes Daddy's juice day. I help him chop up beets, carrots, celery, an avocado, and a variety of other raw vegetables. He feeds them into the top of a heavy-duty white blender, and out flows a purple concoction that he refrigerates and sips throughout the day. It gives him a purple mustache that he forgets to wash off.

Friday is Daddy's weekly fast day. He begins by squeezing a dozen fresh lemons into a large bowl and pouring the juice into several glass gallon jugs of water. He saves old glass root beer containers from the Twin Kiss ice cream shop for this purpose. Then, from morning until sundown, he eats nothing solid, sustaining himself with glass after glass of lemon water. He breaks his fast on Friday evening with a light fruit salad (which I make for him), a mug of buttermilk, and a glass of fresh-squeezed orange juice, laced with a raw egg and four ounces of milk.

Daddy subscribes to a magazine published in Yucatan by a group of mystics who study the Mayan calendar. He begins to study charts and investigate Mayan calendrics. He learns about the 26,000-year astronomical cycle, the precession of equinoxes that ancient Mayan priests charted with the naked eye. He begins to watch the skies himself, to determine the timing of the world's transition to a more advanced stage of development.

"We're moving toward a time," Daddy tells me, "when humans will be able to communicate telepathically, and be in harmony with all times, all places. Seers will be able to watch for signs and wonders of this approaching era. When the winter solstice sun aligns to bisect the Milky Way, this new age will awaken."

I'm not sure how to react when Daddy conveys this esoteric knowledge to me, so I just listen, watch the skies with him in the backyard, and wait for this time to come. I ask Spence what he thinks about all this.

Spence is just home from work, still dressed in one of the fashionable three-piece suits he wears these days. He shrugs. "I don't think it's scientifically accurate. If you want to study the movements of the planets and the stars, you can use my old telescope, but you really need a much stronger lens, a more powerful telescope, maybe something like 'Big Eye' at Palomar in California."

When I tell Daddy about Spence's advice about using a telescope, Daddy just shakes his head and says, "Magnification won't help. It requires an enlightened subtle eye, an eye with a very sensitive vision. Scientists can't replicate that."

Though the event occurred more than a year earlier, it's not until November 1969 that the My Lai Massacre hits home. The evening news breaks, bringing disturbing TV footage into America's living rooms.

I watch with Daddy as viewers across America learn that a U.S. Army company called Charlie has killed between 200 and 500 unarmed civilians in a hamlet near the northern coast of South Vietnam. On the morning of March 16, 1968, a platoon of American soldiers entered My Lai as part of a search-and-destroy mission to flush out Viet Cong guerrillas. The soldiers were advised by army command that anyone found in My Lai could be considered Viet Cong or active Viet Cong sympathizers. Instead of guerrilla fighters, the soldiers found unarmed villagers—mostly women, children, and old men.

The misguided attack was alarmingly brutal. Villagers were raped and tortured before being killed. Dozens of inhabitants, including young children and babies, were dragged into a ditch and executed with automatic weapons before the massacre was halted. America was left with an indelible blemish on its conduct in the war.

As Daddy gets older, he asks me to do more personal things for him. Once a week, I shave his beard. Daddy stretches out flat on his back on the sofa. I spread a towel over his chest, tucking it under his shirt collar like a bib. From the kitchen, I fetch a basin of water, heated on the stove until it's plenty hot. I dip a fresh washcloth into the basin, wring it out, then press it over his beard to soften it while Daddy lies back with his eyes closed, enjoying being taken care of. When the washcloth begins to cool, I remove it, and lather his beard with a shaving brush and cream. I try to be very careful, but once in a while, I nick one of those tricky spots—like where the jawbone juts out like a knob down below his ear. "Oops! Sorry, Daddy." But he doesn't complain.

When the job is done, I douse him with his favorite aftershave. I dump the soapy water out behind the house. Sometimes, when I come back, he's fast asleep, snoring. I cover him up and look around to see what other chores need to be done. There's always something. I smile when I remember what Paloma's mom says about being a housewife. It's kind of like a mantra for her. "When in doubt, do dishes!"

CHAPTER EIGHTEEN

LATE BLOOMER

THE Vietnam War is at its height when Alice and Grace, two sisters who are friends from high school and church, invite me to become a USO hostess. They've been going to the USO for about a year now, hoping to find husbands.

"Why don't you come with us, Lissa? It's a lot of fun. You'll meet lots of cute guys there. Good husband material."

I'm not really looking for a husband, but I would like to get out of the house and have some fun. When I ask Daddy for permission, his response surprises me.

"Maybe you can find yourself a nice husband there. You can get married and live here with me. You can still take care of me, but you'll have a man to support you after I'm gone."

Daddy checks out the USO. He speaks on the phone with one of the elderly lady chaperones, and is relieved to learn that the USO keeps a careful eye on all its hostesses. Besides, the sisters' mother—whom Daddy calls "a good, decent woman"—is letting her daughters go there.

So, on a warm evening in March, I walk into the Baltimore USO for the first time. I've just ridden into Baltimore with my two girlfriends. Alice finds a cramped parking space in a lot just off an alleyway next to the Odd Fellows Hall, a brick masonry building at Cathedral and Saratoga Streets near the main branch of the Enoch Pratt Free Library. The USO occupies the northern section of the Odd Fellows building. At the northeast corner, *I.O.O.F. 1891, 1931* is chiseled into the cornerstone.

Following behind Alice and Grace, I pass beneath a brownstone entryway through a set of modern glass and steel doors. The front lobby opens onto a large dance hall. We step down onto a polished wood dance floor. From the high ceiling far above us at the center of the room, a lighted, mirrored glass ball slowly revolves. A stage looms at the opposite end of the room; a bank of pool tables flanks the dance floor on the left.

Alice and Grace take me downstairs with them to the ladies' room, where they check their hair, fix their makeup, and make sure their slips don't show.

This basement level is a lounge. Here, besides the men's and ladies' rooms, are a bank of old wooden phone booths, wobbly card tables and folding chairs, lounge chairs, a couple of TVs with rabbit-ear antennas, some end tables with lamps and ashtrays, a couple of Gideon Bibles, and a bookcase filled with tattered paperbacks and back issues of *Reader's Digest*.

When I look in the ladies' room mirror, I think I look pretty good, but I feel a little self-conscious. I'm wearing a fuchsia crepe dress I borrowed from Alice. It's printed with big, gaudy flowers, and it has a low ruffled collar that is open to about four inches below the bottom of my neck. It has a tight skirt that comes in close at the waist and hugs my hips and butt.

"You look sexy, Lissa," Grace says.

I'm not sure how to handle that. When we walk back upstairs, I notice some guys looking at my butt. At least, I think that's what they're looking at.

Upstairs one of the soldiers is acting as a disc jockey, playing records on a turntable. At first, I take a seat on one of the folding chairs lining the walls, and watch Alice and Grace dancing with some of the guys they seem to know. Then the DJ announces a dance contest.

"Okay, now, folks, guys and gals, I'm gonna turn up the volume and play you some Iron Butterfly, "In-A-Gadda-Da-Vida," all seventeen-plus minutes of it. So grab a dance partner, get out there on the dance floor, and do your best to keep it rockin' all the way through to the end. The winning couple gets a pair of movies tickets."

The music starts up. Organ, drums, electric guitar. It's rhythmic, but also loud and aggressive. Right away, a guy comes over and holds out his hand. "May I have this dance?" He seems nice, very friendly.

"Well, I don't really know how to dance to this music."

He smiles and sits down next to me. "Me neither. How about I just sit this one out with you?"

"Okay." He seems relaxed and open, which makes me feel more at ease.

The music pulses on, and it's hard to have a conversation.

"Name's Jack." He leans in close to my ear so I can hear him.

I lean over toward him and say in his ear, "Hi, I'm Lissa."

"A pleasure to meet you, Lissa."

The music goes on and on. Sometimes it gets discordant, and the lyrics are eerie, but sometimes the words sound oddly ethereal to me.

"What kind of music *is* this?" I ask.

"I think this qualifies as hard rock. I heard the title of the song is really a slurred version of "In the Garden of Eden.""

All I can think to say is, "Wow!"

The song finally ends, and my friend Grace and her partner, who have been swerving their hips and gyrating up a storm the whole time, win the contest.

The next song is "Sweet Caroline."

"May I have the pleasure?" Jack says.

I'm a little nervous, but Jack is so charming and has such good manners, I say, "Okay," and he draws me out on the dance floor.

The beat keeps slowing down and speeding up. The couples on the floor seem to be having a hard time deciding whether it's a fast dance or a slow dance. Jack and I start fast, kind of skipping and swaying back and forth separately. But when Neil Diamond starts to sing "Hands, touching hands. Reaching out, touching me, touching you," Jack pulls me in close, and I find myself melting into the beat with him.

On the way home with Alice and Grace, I sit in the back seat, my eyes closed, still hearing those sweet lyrics, "Warm, touching warm, reaching out, touching me, touching you. Sweet Caroline, good times never seemed so good." Dancing with Jack was even better than dancing with the wind.

I see Jack a few more times at the USO. Then he ships out to Vietnam, and I never see him again.

In the spring of 1970, I enter the annual Miss Baltimore USO contest. It's an unusual time to be entering a beauty contest. Women's liberation is gaining momentum. Just two years earlier, women gathered from all over the USA to protest the Miss America Pageant in Atlantic City, New Jersey. Feminists were upset because beauty pageants paraded women like "cattle," emphasizing a woman's physical appearance over other qualities. They felt that these contests made women—those who didn't measure up to certain superficial standards—feel inferior. To show their independence, women tossed bras, curlers, girdles, high heels, eyebrow tweezers, and false eyelashes into "freedom trash cans." Some women burned bras to protest being "pushed up" and uncomfortable; some began to wear no bras at all.

I enter the Miss USO contest anyway. I need to prove something to myself. I've been what you might call a wallflower all through high school—no dating, no real boyfriends. Now I need to prove that I am attractive, that I can win something—something *of* my own and *on* my own. To me, it's kind of like pretending, taking a role in a play. I always wanted to be in the plays at school, but Daddy would never let me stay after school to try out. So now I'm going to go for it!

Long, straight hair is in now. Before the contest, I put my hair up on gigantic rollers to stretch out the curls. I comb my hair out long and straight, parted in the middle. It goes way down below my shoulders to the middle of my back.

As I line up onstage with sixteen other contestants, wearing a super-padded bra and plastering my most winning smile on my face, the voices of female activists rumble around in the back of my mind and jeer at me.

First, we file one by one down and back a floodlit runway, modeling a street dress. I got my dress on sale at Ward's; Spence gave me the money for it. The dress has red and white stripes, very patriotic. It's short, just above the knees. With the white heels, it shows off my legs and ankles. I remember how Daddy used to say he turned me on his lathe, and that I was perfect. Well, I guess I'll have to see if the judges think he was right. I'm relieved we're not asked to model bathing suits.

The judges, we are told, will be grading us on poise, personality, personal appearance, posture, and figure as well as our ability to represent the values of the United States Armed Forces.

Next, we go backstage and change into evening gowns. I'm wearing the same outfit I wore for the senior prom—white satin and lace dress, white heels, and long white gloves, unabashedly virginal. After a second runway walk, this time in our evening gowns, we return to the stage for a "chat with the emcee." He's an upbeat local radio personality.

When it's my turn to "chat," I speak in the clear, well-modulated tones I've practiced at home in front of the mirror. All the contestants have been given a set of possible questions in advance, and I've memorized good answers to all of them.

The emcee reads my question, "Who is your favorite American hero?"

I've lucked out, I think. It's one of the better questions.

I recite my practiced reply, "I would have to say John F. Kennedy. He was a great leader, a great president, and a war hero who had a lot of vigor." I say this sincerely, with respect and wistfulness for our fallen president, knowing that I've chosen the words "war hero" and "vigor" to please the top brass in the audience.

Though I do admire JFK, it occurs to me that one of the first woman aviators, Amelia Earhart, might be a more genuine choice for me. Her courage and pluckiness remind me of Jimmie. I've always wanted to be less timid, more athletic, and more adventurous, like Jimmie.

After responding to the emcee's question, each competitor takes one last walk down the runway toward a soldier in dress uniform waiting at the far end, ready to take that girl's arm and escort her down four carpeted steps to a seat in the audience.

I take my final turn on the runway, careful to exhibit good posture for the women fashion editors and remembering to flash a winning smile in the direction of the male dignitaries in the judges' box. I approach the young Marine who is waiting for me. As I take the first step down, one of my heels catches in the red carpeting. The Marine grabs my elbow just in time to keep me from toppling down the stairs.

"Got you," he whispers.

"Thank you," I whisper back. I keep smiling the whole time—not because I'm poised, but because by now, a perpetual smile is frozen on my face.

I sit with the other contestants in one of the rows of folding chairs they've reserved for us near the rear of the auditorium. We all hold hands, trying hard to control our jitters as the judges make their determinations. Only one of the contestants is black. I sit next to her, and she squeezes my hand tight in anticipation.

First to be announced is Miss Congeniality, the contestant receiving the most votes from the other contestants.

"Marion Johnson," the emcee announces. Marion is the one holding my hand. We hug, and she goes up onstage to receive a small plaque. Next to be announced is the second runner-up, a freckled blonde girl; then the first runner-up, a.k.a. the USO Princess, a dark-haired beauty. I had thought maybe she would win.

Then I hear the emcee say, "This year's winner, our 1970 USO Queen, Miss Baltimore USO, is Lissa Power!"

Somehow, I'm up on the stage. A crystal-studded tiara is being placed on my head by the previous year's winner, and I feel tears streaming down my face.

A photographer from the *Baltimore Sun* takes my picture, and a reporter asks me some questions. I'm not prepared for these questions, so I find myself giving some pretty inane answers.

"What are your plans for the future?" the reporter asks me.

"I'd like to travel. I'd like to be a stewardess for Pan Am."

"Why Pan Am?"

"Because I like their uniforms."

When the interview is over, still dazed, I make my way down the broad staircase to the row of old wooden phone booths at the basement level. I call home. My brother answers.

"I won, Spence! I won!"

"You won?"

"Yeah. You seem surprised. Can you get Daddy to come to the phone?"

A pause. Then, "Okay, I'll get him...you mean you actually won?"

"Yes, I won!"

Daddy picks up the phone. "Hello, Lissa. Spence tells me you won the contest."

"Yes, I actually won!"

"I'm not surprised. I knew all along my little girl would win. It was written in the stars."

As I leave the phone booth, I see the other girls, surrounded by friends and family. My friends Alice and Grace are not in attendance. They're out on dates with other soldiers.

I change into my street clothes and wait outside for Spence to come and drive me home. I realize that being the winner sets me apart somehow. There is only one winner. I leave the USO that night feeling very alone.

Over the next few weeks, I find myself basking in adoring glances and sheepish grins from Midwestern farm boys who have come east to be soldiers. I reign, white-gloved, crowned, and bannered, as Miss Baltimore USO 1970. My picture appears in the *Baltimore Sun*, and I'm given a big gold trophy with an engraved nameplate that says *Miss USO Queen 1970*. All the judges and local USO officials have signed an autograph book for me, filling its gold-speckled pages with their congratulations and good wishes. "Treasure it for your grandchildren," the head chaperone tells me.

It's Preakness Week in Baltimore! Gold and black-eyed-Susan banners blossom overnight on lampposts throughout the city, heralding Baltimore's most important horse racing event, the Middle Jewel of the Triple Crown. The Preakness won't be held until Saturday, but today's midweek racing card features the Miss USO Handicap.

As the May afternoon sky clears, the USO directors escort me to Pimlico Race Course, along with my traditional court of ladies-in-waiting. I wear my white satin pageant gown and the glass crystal-encrusted tiara. A red, white, and blue banner crosses my chest diagonally, its stitched-on gold felt lettering identifying me as Miss USO.

After meeting Pimlico's general manager and dining in the clubhouse on shrimp cocktail and minute steak, I'm hurried down to the winner's circle to present an inscribed silver platter to the winning jockey.

"Kiss him," my princess (first runner-up) whispers, and gives me a nudge. The jockey looks well over thirty, and seems worn-out and harried by the mile-and-one-sixteenth ride. I take one look at this short, mud-spattered South American, and decide he could care less about the USO and its simpering Maryland belles. I just pass him the plate, smile for the photographer, and get out of what seems to be a false situation as quickly as I can.

On the Sunday after Labor Day, amid floats and marching bands, I ride through Baltimore in the "I Am an American Day Parade." I'm perched on top of a sleek red convertible's back seat. The car is draped in swirls of red, white, and blue bunting. I'm wedged between my reigning ruffle-gowned USO princess and the second runner-up. Two medal-decked officers—one army, one Marine—are squeezed into the back seat.

Up front, a navy guy steers the borrowed convertible as it creeps along the downtown parade route. An Air Force guy sits next to him. I wave to crowds of people lining the sidewalks. In support of the peace marches I've seen on TV, I give peace signs to the bystanders. During the ride, the princess leans toward me and whispers, "You know, Lissa, these guys in the car with us? They're too young to have earned all those medals they're wearing. Bet they just bought them for show."

The Marine turns in his seat to look up at me. He's the same guy who kept me from falling down the carpeted stairs during the Miss USO contest. He does look pretty young.

"You remind me of my wife," he says. "She has long hair—a lot like yours." He seems sincere, despite what the princess has just speculated about his medals. I decide to take what he says as a genuine compliment.

"What's your wife's name?" I ask him.

"Betsy. Haven't seen her for a while. Looking forward to my next leave." He pulls out his wallet and shows me a much-handled photo of her.

"She's pretty," I say. "You must really miss her."

He looks at the snapshot, gives a quick nod, and puts it away. "Yep," he says, lips pressed so tight they turn white at the edges.

I alternate between throwing kisses to the older bystanders and exchanging peace signs with the young kids.

"Oh, isn't she pretty!" I hear one woman say. As the parade halts along the way, some kids come running out in the street, asking for my autograph. I sign the notepads or strips of torn paper they hold out to me until the parade marshal comes by and yells at me to stop.

"Don't want some kid getting run over here," he says.

For the moment, we're stuck behind a float bearing a green-painted cardboard Statue of Liberty—she must be about eight feet high from base to torch. An attendant is adjusting the torch, which has begun to wobble precariously in the breeze. Finally, the float lurches forward. Though Lady Liberty careens a bit, she extends her right arm firmly, grasps her torch resolutely, and carries it proudly aloft. Our car inches slowly forward behind her.

In April 1971, I get a letter from Paloma, telling me that Gary has become a conscientious objector and they are moving to Canada, where he can dodge the draft. I, too, am conscientious, but I move in a different direction, one that feels safe and familiar to me. Once again, I find refuge in a world that is separate from my peers. While other kids are following the urgings of Timothy Leary to "turn on, tune in, drop out," I sign up for a couple of evening French lit courses at college. Spence pays for them. I don't have a driver's license. Spence has to drop me off and pick me up from classes two evenings a week, but he is really good about it. He agrees to stay at home to keep Daddy company while I'm gone. Daddy is okay with that. I divide my hours between college classes, books, and time alone at home with Daddy.

At home, I start reading the newspapers and watching the news again with Daddy. My mind echoes with the feminist rhetoric I read, and my ears ring with the antiwar slogans I hear chanted during fragments of peace rallies aired on TV: "One, two, three, four! We don't want your ******* war," "Draft beer, not boys," "Hell no, we won't go," "Bring our boys home," "Make love, not war," "Eighteen today, dead tomorrow." I feel like a fake, a plastic Venus floating on the soapsuds foam of post-JFK Camelot nostalgia.

The pro-war slogans, "Love our country," "America, love it or leave it," and "No glory like Old Glory," leave me feeling confused, conflicted, unsure, and unsafe. I wonder what Paloma would do. I need her advice, but I've lost touch with her since she and Gary moved to Canada. I phone her mother in Virginia.

"Oh, I'm so glad to hear your voice, Lissa. I haven't seen the two of them since they moved to Calgary. You know, they stayed here for a while before they left. Paloma was working as a checkout girl at the grocery store. Gary was having trouble finding a steady job. He did get part-time work as a house painter, but he got depressed. He couldn't stop worrying about being drafted for Vietnam. Tried to kill himself by drinking a bucket of paint. Had to have his stomach pumped.

"Then one day, not long after that, they both drove off to Canada. I guess Gary really didn't want to be drafted. Can't say that I blame him." Then the phone goes quiet. Paloma's mom's breathing is barely audible at the other end.

Finally, she says, "Lissa, I'm worried about Paloma. I'm so afraid she might be getting into drugs again. She doesn't answer any of my letters. In fact, the last few have come back marked "Addressee Unknown."

The next week, I'm scheduled to make a Miss USO appearance at an Orioles baseball game, but the event gets canceled because of a peace demonstration.

The USO is perennially low on funds, so the club retains its cracked vinyl sofas, faded pool tables, and battered old TV sets. And now, to me, it seems frozen in time. The walls of the main room—which serves alternatively as banquet hall, auditorium, and dance hall—are lined with smoke-stained portraits of decrepit USO benefactors and chaperones peering out from antique gold frames. The globe mirror lamp continues to revolve and sparkle like a decadent overhang from a bygone dance-marathon era. Shaded lamps on end tables keep the dark corners of the room just luminous enough for the successful vigil of the hawk-eyed matron chaperones.

I don't drift blithely through the year, picturing myself a star-spangled emblem of America's servicemen. I begin staying away from the club as much as possible, avoiding the curious 1940s atmosphere that permeates Baltimore's USO on Cathedral Street. A dereliction of duty to be sure, but one that is reflected in my fellow students' change in attitude toward the military establishment. At first, this change is barely perceptible to me. Then, sporadically, as American youths' beliefs evolve, the nation's streets erupt in peace marches and antiwar demonstrations. As the months tick past, the war in Vietnam becomes more and more unpopular.

It's with a sense of relief that I dress one last time in banner and crown to officiate at the 1971 Miss USO contest; but the onerous crown, once assumed, is not so easily removed. During the ceremony, my hair becomes knotted around the faux diamonds of the tiara. Before a full and uneasy audience, I struggle for what must be a full minute trying to remove the dubious symbol from my head.

All the past year's hypocrisies flash through my mind. I feel exposed—an imposter pretending to be someone I am not. Just who do I think I am, a so-called beauty queen, parading around on this stage in an evening gown while we send unwilling young soldiers to kill and be killed on foreign soil? What ideals have I been trying to represent with my makeup and my crown and my high heels? Am I perpetuating the superficial and unhealthy view of women that so many feminists are calling into question?

At last, I wrench the crown from my head and lay it to rest on the blonde hair of the new blushing, blue-eyed girl seated on the throne. I wince at the pain in my scalp, then stare at the clump of bloody-rooted brown hairs that cling to the crown, looking like an odd hairpiece on the new queen's head. Below, in the darkened auditorium, the audience roars with applause.

In the summer of 1971, when school is out, I go back to the USO. I meet Joe Stoddard at the club. He's just returned from Vietnam, a second lieutenant in the army. He's a good dancer, tall, sad-eyed. When we talk, he seems attracted by what he calls my "good girl" qualities. He tells me I'm the kind of girl he'd like to take home to meet his parents. Says he'd like to take me out next weekend.

Theoretically, the USO has a no-dating policy for its hostesses, which, I've learned, the other USO hostesses completely disregard. In fact, my friend Grace just got engaged to a Merchant Marine she met there.

One Friday evening, Joe presents himself at our front door in his dress uniform, and I introduce him to Daddy. Joe goes out of his way to be polite with Daddy. As we leave for our date, Daddy says, "You'll take care of my little girl, won't you?"

"Yes, sir," says Joe, and I think he means it.

Even so, when we return to the house from our first date, I can see Daddy, dressed in his long johns, peering down at us from his bedroom window.

I stand talking with Joe on the back step, hesitant to let him in so late at night with Daddy waiting for me upstairs. For a moment, I think Joe is going to try to kiss me, but suddenly, he recoils.

"Roaches!"

He sees water bugs crawling up our back door. Our house has been infested with them for years, so I'm used to them, but Joe is horrified. "Reminds me of the jungles in 'Nam," he says. Soon after, he says goodnight and drives away.

As Joe gets to know me better, he seems fascinated with my persistent virginity. He wants me to study Christian Science with him and visit his parents on the West Coast.

From Joe, I get a vague image of the ugliness of Vietnam.

"I picked up two things in 'Nam," he tells me. "Syphilis and fluent Vietnamese." He assures me he's cured of the disease.

He's just signed up as a lifer in the army, and draws a good salary and extras—but because neither Christian Science nor life as an army wife appeal to me, I stop seeing him and continue with evening classes at college.

Months pass, and I rarely go to the USO anymore, but one January afternoon in 1972, when I'm on a mini-mester break from classes, my friend Alice calls.

"Hi, Lissa. How about going with me to the USO this weekend, just for old time's sake?" I agree to go to the regular Saturday night dance, and I meet a veteran whose vacant blue eyes are so haunting, I find them hard to forget.

When Alice and I arrive, the dance is in full swing. I notice a tall, slender blond man—he seems older than the other soldiers at the club—hovering at the periphery of the dance floor. He wears a long dark overcoat and seems to stare across the dance floor at nothing in particular.

It's not long before Alice and I are asked to dance. Dance after dance, the evening slips by. A horny sailor just off the boat pulls me in tight and tries to grind me at the crotch until one of the chaperones intervenes. A timid young farm boy from Kansas leads me out onto the dance floor with cold, nervous fingers. When he clasps my hand in his, his palm is slippery with sweat. As we begin to dance, the fragrance of his fresh aftershave mingles with the acrid scent of his perspiration. At first, his body trembles almost violently; then, slowly, he begins to relax.

When the music stops, he is red-faced. He thanks me profusely for the dance and offers to buy me a Coke, but before he gets back, a straight-backed academy-trained officer cuts in. I can see the Kansas guy hanging out at the edge of the dance floor holding my Coke. And next to him is the tall blond guy I had noticed earlier. Maybe it's my imagination, but the blond soldier seems to be watching me.

When the current dance is over, I excuse myself and head over to the Kansas guy, who's still waiting with my Coke. Before I reach him, the tall blond guy intercepts me. He looks to be about forty-five, the perfect image of a handsome blue-eyed American soldier you might see in an old war movie. Up close, I can see that his skin is pale, almost gray, and his chin is stubbled. His overcoat is unbuttoned and too large.

He stares at me for a long moment, drawing me deep into the vague shadows in his eyes, plunging me with him into some dark, unspeakable horror.

Finally, he speaks in hollow monotones. "In Korea. I was a pilot in Korea. A bomber pilot. I dropped bombs on people."

I try to respond gracefully, as a good USO hostess is trained to do, but his unwavering stare unnerves me.

"That must have been a while ago," is all I manage to say. He seems puzzled by my words.

"Is it a while ago?" he asks, then turns away from me, wheeling abruptly in an about-face, and walks stiffly away to resume his place at the edge of the dance floor.

I spend the rest of the evening dancing with the younger soldiers, still catching, from time to time, the older soldier's solemn stare. I learn later that he is under psychiatric care, that he is supposedly "harmless" and is allowed weekly outpatient visits to the club. His only "bad habit," I am told, is this persistent telling of his personal war story to every newcomer at the club.

I see him on several occasions after that, approaching new club members to tell his story, like a twentieth-century Ancient Mariner trying to expunge his soul of evil wartime deeds, trapped forever in the mercilessly grinding cogs of combat.

In February, I go back to college for more evening courses, and stop going to the USO. I'm too busy with coursework. The Vietnam War churns on under Richard Nixon, and the kids don't like it. The peace movements on campus are becoming more audible, but I don't take part in any peace marches. The noise and the crowds don't seem peaceful to me, and I guess I'm still on the fence about the war. Aren't Americans supposed to be the good guys? Maybe. Aren't communists our enemies? Maybe not. I am confused, and I am a coward. I just want to be safe. I bury my nose deeper and deeper in French novels and try to avoid thinking too much about American current events.

CHAPTER NINETEEN

QUACKERY AND THROUGH THE WIRE FENCE

D ADDY and I are in the sun parlor, in "Florida," as Daddy calls it. He leans back in his cushioned rocking chair, and I take my customary seat opposite him on the watchmaker's stool. There's no cigar today. Daddy's given them up entirely. His reason: shortness of breath.

"Can't walk down the driveway to the mailbox anymore without getting out of puff. And that's just a little more than a hundred feet. Must be the cigars."

Even though the afternoon sun casts light and warmth through the parlor's bank of south-facing windows, Daddy's voice today is distressed and grim.

"I don't trust doctors, Lissa. Doctors are just a bunch of quacks, and I'll tell you why."

I adjust myself on the stool and wait to hear Daddy tell a story he's told me many times before: a tale he calls "Quackery," about the untimely deaths of his pappy and his sister Katie.

Resting his arm on the rocker's arm, Daddy stretches out his open palm to me and says, "Lissa, today you are a golden butterfly, rimmed in pink. Come settle here on the palm of my hand, and rest content while the dreams are flowing."

I move the stool closer and let him close his hand around mine.

"Once upon a time, on a long-ago day, Lissa, Tulip Hill wore a cloak of sadness. The sky was gray, the rain fell steadily, mist surrounded us. On this day, I lost my favorite sister, Katie.

"Katie was the big sister who walked with me on my first day of school. She held my hand firmly in her own and protected me from the older children's bullying and teasing. I still keep locks of her auburn hair, nested in with her obituaries, in a little cedar box at the bottom of my dresser. Will you keep them for me always, Lissa?"

I nod. This is not the first time he's asked me to do this. I know where he keeps the cedar box. I've seen its contents.

"My Katie was just fourteen when she came down with a strange illness. I was sent to fetch old Doc Turner, our family doctor. Well, he went about examining Katie, saw that her tongue was coated white, and said she must have been eating too many crackers. Told her to lay off those crackers, and she'd be fine in a couple of days. Hurried off to his next patient, never asking how she was feeling or if anything hurt. Well, she hadn't been eating crackers. We had no crackers in the house at that time. Next evening, Katie took to her bed and died.

"A few months passed, and another fog set in over Tulip Hill. That fog hung over us for weeks, shrouding the natural light. Day after day, I walked with Pappy out to the fields at sunup, and back home at sundown. We couldn't see the sun. I had to carry my pocket watch along to gauge the hour. Mists filled the hollows. Tall trees hovered over the edges of the fields like white-shrouded specters overseeing our work.

"An invisible pain began to gnaw deep within Pappy's stomach. But Pappy had seven young mouths to feed and another on the way, so he kept on working the fields. The pain got worse and worse, until finally, he collapsed at the supper table in unbearable stomach pain. He took to his bed, his belly swollen and enflamed. Once again, I fetched old Doc Turner. He instructed my mammy to apply a raw potato poultice to Pappy's abdomen, and had him swallow a hearty dose of castor oil.

"Later that night, Pappy's appendix busted open. By sunup, he was dead. So now you can understand, Lissa, why I don't trust doctors. Look at what happened with your mother. Those so-called surgeons cut her up. Sawed off her breast. Gave her a hysterectomy. And when that didn't stop the cancer from spreading, they burned her up with radiation until the skin on her back was burned raw, and her body couldn't take any more of it. That's when they just filled her full of morphine and let her die."

Although I don't contradict Daddy, I do know that his views about doctors are pretty narrow. And regarding the truthfulness of Daddy's stories, I've come to see that the truth may vary with the telling, and that an old man's fragile memories can shift and move with the sands of time.

Because on other days, Daddy changes his story, and tells me how his pappy was crushed to death by a tulip poplar.

"Long ago, a grove of poplars began to grow on the crest of Tulip Hill. Among the most ancient of these was a tulip poplar more than a hundred feet high. Now, it's been confirmed by wiser minds than mine that, from the time of birth, each of nature's creations carries within its innermost core the exact time—day, hour, and instant—that it is destined to die.

"Well, as it turns out, the time of death for this goliath tree was synchronized with that of my pappy. On one predetermined summer evening, as I stood watching Pappy ride home from the fields on his sure and patient draft horse, Dolly, the colossal tulip poplar came crashing down, crushing Pappy and Dolly beneath it. My two oldest brothers, John and William, came running. They toted Pappy's crushed remains up to his bed. John came back to put Dolly down on the spot, and I was sent to fetch Doc Turner. Doc Turner pronounced Pappy dead, and my brothers set about making a coffin for our father from that very tree."

By the spring of 1972, Daddy's health is failing. He's ninety-three now. His feet are heavy and clumsy, and he has trouble lifting them.

One afternoon, driving home from picking up pizza for us at the local Italian carryout, rounding a curve, his foot slips, and he steps down hard on the gas pedal instead of the brake. Daddy drives the 1964 Corvair Monza—the car he bought not long after Jimmie died to replace the ailing 1950 Olds—through the fence at the abandoned Nike Missile Base. He comes home, carrying the cardboard pizza box. The pizza is fine, and he's not hurt—at least not physically—and his car is still drivable.

"Let's have some of this peesha," Daddy says. Because of his missing teeth, his faulty hearing, or maybe because he never learned to pronounce the word correctly, he always calls it "peesha."

But as we share the pizza, I can see that he is shaken, dejected. He runs his right hand through his hair, and begins to pluck out—one at a time—the hairs near the front of his scalp.

I rush over to Daddy, as I always do when this happens, pull his hand away from his head, and plead, "Please stop pulling the hairs out of your head, Daddy."

Daddy strokes my hand and says, "What would I do without you, Lissa, to watch out for me?" And for a while, at least, he refrains from plucking out his hair.

"This is the first accident I've ever had in all my years of driving," Daddy says. "I'm disgusted with myself. Guess I'm not fit to drive anymore. I'm giving up my driver's license. You're going to have to learn to drive so you can take me to the places I need to go."

While I was in high school, I did take the driver's education course, but I've never tried for a driver's license. I'm not like Jimmie; I've been content letting other people drive me around. Anyway, now Daddy pressures me to get my learner's permit, tells Spence to take me out on a Sunday to practice at Sweeney's empty parking lot. Eventually, Spence drives me to Belair for the driver's test. I've studied for the written part, and selecting all the correct answers is super easy.

Next comes the part where you have to drive an examiner around the block. I'm about to switch on the car's ignition when the examiner asks me for the car's registration card. I can't find it in the glovebox or anywhere in the car. The examiner scowls at me and says, "I can't give you the driving exam until you show me a valid registration. You should be carrying that at all times in your vehicle." Spence drives me back home, where we learn that Daddy has left the car's registration card out on his desk.

Daddy apologizes. "I'm so sorry to make my little girl go through this ordeal twice."

Spence sighs, shakes his head, and resignedly drives me back to Belair. This time, I luck out. I'm assigned a different examiner, who seems much more amiable than the last guy. I do pretty well driving around the block, except for getting a point or two subtracted from my score for not coming to a *complete* stop *before* the stop sign.

The parking test comes next. I'm worried. Parallel parking has never been my strong suit, but again, I luck out. As soon as I manage to back the little maroon car just partway into a very large space, my examiner smiles and says, "Good enough." This time, I go home with a brand-new driver's license. I'm still a little nervous about driving, so I let Spence drive us home until I can get more practice on back country roads.

I show Daddy my license. "I'm so proud of you, Lissa!" And so, at the age of twenty-one, I become Daddy's chauffeur.

CHAPTER TWENTY

BABY STEPS

WEEKS go by. My life is going nowhere fast. I need to find a good way to earn money for myself, to become more independent. I remember what the Hutzler's fashion director said to me, and I think maybe I can make a living being a fashion model. I could try contacting that woman, but I don't remember her name, and besides, that was more than five years ago. She's probably not even there anymore. Instead I look up local modeling agencies in the yellow pages, find one downtown that looks promising, and talk to Daddy about it.

Daddy keeps saying, "I need you here to take care of me, Lissa. It's a hard world out there. You'll never find anybody who'll treat you as well as I do."

I get angry with Daddy. I yell at him and say, "The more I do around here, the less I get." I cry, run away from him, out behind the corn crib, which is falling apart now. Beside it, a sapling grows inside the part of the barn where Granddaddy Friedrich used to park his tractor. The slender tree has pushed its way up and poked a hole in the barn roof. I collapse in a pile of fallen boards and sit facing a jungle of poison sumac and other weeds that have grown up thick and tall, choking out what used to be Jimmie's vegetable garden.

Eventually, Daddy comes out to find me. "What's wrong with you? I don't recognize my little girl anymore. Have you gone crazy?"

I don't answer. He shakes his head and goes back to the house. When it gets dark, I come back in and fix supper.

A frantic anger seems to be surging up inside me, a raw energy I don't know what to do with. I try to channel it in some positive way. Desperate to fix up the house, to make things better, I pull my hair back tight in a bun like Jimmie's, tie a scarf over my head, and repaint all the chipped white kitchen cabinets an avocado green to match the teapot I keep on the stove to boil water for tea or instant coffee. With a trowel, I tear up the buckled, gritty bathroom floor tile and replace it with squares of inexpensive linoleum I pick out in the Montgomery Ward catalog and get Spence to buy for me—for the house. At night, I sneak out to Daddy's woodshop and use his jigsaw to cut curved pieces of linoleum to fit around the toilet, then set it all in place with black adhesive. Sweaty and sticky, I am briefly satisfied.

Then I see ads on TV showing a thrifty, tidy housewife lining her kitchen drawers with adhesive vinyl contact paper. Once again, I consult the catalog. This time, I order rolls and rolls of contact paper—marbled avocado green for the kitchen, flocked gold for the bathroom. Once again, Spence pays for these quick-fix home improvements, and I go about cutting, peeling, and sticking contact paper—in kitchen drawers and on pantry shelves, above the kitchen sink and stove, on the walls above the bathtub. Daddy seems to watch me warily, but he doesn't ask any questions, and Spence doesn't complain about the money. I think they both just want to keep me satisfied with the way things are.

Eventually, Daddy agrees to check out a modeling agency downtown. I'm still too new a driver to feel comfortable driving downtown, so we take the number eight bus, walk a block, turn down a Baltimore side street, mount wide marble steps to an old stone office building, and pass through an elegant tile vestibule. Once inside, we are directed by a secretary to the director's office.

We find the agency director—a heavily made-up woman, probably in her forties or fifties, with dyed black hair pulled back in a sophisticated French twist—seated behind a wide desk in a small office. Photos of young models line the walls. Daddy and I sit side by side in leather chairs across from the director.

"Tell me a little about yourself," she says.

I try to think of something that might impress her. "I was Miss Baltimore USO. Just recently, 1970," I tell her.

"That's good, good," she says in a deep smoker's voice, turning her head to one side and blowing out a stream of smoke through a corner of her mouth. She crushes her cigarette against the base of a steep ashtray, and I notice that the dark red lipstick stains on the cigarette butt match the glossy polish on her fingernails.

"Mount Vesuvius," she says, glancing down at the ashtray with an ironic smile. She coughs a deep, wet smoker's cough, then pauses a moment to study my facial features.

She smiles over at Daddy, who is holding my hand. "She's a pretty girl. We can work with her, show her how to use eyeliner and shadow and mascara to open up those eyes."

Daddy tugs on my hand to let me know he's eager to leave.

"I'll have to talk it over with my father," I say. Daddy has already gotten up to leave.

The director lights another cigarette, hands over a packet of information about the agency, and shakes hands with Daddy and me.

We haven't walked a block when Daddy says, "That brazen bat, all painted up like a whore! I'm not going to let her get her hands on my little girl."

A few weeks later, when Daddy seems to have calmed down, he agrees to go with me to a modeling school in Towson. Here, on the top floor of a modern office tower, the director chats with us in a spacious room. We sit in a casual grouping of chairs facing a bank of sunlit floor-to-ceiling windows. Daddy gets along okay with this woman, and gives me his permission to enroll here. To pay for modeling school, I take a job as a nurse's aide at the Masonic nursing home, a.k.a. Bonnie Blink, in Cockeysville. Daddy is very pleased with this.

"When you take care of the old folks there, you'll learn how to take good care of me."

Bonnie Blink—an old castle built in Scotland, dismantled, and reassembled in Cockeysville, Maryland—stands watch over Shawan Road from the crest of a hill.

On my first night, with some trepidation, I drive the little maroon Corvair up a long, steep driveway to the stone-clad home where aging Masons and their wives go to spend their final years. I've been hired to work the graveyard shift, eleven P.M. to seven A.M. It's called that, the nursing director has warned me, because that's when most of the residents' deaths occur.

The nurse who supervises me explains that some of the geriatric residents, who seem pretty normal during the day, tend to behave a little strangely at night. On my first night, the supervising nurse takes me and another new aide, a girl named Stephanie, on rounds in the assisted living ward to show us the ropes and meet an unforgettable cast of characters.

Here, we meet old Mr. Tyson. "Mr. T. is senile," the nurse advises us.

As we pass by his bed, he reaches out and grabs Stephanie by her arm. She shrinks back—but not in time to avoid getting smeared with the feces Mr. T. has hidden in his other hand. Stephanie, whose face has gone as white as the nurse's uniform, is given a break so she can wash up and collect herself. Mr. T.'s behavior is so absurd I find myself trying to suppress a nervous laugh.

While Stephanie is gone, the nurse introduces me to an elderly man with a pacemaker who makes no sign of recognition, and never says a word, as we change his bedsheets. "You'd never know it to look at him now," the nurse tells me, "but he used to be a physician."

When Stephanie returns, we move on to the women's section. We have to lift a short but amazingly heavy old lady nicknamed Turtle onto a potty chair beside her bed. Turtle's gray hair is clipped very short, and with her false teeth removed for the night, she strongly resembles a snapping turtle. When asleep, Turtle snores, and the air escaping her puckered lips makes a popping noise. Turtle shares a room with three other old ladies, one of whom is called Squirrel.

Squirrel likes her hospital bed cranked up to its most elevated position. There she perches, chattering to herself as she rummages through crumpled bits of paper and colored cellophane candy wrappers that she hoards in the folds of her sheets and blanket. When the volume of Turtle's popping and Squirrel's chattering gets too loud, it wakes the other two ladies in the room, who begin to moan in unison like a weird Greek chorus.

Over the first week, the nursing supervisor teaches Stephanie and me how to take a patient's pulse and blood pressure. She teaches us how to change a bedridden patient's soiled bed linens while the patient's still in the bed—roll the patient onto her side; roll up the soiled sheet behind her; unroll and spread a fresh sheet halfway across the cleared section of the bed; lift and roll the patient over the soiled roll onto her other side and onto the clean sheet; finish rolling the soiled linen and take it off the bed; unroll the fresh sheet the rest of the way across the bed; roll the patient once more, so that she's lying flat on her back. Easy enough when the nurse is helping us do it. But when the nurse is called away and Stephanie and I are left to do the same thing for the next patient, we wind up rolling this poor patient, a Mrs. Pettipoint, back and forth more than we should, getting her catty-cornered and nearly off the bed a few times before we finally get it right.

We apologize to Mrs. P., but she only smiles sweetly and says, "It's nice to spend time with you girls. My children never come to visit me."

Stephanie resigns after the first week.

I arrange to work on weekends, so I have two nights off in the middle of the week. On those two evenings, I go to modeling classes. Now I regret dropping out and forfeiting my college scholarships. I'm trying to save my paychecks and put them toward college tuition for the coming fall semester, but right away, I have to lay out money to buy a professional makeup kit, complete with false eyelashes. Spence keeps forking out money for me. He doesn't seem to mind paying for me, but I feel guilty about it. I really do want to be independent someday.

"I'm going to get my college degree someday," I keep saying. "Then I'll pay you back, Spence. I promise."

Beautiful young models instruct aspiring student models like me about skin care, nutrition, the tricks of applying professional makeup, how to do walks and turns on a runway, how to diet, how to dress, and which kinds of bras and girdles to put on underneath it all. The instructors are very tall and very thin.

All the modeling students are given a diet plan, which I take very seriously—too seriously. I make a goal in my head to get rid of all my fat and become model-thin. I carry a pocket-size notebook replete with charts that show me how to calculate calories and serving portions for everything I eat. I compete with myself to take in fewer and fewer calories each day. I learn to fill up on things like quarts of plain nonfat yogurt, piles of steamed cauliflower, a hard-boiled egg.

My skin begins to dry out. My legs start to show indentations around the insides of the knees where fat used to be. Watching the fat melt away makes me feel good. I'm achieving the goal in my head. I'm making progress! I'm obeying the strict rules I've set for myself. For now, I'm safe.

Every day, I measure my waist with Jimmie's old yellow cloth tape measure. I check my weight on the scales several times a day. I buy myself a new white nurse's aide dress at Ward's. I'm so proud of myself. I've gone from a size eleven down to a size seven. I've lost twenty pounds, and still counting!

In June 1972, Hurricane Agnes wreaks havoc from Maryland through New York State, inundating the Mid-Atlantic Region with nearly ten inches of rain. In Maryland, Agnes takes nineteen lives—among those, the father of a girl who graduated from my high school a year ahead of me. Her father drowns trying to drive through the old underpass on York Road in Cockeysville. The local roads are flooded. My supervisor at the nursing home advises me to stay at home until the waters recede.

I spend the flood days at home with Daddy, surrounded by dark storms. I run around the house, setting out pans and buckets to catch rainwater as it seeps through seams in the ceiling, drips down walls, and leaves ugly stains on the wallpaper. Daddy frets that water dripping down through the roof into his woodshop will rust his precious machinery. He wears himself out drying off, oiling, and buffing the woodworking lathe, the table saw, the jigsaw, the shaper, the grinders.

In the evenings, Daddy and I retreat to the dining/living room and pass the time with storytelling. I listen to Daddy's stories about his younger brother, Francis, and about how Daddy saved his brother's life.

"I was the next youngest of eight children," says Daddy. "Francis was the only one younger. Soon as he was born, my mammy told me I should be my brother's keeper, so I always tried to look after him. Francis was always the quiet one."

Daddy keeps a picture of Francis in an oak frame on the table beside his armchair. Francis looks back at us with gentle gray eyes behind gold-framed glasses. His smile is thin and fragile.

"I took Francis under my wing and taught him all I knew about watchmaking. You probably don't remember your Uncle Francis. You were just about a year old when he died. He and I were the only two left, after my brothers Clement and Bradley died out at the old Eudowood Sanatorium. They both got tuberculosis working as shirt pressers at the Empire Steam Laundry on Fayette and Front Streets. They worked hour after hour in a fumy closed room, using gas irons that leaked."

Sometimes, this story, like so many others, changes with the telling, and Daddy takes me down a different rabbit hole, in which these brothers—or at least one of them—developed TB after being exposed to poison gas while fighting on the Western Front in World War I.

"My mammy died when she was eighty-six. I remember she had cooked supper and washed up the dishes, like always. Then, after she'd been sitting a while doing her mending, she looked over at me, and said, 'Well, Stouten, I guess my little day's work is done,' and went up to bed. She died in her sleep that night."

"I think that's how I'd like to go," I say. "Nice and peaceful."

"Well, let's hope you've got a long ways to go yet," Daddy says, and continues his story.

"So, me and Francis, just the two of us, we set up a watch repair shop at the front of our old row house at 629 Franklintown Road. We each had our own watchmaker's bench, facing opposite walls. We sat with our backs to one another. Each bench was equipped with its own lathe, its own glass alcohol burner, and a container of benzene solution for cleaning watches. We bent down close over our work, each of us wearing a loupe screwed into his eye.

"Well, one gray day in autumn, Francis knocked over his alcohol lamp. The flame followed the trail of spilled alcohol, leapt up onto the cuff of Francis's work coveralls, and raced up the long gray sleeve. I heard the lamp fall, and turned around just in time to see my brother go up in waves of flame.

"I lunged over to Francis, grabbed the container of benzene, and moved it away before it could combust. Then I ran to the hall coatrack, seized my own heavy wool overcoat, pushed Francis to the floor, rolled him in the overcoat, and smothered the flame. Smoke and the smell of singed cloth hung in the air, but Francis was okay, with only minor burns up his right arm.

"That time, I was able to save my brother's life."

Daddy pauses in his storytelling to stare out at sheets of rain coursing down the front windows. Then he resumes. "But there came a time I couldn't save him. He got so he couldn't walk right. Didn't know what was wrong. Had trouble stepping down off curbs. Looked like he was drunk. Came to find out he had a brain tumor. Died on the operating table."

After the flood, I go back to work at Bonnie Blink. All summer, I work the graveyard shift. It's weird driving home in the morning when most everyone else is driving in the opposite direction to go to work. It's also hard to sleep in the daytime. Even though I pull down all the paper shades in the bedroom, sunlight seeps in below them. My sleep is sporadic. Vague, unsettling dreams are interrupted by traffic, lawn mowers, and the shouts of kids from a nearby swimming pool.

My supervisor moves me to the independent-living wing where residents are still ambulatory. Here, there's not much to do during the night except give out a placebo—a sugar pill—to one woman if she rings her bell, and make one round toward morning to collect and clean potty chairs that residents set outside their doors at night.

Mrs. Mott, the old woman who gets the sugar pill, rings for it at least once every night. Her room is at the very end of the hall, a long walk from the nurse's station. Each time she rings, I make the long journey, carrying a paper cup containing one white sugar pill.

"Did you bring my calming pill, sweetie?" Mrs. Mott resembles so many of the residents here. Old age has shriveled her stature, sagged her skin, melted her features, distorted her voice, blurred her vision, stolen her teeth, and confiscated most of her hair. She is barely distinguishable as a woman, or even as a human being. Like the Saggy Baggy Elephant, her skin sags everywhere that skin can sag—under the eyes, at the neck, under the arms, at the ankles. Her nightgown covers amorphous bulges. Age has turned her into a blob of unrefined flesh.

Every night, Mrs. Mott and I go through the same routine. First, she examines the pill with a magnifying glass. "Are you sure this is my calming pill, sweetie?"

"This is your pill, Mrs. Mott."

"Well, all right. If you say so." Her hand trembles so much, I have to pour the water for her from the bedside carafe and support her wrist as she lifts the water glass to her mouth.

"My husband was a Mason, you know."

"Yes. That's what you told me."

"Name was Charlie. I sure do miss my Charlie. We were together for nearly fifty years. That's why it's so hard for me to stay calm at night. He was a lovely man."

"Good night, Mrs. Mott. Sleep well," I say.

Each night, as I reach for the wall switch to turn out Mrs. Mott's light, I pause to look at the photograph on her dresser—a beautiful and radiantly smiling young woman—a dead ringer for Rita Hayworth in her prime.

Finally, I ask Mrs. Mott. "Who is this beautiful woman? Is this your daughter?"

"That was me," Mrs. Mott says. "Who took my face?"

That wing is kind of spooky at night when I'm sitting by myself at the nurse's station, staring down the long shadowy hall. Occasionally, a resident will awaken in the middle of the night and come wandering toward me, restless or disoriented. One old fellow gets up routinely at about three every morning, shuffles down to the nurse's station, pulls up a chair, and does a crossword puzzle. I try to chat with him, but he's extremely hard of hearing, worse than Daddy.

One night, I hear a helicopter hovering over the grounds; through the windows I can see its searchlight sweeping across the lawn. A guard comes by with a flashlight to alert me that the police are searching outside for an escaped prisoner.

And one morning, not long before I go off duty, there's a kerfuffle down the hall in Room 16, when the nursing supervisor tries to give old Mrs. Foster an enema. The old lady goes berserk and tries to assault the nurse with a butter knife purloined from the dining hall. I see orderlies called in. A wild-eyed Mrs. Foster is put in a straitjacket and hauled off to Sheppard Pratt—and not for the first time, I'm told.

Another night, I'm told the resident of Room 9 has been moved to an intensive care unit. Passing the foot of her bed, I can see her lying flat on a narrow bed, her massive form rising and falling heavily under an oxygen tent. When I arrive the next night, I'm told she will probably pass tonight, and sure enough, by morning, she is gone.

Every morning at about 5:30, I make my potty chair rounds. Wheeling a clanking metal handcart, I pick up the filled potties residents leave outside their doors during the night. I clean them in the bathroom and deliver them back to the appropriate room no later than 6:45 A.M. As I set each clean potty down, I rap on the resident's door, then move on down the hallway. Each potty is labeled with the resident's last name. I'm careful to return the correct potty to its owner. I've been told the residents make quite a fuss if their potties get mixed up.

The little lady in Room 11, I'm told, never speaks to anyone. Apparently, she has no visitors, no family. Her name is Miss Andersen. She is tiny and birdlike in her movements, always quick to come to her door when I rap on it. Each morning, she smiles and bobs her head in appreciation. On my last morning at work before starting back at school, when Miss Andersen comes to grab her potty, she smiles, places something in my hand, darts back inside, and quickly shuts the door.

She's given me a hand-embroidered lace handkerchief. Nestled inside the hankie is a tarnished silver pin. I will treasure it.

Modeling school graduation is marked by a fashion show for our parents and a photo shoot with a professional photographer. I model a hot pink boiled wool sleeveless sheath dress—a hand-me-down from Paloma's older sister, Phoebe—and a floor-length satin gown the color of black cherries I found packed away in my mother's hope chest. Daddy tells me he bought it for Jimmie for their honeymoon. Nobody in my family comes to see me in the fashion show, but I'm okay smiling and posing for the other girls' parents in the audience.

The photographer puts together a good portfolio for me, wishes me luck, and says he's enjoyed working with me.

I have a final consultation with the fashion school director. She tells me I should have my nails done professionally, and suggests I have red highlights put in my hair.

I keep working at Bonnie Blink until the end of summer. One night, hunger pangs get the best of me. I go off my model's diet and binge on ice cream in the nursing home's kitchen. When I go home, I eat half a loaf of bread, then try to make myself throw it up.

It's then I realize it's time to go back to college. My body is starving, and so is my mind.

CHAPTER TWENTY-ONE

BIDING TIME

IN the fall of 1972, I go back to college part-time in the evenings. I'm trying to complete two majors: French and English.

This year, a little before Halloween, I decide to take on another job. I go through the classified ads in the *Sunpapers* and find that Hutzler's, Baltimore's iconic department store, is taking on additional staff for the upcoming holidays. I apply for a part-time job as a sales-girl at their Towson store. I am able to schedule my work hours for the evenings I'm not taking classes. This should work out; I can fix supper for Spence and Daddy right before I leave, and Spence will be home with Daddy while I'm away in the evenings.

Hutzler's is a high-end Baltimore clothing store, one of the three H's—Hutzler's, Hecht's, and Hochschild's. My family always shops for clothes at five-and-dimes like Woolworth's or Kresge's or at low-er-end department stores like Montgomery Ward. In fact, before getting this job at Hutzler's, the only time I ever stepped inside one of their stores was the summer when I was fourteen and Paloma and her mom took me shopping for a new school dress at Hutzler's downtown.

After my initial training sessions at Hutzler's Towson, I'm assigned to the handbags and music box department, a square space enclosed by four counters on the first floor. My supervisor is a veteran saleslady, a matronly woman who wears a tasteful skirt and sweater set and peers out at me over half-glasses attached to a jeweled lanyard.

Under her watchful eye, I greet customers who come to my counter, show them the merchandise they're interested in, and pull down sumptuous leather handbags from display racks or gingerly remove delicate music boxes from glass cases beneath the counters. If I make a sale, I fill out a sales slip and its carbons in a small notepad, ring up the sale on the cash register, and put the item into a Hutzler's bag of the appropriate size.

For me, the hardest part of the job happens one evening when a customer asks me to put her purchase in a gift box. As I attempt to unfold the cardboard box and awkwardly begin to line it with tissue paper, the woman becomes increasingly impatient, glares at me, and finally yells, "Stop! Stop!" Displaying great frustration, she grabs the box away from me, shouting, "Here, let me do that."

With a self-satisfied flourish, she completes what should have been my task, gives the more experienced saleslady a knowing look, and exits, bearing her package with stiff-backed pride out to the parking lot.

I feel pretty inept as a salesgirl, so I'm not surprised when I'm laid off before the end of the holiday season. I am called back for one day to help with inventory, and wind up spending my day in a large supply closet, clipboard in hand, poking through shelves of miscellaneous merchandise and recording the stock on hand. I *am* surprised to learn that Hutzler's stocks toilet paper. Tallying roll after roll of bathroom tissue and other items seems to reactivate my earlier struggles with counting. I find myself counting and recounting each item multiple times to assure myself that I'm entering the correct numbers on the tally sheet.

Daddy's prostate trouble is getting worse. He gets up more and more frequently at night to pee. The urine doesn't want to come out, and when it does, it stings.

Rather than see a doctor, Daddy submits himself to all kinds of home remedies. He reads somewhere that elevating the bottom of your bed can reduce the urge to go at night. Using two paint buckets, he props up the foot of his bed.

He begins to take daily sitz baths. First, he sets a plastic dish tub in our old cast-iron porcelain bathtub, fills the small tub with hot water, pours in a cup of Epsom salts, and stirs the water until the salts dissolve. Then he strips from the waist down, lowers himself into the salt solution, and soaks his private parts until the water cools. He calls me to help him into and out of the tub.

Daddy also tries applying a heated massager, wrapped in a clean sock, directly to the area of his prostate.

When these therapies fail to solve the problem, Daddy asks me to drive him to a prostate specialist in Mount Vernon. The doctor arranges for prostate surgery. He also informs me that Daddy's spine has collapsed due to old age.

Daddy undergoes the surgery at Union Memorial Hospital. He's released the same day. As I drive him home, he curses the doctor. Tells me they gave him a spinal block, and he was in a lot of pain. Says he could hear an old woman moaning down the hall from him.

After his surgery, Daddy never seems to recover fully. "These god-damned doctors," he says. "They're butchers, I tell you. Should never have given me that spinal block. Can't lift my feet at all now. Can barely shuffle around."

With Spence's help, Daddy puts up handles on either side of the bathroom doorway to hold onto when he has to get up at night. He has me try to hold onto his arm and walk him around the backyard for exercise, but he can only walk a few yards. Day after day, he loses mobility.

Soon, Daddy is no longer able to work in his shop or at his watch-maker's bench. He spends most of his time either seated in his armchair in the dining/living room, in front of the TV, or resting in the Morris chair in his bedroom. He complains that the light has gone out of his eyes; that everything looks dark to him, even when the sun is shining.

On a Saturday afternoon in late November, I take a break from studying and pull out a record album I bought a few months ago, *Jesus Christ Superstar*. I find Daddy resting in the Morris chair in his bedroom, listening to the old self-hypnosis record. "I am that I am, I am that I am" drones on as the record revolves slowly on the turntable. Around the base of Daddy's record player, lined up on the Victorian dresser's white marble slab, an assortment of homeopathic remedies in bottles, vials, flasks, tubes, jars, and atomizers waits. Daddy's minions, at the ready!

I lift the needle and put on the new album. I sit on Daddy's bed, listening with him to the entire rock opera. Daddy says nothing. He seems half asleep, lost in thoughts of his own, until the final number, "John Nineteen: Forty-One," begins to play.

At the sound of nails being driven into the cross, Daddy seems to waken. He sits up, leans forward, and cups both ears to hear the last words of Christ:

God forgive them. They don't know what they're doing.

We are accosted with sounds of raucous, derisive laughter, rising and fading away.

Supernatural voices vibrate, drone, and hum, accompanied by eerie background music. Then Christ's voice calls out again, above the miserable plunking of a single piano:

Who is my mother? Where is my mother?
My God. My God. Why have you forgotten me?

The eerie music and voices continue. Then:

I'm thirsty. I'm thirsty!
Oh, God, I'm thirsty.
Oh, I'm thirsty. I'm thirsty. Oh.
Thirsty.

Voices and background music swell.

It is finished.

The music is more pained and urgent now, shrieking.

Father, into Your hands I commend my spirit.

All sound stops for a brief pause, like the space between two breaths. There is a sweet musical reprise. Then, abruptly, the album ends in dead silence.

Daddy leans his head back in his chair, closes his eyes, and after a few minutes, seems to drift off to sleep. I tuck a frayed old quilt Daddy's mother made around his legs, and tiptoe out to let him nap.

The next day, I find an index card on the desk in Daddy's office beside his red mechanical pencil. On the card, printed in large block letters, is: "I WANT TO DIE." The "N" is printed backward; the perfectionist's handwriting has become dyslexic.

I take the index card with me and go to find Daddy in the dining/living room. He's in his chair, napping in front of the television. I turn off the TV, sit nearby on the sofa, and study for a biology exam while I wait for him to wake up.

I've started a load of wash in the cellar. Suddenly, the old washer jerks into an off-balance spin cycle and begins to make a racket as it walks across on the concrete floor just below Daddy's chair. He starts awake, pulls a soiled white hankie from his pants pocket, and wipes drool from his chin. I use Daddy's index card note to mark my place and close the textbook. I've just started to review a chapter on DNA and the double helix.

"I'm going to run down and fix the washing machine," I say. "When I get back, how'd you like me to trim your toenails for you, Daddy?" I know Daddy loves to relax and soak his feet in his favorite bran and borax foot soap.

"That'd be real nice, Lissa," he says. "Don't know what I'd do without my little girl to take care of me."

As Daddy soaks his feet, I ask him, "Daddy, don't you still want to live to be a hundred? You always said that's what you wanted to do."

"Careful what you wish for," Daddy tells me. "You know, I wanted to be around long enough to see that you and Spence could fend for yourselves. Looks like Spence is doing pretty well these days. Seems to be the golden boy down at the bank. Making good money now. More than I ever made."

I pull one of the chairs in from the kitchen and sit opposite Daddy. I pull his right foot out of the soaking tub, pat it dry with a hand towel, and rest it on a larger bath towel that's spread across my lap.

"And you, Lissa," Daddy continues. "You don't need me anymore. I'm just in your way here."

Beginning with the big toe, I use the pointed toenail clipper attachment to dig out gook from beneath the nail and push back the cuticle. The nail is too long. I pinch the clipper around it, start to clip it shorter.

Then, as always, Daddy shouts, "Ouch! Careful there, Lissa. That's my toe under there."

Then, as always, I say, "I am being careful, Daddy." This habitual call-and-response dialog is repeated for each toe.

"Daddy, don't die," I say. "I need you to tell me stories, tell me right from wrong, tell me I'm your little squirrel ears. You need to be around so we can read each other's mind." When both of Daddy's feet are done, I massage them with Jergens lotion.

"Well, you know, Lissa, I'll always be close by. I'll be a great escape artist, just like Houdini. And I promise you, if there's any way I can wriggle my way out of the locks and chains of death, I'll come back here to be with you. And even if I can't come back here on Earth, I will always be watching you from afar."

As the days pass, Daddy becomes more and more dependent on me. Finally, when he can't go up and down the stairs anymore, he spends his days either in bed or propped up in the Morris chair to eat the meals I serve him on a lapboard that's balanced across the chair's wide, sturdy wooden arms.

Daddy keeps an old bicycle horn beside his bed and honks for me when he needs me to help him get to the bathroom. He leans on me as we walk. When we reach the toilet, I turn him to face me, help him get his pants pulled down, and help him lower his bony emaciated butt onto the toilet seat. Sometimes he asks me to wipe his bottom for him, or pull out a sticky chunk of poop. I get poop on my hands, sometimes embedded under the fingernails. I become obsessed with handwashing. I scrub my hands over and over, many times, in multiples of four. I pour rubbing alcohol over them. I scrub them with a brush. My hands become red and raw. Sometimes, they bleed. It's hard to feel safe these days.

Spence is away all day, working hard at the bank so he can support us financially. I study hard and get good grades. One day, I notice that the bricks are starting to crumble and fall off the top edges of the chimney. Another day, I notice the pendulum on the Regulator kitchen clock has stopped. I wind the clock and push the pendulum with my finger, but nothing I do can make it run again.

CHAPTER TWENTY-TWO

RIPPING OUT
THE LIFE SUPPORT

IT's late at night—just past midnight, according to my wristwatch. I'm at the kitchen table, books and papers spread out. I'm working on a report for French class that examines Flaubert's commentary on nineteenth-century provincial life in *Madame Bovary*. I've just begun to posit that the social context was responsible for Emma Bovary's boredom and eventual suicide when Daddy cries out, "Lissa, come here!"

I run upstairs to Daddy's bedroom. He's sitting up in bed, grasping his chest and breathing fitfully. Between gasps, he says, "Lissa, get me an ambulance."

"What's wrong, Daddy?"

"I'm having a heart attack! Call the fire department."

I do as he says, and within minutes, the ambulance arrives, manned by volunteers. The driver is the pharmacist at our local drugstore. He's assisted by a pretty blonde woman. I recognize her from high school. She used to ride the same school bus.

I'm embarrassed that our house is so shabby. I'm glad it's too dark for them to see how much dust I've let accumulate on the furniture, floors, and stairs.

I ride beside Daddy in the ambulance. The young woman I know from high school—I remember now her name is Cassie—goes about her work, checking Daddy's vitals. I wonder if she remembers me, but I don't say anything.

We pass through Grangerville. The town is no longer the quiet rural crossroads our Oldsmobile transported us through on weekend visits to Grandma and Grandpa's farmhouse, so many years ago. New buildings are going up—banks, restaurants, a video store, a strip mall anchored by a supermarket and a 7-Eleven. A liquor store thrives next to the old hardware store. Some people are calling Grangerville a boom town, and we hear rumors of further expansion.

En route, we get stuck behind a long, slow dairy truck that seems to be returning to the Beltway after delivering milk to the new supermarket that's putting Sweeney's out of business. The pharmacist sounds the siren, the truck pulls over, and we zip past on our way to St. Joseph's Hospital in Towson.

Daddy is whisked off to an emergency room. I stay behind in the waiting room. In the panic of getting Daddy to the hospital, I've forgotten to bring along any reading material from school. I'm wasting precious time. I could have been studying. I soothe myself by reciting, over and over, the opening lines from Ronsard's famous carpe diem poem: *Mignonne, allons voir si la rose qui ce matin avait déclose....* Sweetheart, let us go see if the rose that unfolded this morning....

Between three and four A.M., Daddy is released from the hospital. The doctor comes out to chat with me briefly, telling me it was a false alarm. Not a heart attack. But he recommends that Daddy see a geriatric specialist.

I call Spence, and he comes to drive us home in the Corvair; his new sports car is only a two-seater. An attendant delivers Daddy to the car in a wheelchair. I sit with him in the back seat.

"So, how'd it go? Are you okay, Daddy?"

"Yes. I think I'm all right now, Lissa." Daddy's voice is amazingly calm. "When I first got here, they called in a priest. He gave me the Last Rites, performed Extreme Unction on every part of my body, asked God to pardon me of whatever sins I may have committed. It was good to hear those words after all these years, '*Per istam sanctan unctionem et suam piissimam misericordiam, indulgeat tibi Dominus quidquid per....*' I'm grateful to that priest. I feel as if some burden has been lifted. I'm relieved."

Daddy does have me make an appointment for him with the recommended geriatric specialist, Dr. Tan, a slender Asian man with delicate hands and a gentle demeanor. He has Daddy checked into Greater Baltimore Medical Center for observation.

I visit Daddy after his first round of tests. "How are you, Daddy?"

He's sitting up in bed. "I'm so glad to see you, Lissa. They've been poking and prodding me since early this morning. A man can't get any rest around here."

"So, what did the doctors tell you about your tests?"

"You tell me, Lissa. You used to be able to read my mind."

"I don't think I can do that anymore, Daddy. Guess I grew out of it."

"You used to promise me you'd never grow up, that you would always be my little girl and sit on my lap."

"The nurse tells me you're not eating much of anything. You should try to eat something." Daddy looks thinner and frailer than ever.

"I don't like hospitals or hospital food. I miss your home cooking."

"So, what did the doctors say?"

"They told me I have the most beautiful organs they've ever seen in a ninety-four-year-old man. What do you think about that?"

"That's good to hear," I say and squeeze his hand.

After a few days in the hospital, Daddy stops eating altogether. He begins to fret, and tries to rip out the IVs.

A doctor I've never seen before stops by Daddy's room while I'm there, and asks if he can have a few words with me. This doctor is young, efficient, all business. "Your father's senile. There's nothing more we can do for him here."

"Senile?" The word catches me by surprise. It sounds harsh and impersonal. My daddy, senile? I've never thought of him that way. Some of the patients at Bonnie Blink were senile. But not my daddy.

"Yes. You'll need to take him home. We need the bed space." The doctor shakes my hand briskly and strides off down the hall.

Spence and I spend some time in a hospital business office, signing release forms and chatting with a social worker who's been called in to advise us. She's middle-aged, overweight, overworked. Her eyes are bright blue and kind, but she looks frayed around the edges. Her name is Mrs. Kay.

Mrs. Kay asks us questions about our family situation. I answer as best I can. Spence just responds yes or no. He doesn't believe in giving unnecessary explanations.

Mrs. Kay is flabbergasted that we haven't applied for any kinds of Social Security or Medicare benefits.

"Do you realize that, based on your father's age and situation, the two of you could have been receiving financial support from the government for years? You know, you might want to look into getting some home care for you father."

Spence and I bring Daddy home that afternoon. Spence drives the Corvair. I sit up close to Daddy in the back seat. He's wrapped in a blanket. He's very weak, and tends to list to one side or the other whenever Spence negotiates a turn. I put my arm around Daddy to steady him.

On the way home, we pass scores of well-tended suburban homes, all decked out for Christmas—colored lights strung along rooflines and looped on outdoor evergreens, life-size Nativity scenes, beribboned wreaths on doors. My favorite is a rooftop straddled by Santa's sleigh and eight not-so-tiny ascending reindeer. A jolly Santa stands waving in a sleigh, brimful of presents. It is one week before Christmas 1972.

Daddy is so weak now he can't sit up on his own to eat. I have to prop him up with pillows in the Morris chair in his bedroom. He is unable to chew solid food. I'm not sure how to take care of him.

"Daddy, maybe we should get a nurse to check in on you at home," I suggest. "Or maybe Aunt Essie can come over from next door. She is a nurse, you know."

Daddy shakes his head like a stubborn child. "I don't want anybody but my little girl taking care of me."

I try to serve him some of his favorite foods—steamed fish, canned pear halves—but he doesn't seem to be able to chew them. I cut them up into small pieces and try poking a piece at a time into his mouth on the end of a fork, but he either lets the piece of food sit on his tongue until it falls out onto his shirtfront, or he swallows involuntarily and nearly chokes.

I remember that at Bonnie Blink some of the residents were given baby food to eat. I buy a selection of strained vegetables and fruit. Daddy's favorites seem to be pureed butternut squash and pureed prunes. I tie a dish towel around his neck to serve as a bib and spoon-feed him.

December 23rd is a cold, gray day. I'm on break from college, and spend the afternoon with Daddy in his bedroom. I have him propped up in his Morris chair, wrapped in blankets, but the wind is rising, and I can hear it whistling through the newspapers we use to seal the gaps around the edges of our front door downstairs. I turn up the thermostat in the hallway, and the old radiator in the bedroom sputters, pulses, and rumbles as it heats up.

Daddy doesn't do or say much these days, but he seems to listen intently to everything I say.

"Daddy, would you like me to tell you a story? I think maybe it's my turn to take you with me to once upon a time." I sit across from him on his bed.

I can see a flicker of recognition in his eyes, and the hint of a smile on his face.

"Actually, I'm going to read you a story I wrote for college last semester, for my creative writing class. Would you like to hear it?"

No change in Daddy's expression. I take that for a yes, and begin to read him a story I wrote at the beginning of December called "Passage."

The child felt very small and warm inside her sweater, inside her coat, inside the bus. She pressed her cheek against the frosty window, unfocused her eyes, and watched the passing blur of twinkling Christmas lights. She saw a plastic Santa, sleigh, and reindeer atop a passing roof. She saw strings of lights, rows of winking candles, swirling Christmas trees. Through the pane of glass came strains of music—bells and tambourines and trumpets played by men and ladies in gold buttons, black bows and caps. Her left cheek glowed cold from the press of icy glass. Her right cheek pulsed warm from the chafe of her furry coat collar.

The child sat alone, four seats back, directly behind the driver's seat. She could not see him. He was isolated by a plastic curtain. But she knew he was there. She could see the press of his shoulders against the plastic flap. It was Christmas, the child was coming home, and she was very tired. Her eyelids drooped, her small lips parted, she slept.

It was the child's dream to ride forever on this bus in the soft and twinkling Christmas night, to float through endless passing scenes kept safe for her beyond the window.

The bus jolted to a sudden stop. The child's chin jarred against the pane. Her eyes blinked open to see an old man staggering down the aisle, grasping wildly at the seats, fighting for his balance. He descended the steps slowly, unwillingly entering the cold city street. The driver grew impatient, rocked back and forth against his curtain. The child shivered from the sudden draft of cold and huddled farther down inside her coat. The door banged shut at the old man's back. The bus jolted to a start.

The child sat up, removed her left mitten, and touched the icy window with her fingertip. The glass had grown steamy from her breath, and she began to trace her name across the surface. But her letters were too large, and she ran out of space before her name was finished. She replaced her mitten and erased the entire square of glass with a flattened, red-wooly palm.

She could see the stars now. They were very white and clear. Some were sharpened spears of cold and ice. Others were sparkling spikes of flame and fire. The child made one wish upon them all.

Now the bus was passing the suburbs—the glowing-yellow, clustered suburbs. Many passengers got off at square brick houses with painted shutters. The bus was nearly empty now. The child watched as, one by one, the last passengers rose and filed out—a lady in a cloud of thick perfume, a tall man with umbrella and galoshes in hand, a brown woman whose face looked worn and crispy. They all buttoned coats and lifted collars before leaving the bus.

The bus moved on. The child sighed one small, happy sigh, leaned back against the seat, and continued to watch the roadside as it passed swiftly by. She needn't get off yet. There was still a long way to go.

Soon, the bus crossed a bridge. Now it traveled darkened roads instead of lighted streets. There were no more road signs, no more stoplights. The child peered out at thick black winter woods.

She could not remember having come this way before. She wondered if the driver could have lost his way. Looking forward, she saw only the vacant flapping of the plastic curtain exposing an empty driver's seat. She felt one frosty tear upon her left cheek, one scalding tear upon her right. The air was calm, yet full of wild and wondrous wind to fill each lung with chilling warmth. The child breathed deeply.

Just beyond the Manor Bridge, they found a shattered bus, plunged through the left-side railing of a seldom-traveled roadway and lying on its side at the foot of a ravine. A dazed, undamaged driver was found wandering some miles away. He had taken a wrong turn, leapt free.

Beside the tilted bus, a woman cried. A man looked on. They shivered in the cold and eager dawn.

Beneath the bus, they found a small, bundled body, half-crushed, peering through a shattered window. The left cheek was broken, covered with countless drops of glass and blood. The right cheek was whole and firm beneath a single streak of tear, still warm.

Inside the bus, a single, small, silent child rode endlessly into a soft and twinkling Christmas night. The End.

When I finish reading my story, the bedroom has grown dark, and Daddy has fallen asleep in his Morris chair.

CHAPTER TWENTY-THREE

RED SLIPPERS

B Y Christmas Eve, Daddy is bedridden. I have to put a rubber mattress liner under his sheets and keep absorbent bed pads— that look like large, unfolded rectangular paper diapers—tucked under him.

Spence and I don't do anything special for Christmas this year. We don't buy each other presents. I don't send Christmas cards or bake cookies. We don't put up a Christmas tree. I don't play the piano. I don't sing "I Want a Hippopotamus for Christmas." The only present I buy is one for Daddy.

Aunt Essie stops over with a plate of homemade cookies, arranged under a red paper napkin on a plastic platter shaped like an indented Santa Claus. The weight of Daddy's condition in the bedroom upstairs casts a heaviness throughout the farmhouse.

Daddy doesn't even eat baby food anymore. I do a trick I learned at Bonnie Blink. I concoct a high-calorie, high-protein milkshake— whole milk, ice cream, and dry milk powder—in a blender, and get Daddy to suck it through a bent glass straw. For hydration, I hold ice cubes wrapped in a washcloth to his parched lips. He suckles at the washcloth like a baby.

I change his bed pads and sheets throughout the day and night. I give him sponge baths in bed, and rub his skin with lanolin. I roll him and prop him in different positions to prevent bedsores.

On Christmas Day, I wake early on the sofa in the dining/living room. I've taken to sleeping there instead of in my bedroom. I don't know why. It just seems safer there, farther away from Daddy's dying. I make coffee for myself and go upstairs to check on Daddy.

I clean him up, dress him in fresh long johns, and get him to swallow a sip or two of milkshake. Then I prop him up in bed and bring him his Christmas present. I place it on his chest. I haven't bothered to wrap it. It's a pair of red bedroom slippers. Red is still our favorite color.

"Merry Christmas, Daddy," I say, and kiss him on his forehead.

Daddy clutches the red slippers to his chest, tears in his eyes, and says, "My little Lissa, my little Lissa."

It is two days past Christmas, in the middle of the night, and Daddy is dying. I call to Spence in his bedroom, pound on his door. Finally, he answers.

"I think Daddy's dying. What should I do? Should I call the doctor?"

"You can try if you want," he says. But Spence doesn't get up.

I call our local doctor. His wife calls him to the phone. The doctor tells me he doesn't make house calls.

I go back upstairs and pound on Spence's bedroom door. I shout through the closed door, "Spence! Spence!"

"What do you want?" He sounds cross.

"I called the doctor. He says he doesn't make house calls. What should I do, Spence?"

"Go back to bed. There's nothing we can do until morning. Now let me get some sleep."

I go back to Daddy's bedroom and sit in the Morris chair beside his bed for a while, until I hear the death rattle begin in Daddy's chest. It's something I've read about in novels, and I'm a little surprised that such a thing really exists, really happens.

Then something, I don't know what (is it cowardice, panic, the selfishness of youth?) prevents me from staying there to watch my father die.

I take Daddy's hand in mine one last time and say, "You'll have to do this by yourself."

I know that he hears me, that he understands what I have said. I can see, quite clearly, two tears roll down his cheek. For a moment, his hand tightens around my hand. Then he releases it.

I sleep fitfully on the sofa downstairs. My mind is saturated with a rapid flow of dreams and fluid visions. I am seeing into Daddy's mind as he lies dying. I see Fringe-A-Frock exploding. I hear the distant echo of the words *Urchie's dead*. I hear Moses Queen's laughter echoing in Fallen Angel Swamp.

Tonight, winds roar around the wooden clapboard farmhouse, rattling the windows. But it's not our farmhouse. It's a different one, the one on Tulip Hill. It is on nights like this that Daddy comes up with some of his most important inventions. I see the boy Stouten put aside his schoolbooks, climb into bed, and run his fingers lovingly over watches and watch parts he keeps in an old cigar box under his bed. With young Stouten, I fasten my eyes on the two prettiest things he's ever seen—his mother's smile and the workings of a watch.

It is long past midnight when Stouten turns down the wick, extinguishes the kerosene lamp on his bed stand, and drifts off to sleep. Dreams come to him, and now to me—apparitions of inventions past, auguries of inventions future—gears meshing, pistons sliding in cylinders, steam pressure building and releasing to drive the engine that powers the world.

Now, more intricate visions arrive—escapement mechanisms with balance wheels and hairsprings, the controlled expansion and contraction of the delicately coiled hairsprings—watches ticking like mechanical hearts, counting out the hours until the first light appears above the swampland east of the Loco Moco River.

The dream shifts forward in time, and I see my Uncle Francis burst into flames. I see Daddy wrapping his younger brother in his overcoat.

And now, and finally now, I see an old man and his little girl sitting on white marble steps in front of a brick row house, bidding goodnight to a world of once upon a time under the watchful eye of Natty Boh.

Early in the morning I return to Daddy's bedroom. His body is there, but I can tell that Daddy's not in there anymore. My mind seems paralyzed, locked, frozen. I am seized with a terrible sense of confusion, vertigo.

I run from the bedroom, down the stairs, and, in desperation, phone Aunt Essie next door. She is a nurse. She is Jimmie's sister. She will know what to do.

I take Aunt Essie up to Daddy's bedroom. She says she needs to prepare the body.

At first touch, she says, "He's stiff. They're going to have to break his legs to straighten him out."

"I'm sorry. I'm sorry." I begin to sob. I'm filled with guilt. "The doctor wouldn't come. I didn't know what to do."

I run down and phone the doctor again. "My father is dead," I say. It feels like a confession.

"You have my condolences. You'll need to notify the coroner."

I run back upstairs. I pound on Spence's door.

I go back to Daddy's bedroom. Aunt Essie is bathing the body.

"It's all right, honey. I've pulled him straight."

Spence is up now.

"Spence, the doctor said we have to call the coroner. I don't know the coroner's phone number. What should we do? Aunt Essie's here."

Finally, something clicks in Spence. He becomes my big brother again.

"It's okay, Liss. I'll take care of it."

The rest of the morning spins past in a crazy blur. Spence calls the coroner. The coroner comes and writes a death certificate. Sometime

before (or is it after?) the coroner's visit, I don't know when, I'm startled to hear a tap at the kitchen-door window. It's a police officer.
He sits across from me and Spence at the kitchen table, asking us
questions, filling out a police report.

Guilt comes crushing in on me as I hear myself say, "I wasn't with
him when he died. I found him this morning, around six o'clock."
Have I broken the law? Does he think I've killed my own father?

"Sorry to trouble you like this," the officer says. He must see the
anguish on my face. "But in situations like this, we have to make a
report."

He finishes the report. "Take care, you guys," he says, pats me on
the arm, and leaves.

We arrange to have a Roman Catholic funeral mass held for Daddy
at an old stone chapel in Baltimore County with an elderly priest. I
think this is what Daddy wants. Then we have his body transported
for burial in the family plot at St. Ignatius, in St. Mary's County.
Throughout it all, I seem to be watching myself from a distance.

I see a young woman, walking dazed like a zombie beside her
brother away from a fresh grave, past rows of gray monuments,
engraved gravestones, and solemn stone angels. But this young woman's hair is short, very short, like a boy's. She has cut off the two long
braids herself, wrapped them in tissue paper, and placed them in her
father's dresser drawer, nestled alongside another young woman's
auburn curls in a cedar box.

Relatives come to pay their respects. She hears them whispering
among themselves, saying things like, "She's really taking it hard,"
and "Is she okay?"

At the edge of the graveyard, I stumble on a loose rock in the
pathway. Spence grabs my wrist to keep me from falling. We get into
his sports car, and he drives me home.

Some believe that the soul must make a journey after death. Tonight, I take that journey with Daddy's soul. He is floating somewhere, looking down on his watchmaker's bench. I watch with him through darkening glass panes. With him, I see crows swirling and descending from the sky. But they are not crows; they are instead large ashes, rising above a flaming trash barrel in the yard, spinning, then slowly descending to rest upon the frozen grass. Daddy and I see remnants of burned newspaper pages, year after year, still smoldering red at the edges. Their photos are blackened, their words swallowed and obscured. Man's messages to man are immolated and transformed into twisted shadow birds of sorrow, or of prey.

Daddy was ninety-four. I am twenty-two. The year has ended.

CHAPTER TWENTY-FOUR

AFTERMATH

In February 1973, after Daddy's death, I return to college full-time and immerse myself in American literature—Faulkner, Steinbeck, Hemingway, Flannery O'Connor, Carson McCullers—and in French literature: Proust, Gide, Sartre, Camus, Robbe-Grillet.

Reading Sartre jolts me, fills me with anxiety and despair. His words lead me to believe that my life means nothing unless I give it meaning. I must accept individual responsibility for every action I take. I cannot depend on someone else's rules. I must define myself, create myself through every decision and choice I make. Only in this way can I be authentic and free.

In March 1973, the last American combat soldiers leave South Vietnam. For our country, the war is officially over. But at what cost? To what end? Again, the counting comes! And what are we left with when the numbers are counted, the tallying done, the balance sheet drawn up? Of the more than three million Americans who have served, nearly 58,000 are dead, more than 1,000 are missing in action, and 150,000 are seriously wounded. And these are just the tallies in the American column of the balance sheet.

I continue into summer, taking back-to-back semesters. I'm preparing to spend my junior year abroad in France. I read *A Moveable Feast*, Ernest Hemingway's memoir about his years as an American journalist in 1920s Paris, struggling to become a great writer. I imagine myself mingling with other writers in cafés, gathering with the literati at a salon, flourishing under the roof of a benevolent and inspiring host or hostess, being recognized by like-minded artists, and becoming the next great expatriate American writer.

I sell the Corvair to my friend Alice's father for $200; he's a collector. I get a passport and a student visa. As a going-away present, Spence buys me a vintage 1940s British fireman's jacket at Sunny's Surplus. Coarse blue wool, NFS (for National Firemen's Service) embossed on its double-breasted silver buttons, it matches one he bought for himself that I've long admired. Wearing it, I think, will make me appear strong, intrepid. I leave most of my things behind and pack only one suitcase—a couple of changes of clothing and a huge Larousse French-English dictionary.

In October 1973, I depart for France aboard a champagne flight to Paris. All of this is funded by Spence. He's been incredibly generous with me since Daddy's death, financing me, encouraging me. He makes good money now.

I remember asking Spence once, not long after Jimmie died, "Spence, do you ever think you're going to be famous?"

"Nope...well, maybe once...nah, not really."

"Well, I do, Spence. I've always thought I'm going to be famous one day."

Now Spence says to me, as he sends me off, "If somebody's going to do something important, then maybe it should be you."

I think Spence is motivated, even driven, by words Daddy drilled into his head over the years: "You must always take care of your little sister. She's just a little girl."

I fly from Dulles to JFK, then from JFK to Paris. Spence has bought me a first-class ticket. As the plane crosses the Atlantic, champagne flows endlessly. I drink too much, and the alcohol, combined with the dose of Dramamine I've taken to prevent motion sickness during the flight, has put me in a groggy, dreamlike state. I can hear Daddy's voice saying, "You're coming, and I'm going."

Throughout the long plane flight, I sleep and wake, sleep and wake. Suddenly, it's morning, and I'm in Paris! Even though I'm bleary, jet-lagged, and disoriented, adrenaline propels me from Orly Airport to Gare de Lyon. Here, I buy a ticket for the next train to Clermont-Ferrand, where I will be attending classes at the Faculté des Lettres.

Like so many of the buildings in Paris, the Gare de Lyon train station is built on a grand scale, an elaborate concoction of Belle Epoque architecture. At one corner, a massive clock tower greets me, and I am reminded of Daddy's Bromo-Seltzer Tower in Baltimore.

My train won't be leaving for several hours, so I make my way into the station's magnificent restaurant, Le Train Bleu. Its interior is breathtaking. I enter, and am at once enfolded in an extravagantly appointed rococo décor, an ostentatious swirl of red velvet, gilt moldings, and painted frescos depicting historic French scenes. Pendulous chandeliers cast romantic lighting on the parquet flooring.

I take a seat alone at a wood-paneled booth upholstered in maroon leather, and order a café au lait and a ham sandwich, un sandwich au jambon. I've kept my hair short, sort of a brunette version of New Wave actress Jean Seberg's cropped hair in *Breathless*.

Soon after, a Frenchman, wearing a corduroy suit and a black turtleneck sweater, approaches my table and asks if he can sit with me. Though he's not exactly Jean-Paul Belmondo, I say okay. He makes a quick bow, settles into the seat across from me, introduces himself as Paul Duval, and asks my name.

"Je m'appelle Lissa."

Monsieur Duval seems neither young nor old. He has a smooth mustache, a receding hairline, and wears his hair oiled and combed straight back. His face is curiously rodent-like, and extends itself into a classic Gallic nose reminiscent of the one I've seen in photos of Charles de Gaulle. His smile is oddly feral and his teeth are quite yellow, almost as yellow as Daddy's. With a seamless flow of movements, he draws a blue packet labeled Gauloises from his pocket, lights a short, unfiltered cigarette, snaps his fingers for a waiter, orders a Pernod, and offers to order me a drink, as well.

"Non, merci," I say, and begin my first real conversation in France.

"What's Pernod, M. Duval?" I ask.

"Call me Paul."

The Pernod arrives, and Paul holds his glass up to the light.

"You ask me, what is Pernod? Well, Lissa, to answer that question, one must employ several of the senses. First, one must look at it. And what does one see? What is the color of it?"

"It's very yellow," I say.

"Yes, my dear. More brilliant than the sun, and more radiantly clear."

He passes the rim of his glass under my nose. "Next, one must sniff it. And what does the nose tell you, my dear?"

"I think I smell licorice."

"That's it." He swishes the glass gently around under my nose. "The nose reveals to you a mélange of licorice, anise, garden herbs, carnations, and fennel. Now taste it." He hands the glass to me.

I shake my head. "I don't think so."

"Here. Place just the smallest of drops on the tongue."

I take a very small sip. "Umm," I say, so as not to hurt his feelings. But I really don't like the taste of licorice.

"It's exotic, n'est pas? Powerful. Bittersweet."

By now, the waiter has arrived with my sandwich. I take my first bite. It is such a delicious sandwich! Unlike anything I've tasted before. A fresh, crisp, skinny baguette, spread lightly with butter and layered with thinly sliced ham and a soupçon of Dijon mustard.

"How do you like it?" Paul asks.

"C'est formidable!"

Paul tries to persuade me to come spend a few days with him at his country home. He tries to paint a seductive tableau, describing its abundant orchards, limpid fish pond, and tranquil sunsets.

"Non, merci," I tell him. "I have to catch a train."

He looks disappointed. He implores me to reconsider, but I insist, "No, no. I must go. I'm expected at the dormitory."

It feels good to say no, to know what I want and what I don't want, to do what I want, to assert myself, to take care of myself, to be responsible for myself. I feel the release of an unidentifiable constriction. I experience something I have never felt before, a palpable wave of self-determined new beginnings. Everything is possible. This is where everything begins!

In the early afternoon, I board the train to Clermont. It whisks me south, past waves of French countryside, stopping at Nevers, Moulins, Vichy, and Riom/Chatel-Guyon. It's nearly six P.M.—or 1800 hours, as they count it here in France—when I step off the train in Clermont, carrying my suitcase.

Disoriented, I cross a series of train tracks. Suddenly, I see a train coming right at me. I must be crossing at the wrong spot. At the front of the approaching train, I see the engineer gesticulating at me. I hear the clang of a warning bell and the grinding of brakes to slow the train. At the last instant, I race across the tracks, just in time to avoid being hit.

I hurry through the station and get into one of the cabs waiting outside. I give the cab driver the address of my new dorm. He drops me off at Place de Regensburg, and removes my suitcase from the trunk. I pull out one of the unfamiliar franc notes from the wad of bills stuffed into my coat pocket. Spence got the French currency for me at Maryland National Bank before I left home. When a huge smile spreads across the taxi driver's face, it dawns on me that I must have really over-tipped him.

The driver points toward my destination: just across the square to a dormitory, built to accommodate young workers from the surrounding countryside who have found jobs in Clermont. The dorm also houses foreign students like me. It has two slim and distinctly separate towers—one for young men, one for young women—joined by a lobby on the rez-de-chaussée. I ring the buzzer at the door, the concierge buzzes me in, and I cross the threshold.

A curious vibration rises up my spine and explodes out the top of my head. A new door flies open, and through it shines a pure, white light—so very bright, and yet it doesn't hurt my eyes. I soar beyond *once upon a time*—to here, to now, where everything begins.